THE AUTH

Roy Fuller's early life is recounted in his three quite recent volumes of memoirs, *Souvenirs*, *Vamp Till Ready* and *Home and Dry*. He was born in 1912 in Failsworth, Lancashire, but educated and articled to a solicitor in Blackpool. Soon after qualifying he moved south, eventually becoming a solicitor with the Woolwich Equitable Building Society, with whom he spent the rest of his professional life. In 1969 he retired as solicitor to join the Woolwich Board. He was Professor of Poetry at Oxford from 1968-73, and a Governor of the BBC from 1972-79.

During the war he served in the Royal Navy and became known as a poet through his two wartime books of verse, *The Middle of a War* and *A Lost Season*, both published by The Hogarth Press. He began as a writer of fiction after the war with a novel for children, and continued with three crime novels. Six 'straight' novels followed at fairly regular intervals, but he has not published a work of fiction since *The Carnal Island* of 1970. (This, along with *The Ruined Boys* and *My Child, My Sister*, is also appearing in Hogarth paperback.) However, he has gone on writing poetry. His monumental *New and Collected Poems 1934-84* came out in 1985, followed by *Subsequent to Summer* in the same year and *Consolations* (1987).

He married his wife Kate in 1936 and they have one son, the poet and author John Fuller. His brother, another John Fuller, is well known in the gastronomic world as a former head of the Scottish Hotel School, and the author and editor of many works on cooking and catering education.

IMAGE OF A SOCIETY

Roy Fuller

New Introduction by Jeremy Lewis

THE HOGARTH PRESS
LONDON

Published in 1987 by
The Hogarth Press
Chatto and Windus Ltd
40 William IV Street, London WC2N 4DF

First published in Great Britain by André Deutsch Ltd 1956
Hogarth edition offset from original British edition

British Library Cataloguing in Publication Data

Fuller, Roy
Image of a society.
I. Title
823'.912[F] PR6011.U55

ISBN 0 7012 0689 6

Printed in Great Britain by
Cox & Wyman Ltd
Reading, Berkshire

INTRODUCTION

At one point in his autobiography, Roy Fuller takes George Orwell to task for writing conspiratorial left-wing 'bosh' in *Coming Up for Air* about the nefarious doings of a building society: Orwell had, he tells us, displayed his 'usual disregard for probability and fact' in portraying the society as some kind of all-pervasive, tentacular agency of exploitation. As a writer, Mr. Fuller has much in common with George Orwell, including a plain, commonsensical prose style, a feeling for the modest, telling details of everyday life, and a very English and undogmatic inclination to the left of the political spectrum. Where he differs from Orwell, and from so many modern writers, is in his readiness to write about work, and the experience of work, from the point of view of a regular practitioner rather than a somewhat disdainful and – as his understandably irritated outburst suggests – ill-informed outsider.

It's a sad irony of present-day literary life – and one that, no doubt, provides useful ammunition to those who believe that 'the arts' have precious little to offer, or to do with, the man in the street – that although an ever-expanding proportion of the working population spend their working lives in offices, shuffling pieces of paper about, dictating long and horribly complicated internal memos, and sending urgent electronic messages flashing round the world, office life and the business world feature hardly at all in the serious modern novel. There are, I suspect, two particular reasons for this: a prevailing contempt and suspicion of business life, shared by gentlemanly or bogus-gentlemanly High Tories and censorious left-wingers (two traditions which, surprisingly, have much in common, and come together, perhaps, in a figure like George Orwell); and the exaltation of English Literature as a subject of academic study, to the extent that literary criticism now seems to occupy – for no very convincing reason – the same kind of intellectual pre-eminence that was once afforded to the classics. School teachers and those who teach in universities tend to instil into their charges a lofty contempt for the worlds of industry and commerce, making loud noises of disapproval while wherever possible enjoying the fruits thereof; among those who teach Eng. Lit. in particular there is a tendency to the incestuous notion that literature is – or should be – written by 'professionals' (i.e., academics teaching Eng. Lit.) and can only be properly understood or 'decoded' by fellow 'professionals' (i.e., other academics and their former pupils in the literary world). Not surprisingly, perhaps, many modern literary novels tend to be written by dons or quasi-dons, and consist of scenes from academic life, or opaque broodings on the nature of fiction or the problems inherent in writing a novel, or – when a skittish mood is upon their creators – of elephantine flights of fantasy; and whereas a Wells or a Dickens or an Arnold Bennett brought an informed affection as well as a sense of outrage or injustice when writing about the working lives of clerks or shop assistants or those who toil in the Circumlocution Office, the modern novelist all too often seems to lack the knowledge, the experience or the sympathy that would enable him to write about the ways in which a sizeable part of the population spends the inside of the working week.

Roy Fuller was articled to a firm of solicitors in Blackpool immediately after leaving school at the age of sixteen in 1928, and spent much of his life combining a very varied and productive literary career with his work as the solicitor for the Woolwich Equitable Building Society – a *curriculum vitae* that, no doubt, excites among literary folk the same slightly shocked tremor of unease as Wallace Stevens's undeviating devotion to the affairs of the Hartford Accident and Indemnity Company, or T. S. Eliot's unhappy spell with Lloyds Bank (from which, it will be remembered, he had to be rescued by a posse of fellow writers and well-wishers). Roy Fuller has written that 'in literature, truth about life cannot be separated from truth about society', an observation that probably owes more to his practical sense of things than to the Marxism he espoused from his schooldays and through the 1930s: far from assuming that commercial and office life is too dull or too wicked or too far beneath contempt to merit the attention of the serious writer, he knows – like those of us who, for better or for worse, spend our days in such places – that even the dreariest-seeming office is, like a rock-pool or the underside of a stone, aswarm with unsuspected life, a universe in miniature, peopled by tyrants and time-servers, plodders and human dynamos, driven on by ambition or greed or fear or merely a modest desire to keep one's head down and get through the day as best one may; and that each one of them, like a microcosm of society at large, has its own folklore and politics and awe-inspiring hierarchies – so compelling to those within, and so meaningless to the world at large – and that in them high dramas of rivalry and revenge, of duplicity and cowardice, co-exist with the most touching, melancholy manifestations of those consoling, self-protective myths that most of us survive by. First published in 1956, *Image of a Society* must be unique among novels in being set in a North Country building society; and in it Roy Fuller not only proves – if proof were necessary – that the office can be as productive of first-rate fiction as any other aspect of life, but re-enfranchises the world of nine-to-five as a legitimate subject for the novelist.

As we all know, office life is much exercised with power, and with rival claims to supremacy: so too is *Image of a Society*, though Mr. Fuller – while describing with a ruthless precision the mechanics of managerial ambition – is more concerned with its pathos and, ultimately, its tragic aspects than with the kind of slick one-upmanship that aspiring middle managers read about in manuals of office practice or in business-page biographies of over-abrasive, cigar-puffing contemporary tycoons. On the face of it, he evokes what seems, by current standards, a courteous, slow-moving community, in which the managers join one another for biscuits and tea in mid-afternoon, remember to call the directors 'sir', and inhabit a solid, vanished world of mahogany and polished brass, of

Victorian provincial clubs and local self-regard. As such, *Image of a Society* has, at the very least, a considerable historical and sociological interest; but what makes Mr. Fuller so striking and so sympathetic a novelist is his eye – kindly but unflinching – for the ways in which we sustain our self-esteem and play out our parts before our colleagues and superiors, and the petty triumphs and evasions and duplicities that form the stock-in-trade of any kind of institutional life. An excellent example is provided early on, when the House Manager is interrupted while taking his tea:

> Ramsden's house telephone rang. He put down the remains of his jam puff and picked up the receiver.
>
> 'Hello,' he said shortly. Then his tone changed to one of efficient sweetness. 'Yes, Mr. Blackledge,' he said. 'Yes, right away.' He put the receiver back, looked at Willie and then at his scarcely touched mug of tea. 'God's perishing teeth,' he said. 'Why do they always want me at tea time?'

So Witt, the Saddleford Building Society's solicitor – a man who, more than most, finds it hard to sustain the necessary suspension of disbelief – finds 'his face cramped with a false expression of interest' and, like so many of us, 'in his office, shrinking from the naked contact with another personality, he would often deal with a situation which demanded a telephone call or an interview by deliberately procrastinating or writing a memorandum'; or the ebullient Blackledge, who wants above all else to be next in line for the job of General Manager when old Matheson retires, agonises over his rating in the company car park, but comforts himself with the belief that, when it comes to timing his arrival in the office, he has struck just the right note ('There was a sane and balanced practice in these matters: one ought to demonstrate that one was not the slave of the clock, at the same time making sure that Matheson did not enquire for one in vain'); while his rival Gerson, the cool-blooded figures man, who 'had not, as he knew, a very good brain, and so . . . had trained himself to a pitch of almost terrifying scrupulousness', is spotted advancing his career in the 'Directors' and Senior Executives' Lavatory', where 'he spoke to the other man [one of the Society's directors] in deferential tones and even, out of deference, accommodated the tempo of his ablutions to his companion's, so that he reached out for a towel a moment after the other.' Insights like these, exciting as they do an uneasy wince of self-recognition, are all the more impressive for the mild exactitude with which they are recorded.

The novel's central figure, Witt, is younger than his colleagues and altogether more detached about the Society and his part in it. He is an aspiring writer, still living at home with his elderly parents, and, like many intellectuals, he feels restless in the world into which he was born, and finds it hard to give his work the kind of commitment that comes all too easily to a Blackledge or a Gerson: his attitude to his employment is, at best, ambivalent, nursing as he does a 'constant if largely unconscious hope that the Society would be injured, that its borrowing members and employees would revolt against it, that its massive millions and its part in the social fabric of the times would somehow or other be undermined'. Doubtless Witt has much in common with his creator: for all his sympathetic understanding of institutional life, Roy Fuller admits that, as a solicitor whose real interests lay elsewhere, he was competent but uninvolved, displaying a 'lack of true interest, of the common touch, of the energy to avoid the merely routine when the merely routine would serve'. Be that as it may – and it's hard to avoid a slight suspicion that, despite its fundamental truth, Mr. Fuller's former colleagues would charge him with undue professional modesty – Witt's own attitude to the Society, for all its moral arrogance, perfectly captures states of mind familiar to us all:

With his nominal superiors – the directors and the General Manager – he exerted all his concern to assure them of his conscientiousness, and not the least element of acting in this was his private knowledge that he really was not conscientious . . . Nor were his feelings in these connexions altered in the slightest by his clear realization that he despised his work and fundamentally despised all those who had surrendered to it more than a superficial allegiance. Years ago he had thought that the sanctions and coercions of his professional life could never touch the realities of his existence – his writing, his reading, his private morality. Now he knew, though in a fashion he continued to struggle against the knowledge, that merely to get one's bread in the world of Hepworth and Gerson, let alone achieve butter on it, meant a life of such compromise as to make it indistinguishable from lives too ignorant and ignoble to know that the problem of compromise could exist.

But *Image of a Society* is more than just a perceptive and – as past misjudgements on the mortgage front come back to haunt their perpetrators – exciting story of institutional rivalry and intrigue. Roy Fuller is a master of quiet, undemonstrative realism, working outwards from the closely observed detail to the cumulative effect. Like Arnold Bennett before him, he provides a grainy, vivid picture of middle- and lower middle-class provincial life so convincing and so tangible and of such absorbing interest that it's hard not to share J. B. Priestley's wish (conveyed to its creator over dinner one night) that the novel had gone on a good deal longer than it does. Saddleford's grimy main square, with its banks and offices and the Station Hotel and the lime-streaked statue of John Bright; the bar of the Queen's Hotel, with its high stools and horse brasses and bowls of roasted peanuts, where an increasingly uneasy Blackledge restores his flagging spirits with a dash of bogus bonhomie; the gloomy, draughty suburban house in which Witt visits his anodyne girl friend, sipping hot chocolate before an unforthcoming fire, unbuttoning her shirt in a lacklustre way, and waiting for her somewhat strident parents to return home from an evening out; the London hotel in which Witt and – but to say with whom, or why, he stays in the London hotel would be the act of a cad: all of them evoke a world that seems, from the vantage point of the 1980s, extraordinarily different and distant, and is yet immediately recognisable. As a portrait of the way we lived then – and now – *Image of a Society* is hard to beat.

Jeremy Lewis, London 1986

TO KATHLEEN SYMONS

Fiction must almost be in vain
For whom the real will entertain;
But this, so it may also live,
Begs all the interest you can give.

AUTHOR'S NOTE

Because of my regard for building societies and for my friends who work for them I emphasize the obvious: that there is no Saddleford Building Society, nor have its directors, staff and affairs any counterpart in reality. Entirely fictitious, too, is the company and its property with which this story also deals.

I

In the basement of Saddleford House, Ramsden, the House Manager, sat gazing through the door of his tiny office, cleaning his earhole with a paper clip. He could see the gates at the bottom of the lift shaft and, through the gap at the side, the store for surplus furniture, discarded mahogany partitions and outmoded advertisement signs. Along the sides of the gap were Ramsden's bicycle and a stack of rather battered bronze plaques bearing the legend 'Saddleford Building Society. Established 1862'. Ramsden put the paper clip down and pulled out his watch. It was twenty to four. He drummed on the desk with thick fingers: the back of his hand looked as if he were wearing a glove made of ginger fur. Into the fur, from the arm, extended the faint azure of an old tattoo pattern.

The lift machinery sent out a faint hum, and soon the lift slid into the basement aperture. Ramsden threw himself into a negligent but exasperated attitude. A small man in blue overalls burdened with the complications of a pint mug and a plate with a jam puff on it extricated himself from the lift and came into Ramsden's office.

'I'm sorry I'm late, Mr. Ramsden,' he said, putting the mug and plate on the desk.

'I always have my cup of tea at three-thirty,' said Ramsden.

'I know that,' said the other obsequiously. 'There were a queue.'

'Don't you go round the back?' asked Ramsden.

'Yes, Mr. Ramsden, but them canteen women went on serving the queue.'

'You're too weak, Willie,' said Ramsden. 'You want to make your personality felt.'

'Yes, Mr. Ramsden.'

'And I hate jam puffs.'

'I'm sorry, Mr. Ramsden. There were only custards and jam puffs and you had a custard yesterday.'

'Well, I could have had a custard again.'

'I'll go and change it,' said Willie, making to take the plate.

'Oh, stop fidgeting,' said Ramsden. He sipped his tea and took a bite of the jam puff. 'Did you clean Mr. Gerson's windows?'

'Yes, Mr. Ramsden.'

'I'll give you a tip, Willie my lad. You want to watch Mr. Gerson. Please him. See his windows are kept clean. Don't wait for the right day to come round, don't wait till he complains. It's me that's got to take the can back, remember. Mr. Gerson's a particular man.'

'Yes, Mr. Ramsden.'

Ramsden chewed and kept his eyes on Willie as he had, half paternally, half bullyingly, chewed and kept his eyes on ratings when he was a chief petty officer in the Navy. 'What would you think,' he said, 'if you were a traveller for a big firm selling scouring powder and you called on the House Manager of a big building society and you were shown downstairs into the basement and into an office this size?' Ramsden made a small gesture with his mug.

'I don't know, I'm sure,' said Willie.

'You'd think it were a bloody poor do,' said Ramsden 'The Saddleford Building Society and it puts its House

Manager below ground in a hole you couldn't sling an 'ammick in. Look at it from the Society's own point of view: it's bad propaganda, it creates a bad impression.'

Willie had heard all this several times before, but he nodded his pale face absorbedly. Indeed, he was not uninterested in the status of the House Manager's office: in twelve years Ramsden would be retiring—perhaps even before then he would die, for he drank a lot of beer and took no exercise—and he, Willie Ashworth, might well be the House Manager, with one of his staff of cleaners bringing him tea at three-thirty.

'Of course,' Ramsden was saying, 'the Society's expanding, it's short of room. But then there aren't many chaps work here that have to see people from outside. I'm seeing people all the time. There's the travellers, as I've said, and the new cleaning women I take on, and all the outside contractors. They ought to make room for me upstairs. They could make room. Now if they took those two chaps in the Internal Audit Department——'

Ramsden's house telephone rang. He put down the remains of his jam puff and picked up the receiver.

'Hello,' he said shortly. Then his tone changed to one of efficient sweetness. 'Yes, Mr. Blackledge,' he said. 'Yes, right away.' He put the receiver back, looked at Willie and then at his scarcely-touched mug of tea. 'God's perishing teeth,' he said. 'Why do they always want me at tea time?'

'Shall I go and get you another mug of tea, Mr. Ramsden?' asked Willie.

'No, Willie. Don't know how long I'll be.' Ramsden walked over to the lift, got in, and pressed a button.

This was the lift shaft at the rear of the building: it cut through a series of similar and undistinguished corridors lined with the staff lockers. At the ground floor level Ramsden glimpsed, through glazed doors, the clerks at work in the vast hinterland behind the banking hall. As he swam upwards through the first floor one of his own staff passed carrying a bucket and wearing a safety belt, on the unending task of cleaning Saddleford House's 374 windows. The lift stopped at the second floor and Ramsden made his way round the corridor to the front of the building. Here, the final section of the corridor was barred at either end with swing doors marked 'Private': Ramsden always referred to it as the quarter-deck. Cream distemper gave way to a dark glossy panelling, plastic floor covering to carpet, the wall lights were someone's dream of a baronial hall. Off the corridor were the offices of the principal executives, at the end of it the boardroom. Ramsden, removing with his finger nail a raspberry jam seed from a tooth and wondering if an opportunity would occur now to broach the question of his undignified quarters, knocked on the door of Blackledge's room.

The front of Saddleford House, its original brown stone almost black with Saddleford grime, formed one side of a square of which the others were the railway station, a row of banks and offices, and the Station Hotel and the bus terminus. The square was cobbled and in the middle, its sightless eyes turned towards the station's classic pillars, its thick finger holding, like a child who has just learned to read, its place in a book, sat a statue of John Bright. From the window of his office Stuart Blackledge watched a pigeon fly from a cornice of the Yorkshire Penny Bank to the arm of Bright's stone chair and, with a little tilt of its tail, deposit a dropping on the lime-streaked plinth. Blackledge's teeth were clenched on a

Dunhill rough-grained briar, his hands, resting on the back of his hips, threw behind him the folds of his black jacket. He was beginning to put on a little weight: there was no space at all between the small knot of his grey silk tie and the stiff cut-away collar and between the collar and his neck. His face gave promise of turning red, and the hair brushed back over his ears was already shot with grey in the light from the window.

He was wondering, for a moment, why the end of the working day, the slight fading of the light holding the promise of artificial light, drinks, food, companionship, was failing to rouse in him a pleasurable response. He sent up a little smoke signal from the bowl of his pipe and felt the strong muscles in the small of his back, but was not reassured. Then he recalled that he had left his house in the morning on bad terms with his wife Rose. He could not now remember the cause of the quarrel or imagine that their relationship was capable of engendering one even: he was filled with such goodwill that he felt himself unjustly accused, martyred. Behind the Station Hotel distant slender factory chimneys trailed a smoke that quickly merged into the grey sky. A few exclamation marks of rain appeared on the window and his lips pouted round the stem of his pipe.

Ramsden's knock was followed, after the correct interval, by his entry. Blackledge turned round and went to sit at his desk. He knocked his pipe against the signet ring on the little finger of his left hand so that the ash fell into an enormous ashtray, and looked at Ramsden across the leather blotter, the yardage of glass and the silver inkstand.

'Ramsden,' he said.

'Yes, sir,' said Ramsden.

'Is the canteen ready for my talk? The blackboard there? I may use it.'

'Yes, sir.'

'You'll see that those women don't start washing-up until I've finished?'

'Yes, sir,' said Ramsden again, trying to think why the Mortgage Manager was concerning himself with these petty details, which had naturally all been settled by Haigh from the Establishment Department who was responsible for the arrangement of this educational scheme for the staff. Ramsden, with slight alarm, wondered whether Blackledge's questions were not the feint before the smashing blow—a typical Blackledge tactic—and tried to bring to mind his recent misdeeds and omissions. The matter of his change of office vanished from his agenda.

'Last year I had to send someone to stop the clatter.' Blackledge began to fill his pipe. 'By the way, Ramsden, how are the contractors getting on with the garage?'

'Not too badly, sir. They should have finished by June.'

Blackledge's eyebrows shot up. 'As soon as that?' He put the pipe between his teeth. 'Let me see, there will be room for twelve cars, won't there?'

Ramsden agreed. The site on which Saddleford House was built fell away slightly at the rear and, there, part of the basement had been designed as a garage. Recently the space had been reorganized and when the alterations were finished would accommodate the cars of twelve officials of the society instead of the previous seven.

'You've got the five new names?' asked Blackledge.

'Yes, sir.'

'And re-allocated the spaces?'

'Re-allocated the spaces?' Ramsden repeated.

Blackledge looked severely at the gilt-framed prints of old Saddleford hanging on the panelled walls. 'People won't necessarily want to keep the numbers they were probably quite fortuitously allotted in the past, you know, Ramsden. This is an excellent opportunity to rationalize the whole situation. Take my own present number—five. When I joined the society in 1936 it so happened that number five was vacant and therefore it was given to me. Damned awkward number—behind that pillar.'

'Yes, sir,' said Ramsden. 'I got the five new names from the Premises Manager: I hadn't thought about re-allocation—I'll talk to him about it.'

Blackledge fixed his light grey eyes on Ramsden's ginger-fringed ones. 'I don't believe it's quite a Premises Manager matter,' he observed coldly. 'I think I had better deal with it.'

'Yes, sir,' said Ramsden uneasily.

'Let me see,' said Blackledge, 'the General Manager will keep number one, of course. I shall have number two, Mr. Gerson number three, the Assistant Secretary number four—I'll jot the names down tomorrow, Ramsden, and let you have them.'

'Very good, sir. And if the Premises Manager asks me——'

Blackledge cut him short. 'If the Premises Manager has any questions he must come and see me.'

Ramsden shuffled his feet and half turned to go. Blackledge's voice brought him round again—a voice now pitched lower, slightly honeyed, warm.

'Ramsden,' said Blackledge, 'you're an expert. I'm thinking of buying some rose bushes: what kind ought I to get?'

Ramsden came a little nearer to the desk. 'Didn't know you were a gardener, Mr. Blackledge,' he said.

Blackledge let himself be patronized. 'I'm not. Far from it. Beginning to get interested though. Now those rose bushes——'

'Well, sir,' said Ramsden. 'it all depends on what you want. But why don't you go in for these hybrid polyantha . . .'

Blackledge permitted Ramsden to speak enthusiastically for several minutes and then suddenly looked at his watch. 'Good Lord!' he said. 'I must go and talk to those children. Thank you, Ramsden. Most valuable. I won't forget what you've told me.'

Ramsden marched along the corridor with the glow of a man who has done himself conversational justice. And then, as he descended in the lift to his cold tea and the remains of the jam puff, he said to himself: I wouldn't trust that bastard as far as I could throw him.

Walter Haigh, the Establishment Department clerk in charge of the mechanics of the annual staff educational course, wore glasses and a suit which had frayed round the button holes and down the lapel seams and which his wife had carefully but unskilfully mended with thick cotton. He had three young children and soon after the war had bought a house with the help of a mortgage from the Society. His unspectacular appearance concealed an intense ambition to move out of his lowly position. In the meantime he gave his life value by regarding it as dedicated to the ideal of service to others. He was chairman of the Saddleford Building Society Staff Christian Union.

In the canteen, at the end farthest from the service

hatch, chairs had been arranged in rows in front of a table and a blackboard. Haigh stood at the back and counted the heads of the score of young men and women already occupying the chairs and giggling a little. It took him back to the days when he was a W. T. instructor in the Army. When he had made sure, by counting the heads three times, that no one was missing, he walked rapidly down the stairs to Blackledge's office, and poked his head round the door.

'All present and correct, sir,' he said twitching his nose to ease the pressure of his glasses.

Blackledge rose leisurely, concealing his irritation. He had no business to be irritated by this Haigh figure, by the cheap shabby suit, the ill-fitting glasses, the bogus accent which Haigh had acquired with his eventual commission in the Army ('pat', he would say when pronouncing 'put', knowing it was wrong to say 'poot'). And then he remembered what Rose had said to him as he left the house that morning, said reflectively as of a stranger: I never used to think you an irritable man.

As they went along the corridor, Blackledge pulled down the points of his waistcoat masterfully and said: 'What are they like this year, Haigh?'

'Not a bad lot, sir, actually.'

Blackledge strode past the lifts and bounded up the stairs, leaving Haigh a yard or two behind him. But when he reached the fourth floor he was breathing heavily and he felt the blood throbbing in his temples. It was hard for him to realize that he was over forty.

The chattering ceased as he walked to the table. His eyes swept the rows and he said: 'Ladies and gentlemen.' He was conscious that in using this form of address he was bestowing an unmerited but welcome honour.

'Ladies and gentlemen. As you know, I am the Mortgage Manager of this society. I am here to introduce and commend this little educational course to you because originally it was my idea that such courses should be held. Don't let me frighten you by using the word "course". There are no examinations or tests in connexion with the visits you will make during the next few weeks to the various departments of the society. All we want you to do is understand a little better how this organization works and what it does.'

Out of the corner of his eye Blackledge could see Haigh sitting in isolation on the left: as the man made his nose-twitching gesture Blackledge determined to tell the Establishment Officer there was no need for Haigh to stay during this introductory talk. It was mere officiousness and time-wasting.

'There was once a man who worked at a conveyor belt in a factory. His job was to tighten a bolt on a piece of machinery as it came past him. He was good at his job and when he had held it for fifty years the directors of the factory asked him if there was anything particular he would like as a reward for his long and faithful service. This man said yes, there was: he would like to be taken to the end of the conveyor belt so that he could find out what he had been helping to make these fifty years.'

One or two sharp boys laughed: Blackledge expected no better response. On the whole it was poor material that they were getting from the state's inordinately expensive educational establishments. 'We don't want you to spend your time with us like that wretched man.' Blackledge twisted his signet ring. 'Now what is a building society? The Building Societies Acts—the Acts of

Parliament that govern all we do here—state that the purpose of a building society is to raise a fund so as to make advances to its members on the security of freehold or leasehold property. A building society, curiously enough, doesn't build. It obtains money from its investors—from its shareholders and depositors—and lends that money to its borrowing members to enable them to buy the houses they live in—or sometimes to buy shops or farms or even blocks of flats.

'The first department you will visit will be the Accounts Department. There you will see how the money comes to us from our investors and how their accounts are taken care of. Then you will visit my department, the Mortgage Department, which I can't help thinking the most important in the society.' This time even the sharp boys did not know whether or not to laugh. He went on quickly: 'The Mortgage Department, of course, deals with the lending side of our business. Then I think you will have a look at our Legal and Securities Department, and our solicitor, Mr. Witt, will tell you something of his side of affairs. Now I don't want to go on reciting a lot of names that you can't possibly remember, and I think it would be best if I sketched a diagram of our whole organization and indicated what places and persons you will have the opportunity of seeing.'

Blackledge took a piece of chalk and wrote at the top of the blackboard THE BOARD OF DIRECTORS. Underneath he drew a short vertical line and underneath that wrote GENERAL MANAGER. He felt at his back, like the breath of some bored but potentially unruly, captive beast, the gaze of the twenty-two juniors, and thought what he always thought but forgot during the ensuing year, that really this job brought little prestige, was very wearing, and that it was time he delegated it to his assistant manager.

In the Directors' and Senior Executives' dining-room the General Manager, Herbert Matheson, sat alone at the head of the long table taking his tea. An early edition of the *Saddleford Argus* was propped up in front of him. He was a small, neat man with a long nose: the immaculate parting of his white hair was very pink and he wore a blue bow tie with white polka dots. He popped the last fragment of bread and butter and jam into his mouth and then licked his knife. He had joined the Saddleford Building Society fifty years ago as the office boy.

Bearded father-figures, long-dead former directors of the society, looked down from the walls. In an enormous glass-fronted sideboard crystal and silver gleamed through the grey light. Matheson took a chocolate éclair and poured himself another cup of tea. His eye ran down the births, marriages and deaths column: among the deaths were several names he knew. He bit two inches off the éclair, suddenly conscious of his good digestion and the long life before him. He looked up and smiled his gentle smile when Blackledge came through the door and sat down beside him.

'All alone, sir?' asked Blackledge, unnecessarily, aware as always of his virtue in calling Matheson 'sir'.

Matheson, still smiling, put the jam within Blackledge's reach.

Blackledge poured tea. 'I've been giving my annual performance for the start of the Departmental Visits course,' he said. 'Thirsty work.'

The General Manager lit a cigarette with little puffs,

as if after fifty years he were still an amateur of smoking. 'What happened to that photograph of old George Sutcliffe you were going to have framed?' he asked.

'It's hung in the Chairman's room, sir,' said Blackledge. There was no doubt that Matheson paid less and less attention these days to what one said: perhaps he was getting deaf.

'Is it really?' said the General Manager. 'I'd never noticed it.' Blackledge passed him an ashtray. 'Thank you. It's extraordinary that that should be the only photograph of George Sutcliffe ever to come to light. He was General Manager when I first came. He still rode to work on a horse—he had a house at Bellsgate, not far from you, Blackledge. I used to have to watch for him in the mornings, run out when he arrived and lead the horse to the stables at the back of the Saddleford Arms. The offices were in Manchester Place then—where Woolworth's is now. George Sutcliffe died in 1913—collapsed while he was taking his young men's class at the Caroline Street Sunday School. The end of an epoch.'

Blackledge listened with an air of interested concentration which he assumed with scarcely any effort—which, indeed, was almost genuine. The thought of the unbroken line of General Managers, stretching back to 1862, aroused in him a warm and generous feeling. And something was giving him cause for happiness, too, despite the task that lay ahead of him of making peace with Rose when he got home. He extracted a whole strawberry from the jam on his plate, balanced it on the soft part of his folded bread and butter and took a bite. Of course, it was the settling of the garage business, quite a nagging little worry during the last few weeks, which now gently glowed, like the first whisky of the evening, in his solar plexus. In the garage as it had previously existed the allocation of space had been settled by the accidents of history. That the Establishment Officer should have had space number two was accidental and no one attached any significance to it. Gerson had number three, his proper place in the hierarchy. Blackledge's own number, five, was by chance so far down that it could not be imagined that it represented his seniority. But once he had learned that the garage was to be reorganized it obviously became vital to ensure that the numbers corresponded with reality.

If one supposed that the General Manager himself were consulted there could be no doubt that he would, automatically almost, assign Blackledge to the second, Gerson to the third place. Naturally it was too trivial a matter for the General Manager to be brought into. But it was not too trivial that Blackledge could leave it to the Premises Manager, whose imperfect understanding of the situation might allow him to let the garage places stay in their old order or even carelessly—wilfully, conceivably—reverse the respective positions to which Blackledge knew that he and Gerson were in truth entitled. Now he had stopped the leak, with a simple but masterly strategy.

'George Sutcliffe's successor had one of the first motor cars in Saddleford,' the General Manager was saying, 'though I don't remember him coming to the office in it until after the war.'

Blackledge gazed calmly at Matheson's pale face. He could recall the time when he imagined that the succession might be accelerated by the General Manager's death in office, that the pallor, the delicate movements, denoted imperfect health. In those days Matheson's retiring age seemed almost as remote and improbable as one's own death. Yet the time had passed—rapidly, it seemed in retrospect—and Matheson was now sixty-four and there was no cause to day-dream of his demise. Next year he must retire—the society's conditions of service required it. Sometimes Blackledge would wake in the night and be transfixed by the thought that in Matheson's case the directors would advance the retiring age, permit him to stay on as General Manager until he were, say, seventy. In the more rational morning he knew that this could never be. But the thought nevertheless continued to recur. And again he would sometimes frighten himself by imagining that the directors would appoint not himself but someone from outside the society as Matheson's successor: and he would mentally survey the talents and qualifications of promising men that he knew from other building societies.

But these were the rare bad moments to which the ambitious man was as naturally prone as an athlete to pulled muscles: for the most part Blackledge, believing in his worth, knew himself fated now, after the long years of planning and propaganda, to become in a little while the society's chief executive. And he saw clearly and excitingly the new era stretching ahead of reforms and power and increased income.

The General Manager said: 'That photograph flattered George Sutcliffe, though you might not think so. In actual fact, with his beard and the close-cut dark hair, he looked like the figure on a packet of "Monkey Brand". But I don't suppose you remember "Monkey Brand", Blackledge?'

'No, I don't,' said Blackledge.

'It was a sort of cleaning substance in a cake. Used to clean everything—except textiles. There was a comic song in my young days, about a housewife: "They call her 'Monkey Brand' because she won't wash clothes." That was a line from it—quite funny at the time when everyone used "Monkey Brand".'

Blackledge smiled accommodatingly. More and more these days he realized that the society's great progress had been made almost in spite of Matheson. He was getting senile: these absurd one-sided conversations about the past were quite common, indeed, almost the only possible way of passing the time with Matheson. And what did Matheson actually do in the office? Blackledge asked himself. The old man could drop out of the society and no one would know he had gone.

Matheson stubbed out his cigarette slowly and daintily. 'I wonder what happened to "Monkey Brand",' he said concernedly.

Blackledge played his part. 'I suppose detergents will be forgotten some day,' he said.

The General Manager rose. 'If Gerson comes in to tea while you're here, tell him I've gone home, will you? He wanted to see me. It will have to be the morning now.'

Matheson had never really become accustomed to the internal telephone system. 'Yes, sir,' Blackledge said. He watched the General Manager go out, shook his head pityingly, and then looked to see what cakes were left.

Philip Witt's office and the rooms that housed his small staff were at the rear of the ground floor of Saddleford House, so as to be conveniently near the great strongrooms in the basement containing the 40,000 bundles of deeds of the properties on which the society had made mortgage advances. Witt's title was Head Office Solicitor: his department controlled the deeds, looked after the society's domestic legal affairs, and kept an eye on the work of the solicitors on the society's panel throughout the country who acted for the society in its ordinary business of mortgage lending.

Witt's office was dark: the windows were screened from the side street by half curtains of billiard-table green running on brass rods. Opposite his desk towered a mahogany bookcase which had been in the society's possession almost from its foundation, and beside it was a large iron safe, pitted with erosion. Witt signed the last of his letters and handed it to his secretary.

'Will that be all, Mr. Witt?' she asked.

Witt smiled, and the effort made him feel virtuous. 'Yes, Miss Whitehead.'

'Good night, Mr. Witt,' she said.

He said good night and when she was out of the room stretched his legs under the desk, put his hands behind his head and closed his eyes. His face was very smooth, his pallor had an olive tinge: against it the moustache seemed incongruously luxuriant and brown. He thought of his preposterously sleepless night and his careful negotiation of the day, using what energy had been left to him with the parsimony of a working class housewife at the end of her week. And now, when at last he could go home and allow himself to fall into the mindless stupor for which he had craved all day, he saw that his private life could in reality afford him no relaxation, and the evening stretched before him like a boring mountain which yet required stupendous qualities of nerve to ascend.

Often he seemed to himself much older than his thirty-three years: even after a good night his heart might at any time start alarmingly to palpitate and he would put his hand against it, feeling the unreasonable hollows under his breast and knowing, with a wry despair, how far his body was from being the decent machine for carrying him adequately through existence. In such moments he might even dream of a régime of exercise as of a marvellous physician or of a new life away from the affections that had made him what he was.

The internal telephone rang, startling him. He picked up the receiver almost guiltily. At the other end was Blackledge's voice. 'Philip? I was going to have a word with you at tea time but I seem to have missed you.'

Witt said: 'I had a cup of tea in my room.' He made the confession reluctantly, as though Blackledge might deduce from it the disgraceful secret of his insomnia, the oppressions of his private life, everything that gave the lie to his conventionally successful pose as solicitor to the society.

Blackledge passed the clue over. 'Ah,' he said. 'I wonder if you could spare me a few moments now?'

'Yes,' said Witt. 'I'll come up.'

'Will you?' said Blackledge, indicating simultaneously that he wished to infer that Witt was conferring a favour on him by saving him the journey to Witt's office, and that he thought his seniority nevertheless demanded that any journey should be made by Witt.

'Certainly,' said Witt.

It was five-thirty and the corridors were choked with the homeward rush of clerks. There was a smell of plastic raincoats, face powder, cigarette smoke. Witt edged his way to the lifts against the stream, his exhaustion making him preternaturally aware of every face, every tone of voice. He saw once again how his weaknesses turned his life into art and felt a sudden warm affection and pity for this mass of humanity, seeing vaguely but surely how he could find the words to depict the rush through the grey evening to the separate worlds of love, habit and pain.

The second floor was already deserted and outside the lift gates a charwoman was expunging the dust of the day with arcs of her wet cloth. A phrase began to form in Witt's head but before it was fixed in his memory he was opening the door of Blackledge's office. The smoke from the Mortgage Manager's pipe hung in wreaths against the last gleam of sun which shot through a low aperture in the clouds and brightened the window panes.

'It's very good of you, Philip,' Blackledge said. 'I'm not keeping you, am I?'

'No,' said Witt, conscious of his pallor in the light and moving a chair out of it before he sat down. 'Of course not, Stuart.' He wondered if Blackledge's solicitude for others seemed as false to everyone as it always did to him.

Blackledge threw himself back in his seat and smiled winningly as though to indicate that what was to follow was not business but the beginning of leisure, the pleasures of the evening. He said: 'I want you to give me a child's guide to this business of lending on separate flats, Philip.'

'That's an old story,' said Witt, trying to keep the weariness out of his voice.

'I know,' said Blackledge, ingratiatingly, 'but I always forget it. Let me put you in the picture. Cecil Hepworth is going to build three blocks of flats just outside Manchester. A nice site and I think he'll get the buyers. It's good business and I want it for the society.'

'The Board won't advance on individual flats.'

'They haven't advanced on separate flats since the

war,' said Blackledge. 'But then very few have gone up. We've certainly never been offered any as good as these. There's absolutely no objection from the security point of view. But I've got to sell the Board a way out of the legal snags. Now what are the points—in two words?'

'Well,' said Witt, 'it's quite clear that you can have a freehold interest in the floor of a building. The difficulty is to protect the owner of the one floor against the possibility of the rest of the place falling into decay.'

'Can it be done?' asked Blackledge, pointing the stem of his pipe as though to the heart of the question.

'Not practically. There's no doubt at all that the better way is to create long leasehold interests in the separate flats—99 or 999 years. You see that the leases are properly drawn to contain covenants by the leaseholder to support the flat above and maintain his own so that it doesn't fall in on the flat below.'

'And you can't do that with freehold flats?'

'No. The burden of the covenants can't be passed on to subsequent owners of the flats. Even if you make them leasehold the owners are only liable under their covenants to the freeholder.'

'My God, Philip, you make it sound complicated!'

'It's much more complicated, really. This *is* the child's guide.'

'Well, now,' said Blackledge, knocking the bowl of his pipe against his signet ring. 'What's the answer? There must *be* an answer: flats *have* been built and sold separately.'

Witt felt his voice lying behind his tongue, like some frightful obstruction which he could not regurgitate. It was not only his exhaustion which called for this heroic effort to behave normally, even more it was the monstrous ennui the subject induced in him. Before he spoke, his brain made a feeble effort to retrace the complicated and compulsive steps that had led him to this building, this chair, this conversation. 'I'm afraid I take a simple view of the thing,' he said. 'If flats are well-built, in the right situation and sold to reasonable people, they don't usually fall down—at any rate during the currency of a building society mortgage.'

'In other words,' said Blackledge, 'Colonel Bogey the legal problems.'

'You put the point precisely,' said Witt.

Blackledge assumed a grave air to conceal his delight at having grasped the issue: it had become a part of his nature always to show the world, as befitted his position in it, a dignified exterior. 'I'm much obliged to you, Philip. I don't think we need go any further.'

Witt thought of asking Blackledge if he were satisfied that flats which were probably going to be sold to workers in the perilous textile industry justified the by-passing of the legal difficulties and then decided that it was insufficiently his business to justify the effort it would cost him. Besides, it was clear that Blackledge had made up his mind, and he never changed it. He rose, and said good night.

'Good night, Philip,' Blackledge said, and before the other was out of the room his hand went to the telephone. He dialled the number of his home, and while he listened to the ringing tone he slewed his chair round so that he could see his reflection in the darkening windows, the white collar, the touch of silver at his temples. The little instrument in his hand reaching secretly across the miles into the atmosphere he knew so well gave him a sense of power and pleasure. At last he permitted himself to smile.

The ringing tone stopped and he heard his wife's voice. 'Rosie,' he said.

'Hello, darling,' she said, and he remembered the tension between them when he had left that morning. But he knew from her voice that for her, in miraculous accord with his own mood, the tension had dissolved.

'What about meeting me in the Queen's in half an hour? Ring for a taxi.'

She hesitated for a moment and then said: 'Anything the matter?'

'No. Just feel like a few drinks—with you.'

'What about dinner?'

'We'll have it at the Queen's. Nothing spoiling at home?'

'No.'

'Phone for that taxi, then.'

'All right, darling.'

'Is it?' he said, warmly solicitous.

'Yes, darling. It will be lovely.' She hesitated again. 'Do you really want me to come, Stuart?'

Already in imagination he was in the cocktail bar of the Queen's, poised masterfully on a stool at the counter, a cigarette between his fingers, the same fingers round the frosted glass of a Martini, the other hand reaching for a roasted nut, seeing in the mirror behind the bottles his own beauty and Rose's. 'What, dear?' he replied, absently.

'I wonder whether it's because of me or of you——' she said, and then broke off. 'I'll tell you when I see you.'

'Soon,' he said, his hand reaching out for his memorandum pad. 'Good-bye, dear.' She said good-bye and he replaced the receiver. He started writing on the pad: 'Flats should be leasehold, to ensure maximum effect of covenants for support and repair: but question fundamentally simple one. . . .' When he had finished he tore off the sheet and put it in his wallet. He rose. There was nothing to tidy away on his immaculate desk: he switched out the reading lamp and went along the corridor to wash his spotless hands.

II

On the main road south of Saddleford, less than two miles from the centre of the town, the Witts' house stood by itself behind blackened trees, in a district no longer fashionable, invaded even thirty years ago by cinemas, shops, offices. On either side of the yellow-grey stucco pillars that framed the front door were the bay windows of the drawing- and dining-rooms. Almost hidden by the bottle-green velvet curtains, Emily Witt was looking out of one of the windows along the shrub-lined path towards the gate. The scene was illuminated for her by a street lamp and the trams that hammered by beyond it. Once she used to watch for Philip's father through this first darkness, the house clean and orderly behind her, but at last she had ceased to feel the slight, almost pleasurable anxiety about his evening return from work: then Philip's schooldays had brought her again to this place beside the curtain. Now her son was a mature man but the anxiety had never left her and his return each day was a small miracle of recurring happiness and care. She was an old woman, for she had borne Philip at thirty-five.

Her pulses leapt as his thin fingers stooped to unlatch the gate and she stepped quickly away from the window.

By the time she heard his key in the front door she was sitting by the fire, her hands clutching a tray cloth she was embroidering, concealing the heavier breathing her movements had induced.

In the hall Philip Witt scarcely hesitated before going into the room where he knew he would find his mother. In his twenties he would, exhausted as he was, have gone straight to his room and locked it, prepared, strong enough, to endure his mother's reproaches for his neglect and almost anguished concern for his health. But he no longer fought against the inevitable boredoms and exacerbations of his life. And having given his mother the victory in her battle to treat him still, in his manhood, as a frail life which she could in some measure control, he found that she behaved in her triumph more reasonably than during the years of their struggle, so that their relationship had become bearable and he often forgot how much territory he had renounced to her.

'Hello, Mother,' he said, and gave her almost easily the kiss which once had seemed the betrayal of an ideal. She kept her eyes on her work, as her conquest of him and the time of their being together stretching indefinitely into the future permitted her.

'Hello, dear,' she said. He sat in the easy chair opposite her and watched her while she made a stitch. The third chair at the fire between them, straight backed, with wings, covered in the green velvet of the curtains, a linen antimacassar over its back, was his father's. 'Were you kept at the office?' Mrs. Witt asked, looking up at last.

'Yes, Mother. Stuart Blackledge had a conundrum for me.' It was a word of his father's, 'conundrum': he thought how easily he took on the colour of whatever background he was placed against.

'And of course you've got to please Mr. Blackledge.' The office became translated by his mother's mind into the terms of an infants' class. 'Isn't it next year he becomes General Manager?' she added.

'You shouldn't say such things, Mother—certainly not to outsiders. Matheson retires next year: it's by no means settled that Blackledge will take his place. They may appoint someone from outside.'

'They would never do that, now would they?'

He let her squeeze the topic out a little further. 'No, I don't suppose they would.'

'He likes you—Mr. Blackledge?' she asked.

'Likes me?' He laughed. 'It doesn't matter whether he likes me or not.'

'It does,' she said seriously. 'You've always been a little independent, dear.'

'I don't think Blackledge likes anyone except himself.'

'There, dear,' she said. 'You are too critical. I think you ought to go out of your way to be really pleasant to your future boss.'

'I don't fear him,' he said, 'and I'm only pleasant to those I fear.'

She looked at him mildly, ignoring his last remark because she did not understand it, and said what she had longed to say all the time but had tactfully put off because she knew how it upset him. 'I think you're looking a little bit washed out, dear. Why don't you lie down before your meal?'

'Yes, Mother. I'll do that.'

He wondered, as he mounted the stairs, why we are irritable when our wishes are voiced by others. He did not switch the light on in his room. The white honeycomb quilt on his bed shone in the diffused illumination from the road. The quilt, the heavy walnut bed, the wall-paper with its trellis pattern, the beige tiles of the 'modern' fireplace his mother had had installed during his adolescence thinking to cater for his taste, the lino-leum surround to the floral carpet—these things, he knew, almost blotted out the shelves of his books, the multitude of notebooks locked in the chest of drawers. It was cold, and creeping fully-clothed under the quilt and eiderdown, he lay unrelaxed, feeling himself far from sleep. And yet already the natural evening growth of power in his libido, he thought, had removed some of his exhaustion and was increasing his power to live. It was only in the evening that he approached his true self. It was just, then, that his daytime occupation should be carried on by the anti-self, should be hateful and laborious.

He felt his hands becoming warm against the silk of the eiderdown. The evening stretched before him like a long peaceful epoch he could spend in the empire of his own mind. He went over the journey from his office up to Blackledge and remembered the lost opening sentence of his story: *When he took up the breakfast tray he found his wife strangled in their bed.*

Philip's imagination began tracing out the implications and possibilities of that plunge into a hideously fantastic but truly real situation. Soon he fell into a light sleep where the creatures of his creative powers, now totally unrestrained, made him twitch and gasp under the coverlets.

After dinner Philip's father returned to his evening paper in the sitting-room. Philip followed him irresolutely. Mrs. Witt went, as she always did, to help the old servant with the washing up. Mr. Witt sat in the chair he had sat in as long as Philip could remember: Philip sat in the chair which custom had also sanctified as his. His book lay on the arm but he did not open it: he stared at the fire, observing out of the corner of his eye his father's legs emerging from the spread newspaper.

His father wore boots, well polished, the toes rather pointed, the uppers very soft. Above the boots Philip could see the bulges in his father's socks where long underpants had been tucked in. Beyond the silence of the room was the occasional grind of a tram from the road. Then Philip heard, with disgust, the noises of digestion in his father's stomach. Mr. Witt coughed and rustled his newspaper but continued reading it.

Philip's toes curled with exasperation: he made a dozen resolves to walk out of the room, the house. But he stayed paralysed in his gaze, not even daring to light a cigarette. Why did not his father speak to him—about his own business, Philip's day at the office, the local news? The truth was his father still regarded him as a boy, whose life and opinions were too trivial to be received seriously. Or, worse, his father looked down on the weak man into whom the boy had grown. His father's digestion proceeded, with power and mastery—like everything he did—and Philip envied it, hardly daring to admit to himself that he despised the health and extroversion it denoted.

The newspaper remained spread and elevated when Mrs. Witt came into the room. She proceeded with exaggerated quiet and self-effacement to her chair, and gave Philip a gentle, conspiratorial smile which indicated her appreciation of his presence and her pleasure at the improved tone to his looks which his rest and the meal had brought. Her son pretended not to have seen the smile, and immediately reproached himself for the pretence. But still he could not bring himself to look at his mother as she fumbled cautiously for the materials of her embroidery. The silence descended again, the trivial, stupid, tense silence of a family.

At last Mr. Witt put down his newspaper. 'Well,' he said, as though his remark were the climax of a long and amiable conversation, 'are we going to have a few hands of solo?'

It was his mother's complexion which Philip Witt had inherited: his father's face was red, with tones in the cheeks and chin that were almost blue, as though it had been painted by an artist with theories about the nature of light. His hair, still with much black among the grey and growing in tight waves, fitted his head closely like a skull cap. Archie Witt's tall, vigorous figure had grown stout in middle and old age. An ironmonger's shop in a poor part of Saddleford had passed to him as a young man on his father's death: his industry had made the business the leading one in Saddleford, with two shops in the town's two best shopping streets. 'Witts' was a household name in Saddleford, but the man himself had remained without the desire for other than business prominence. He was a member of the Conservative Club but never went there: he lunched at the Queen's but was on no more than casual terms with its prosperous clientèle: he had worshipped at the same church ever since he was a boy but had never played a part in its organizations. Almost every evening he came home to take his place at the head of what might have been a large family, its generations expanding, its tentacles fastened to half Saddleford's life, but which in reality had remained rudimentary and sickly.

'Perhaps Philip is going out,' said Mrs. Witt, looking anxiously at her son.

'No,' said Philip. He thought how easily, in theory, he could have said 'Yes, I am, I'm afraid.' The stultifying boredom that he suffered during the day had its reasons—his talent and lack of talent, his station in life, his upbringing. But there was no need beyond his own weakness for the boredom to be prolonged into the evening. With a rush of courage that even brought a little colour to his face, he actually added: 'Not yet, anyway,' and saw the look of pleasure that his denial had caused his mother to assume die rapidly out. He kept his face averted from his father.

'Get the cards out then, Mother,' said Mr. Witt, in the half-bullying, half-humorous tones he always used with his wife. It was a command not only for Mrs. Witt to go to the bureau drawer, but also for Philip to arrange the card table—arrange it close to his father's chair, with two straight-backed chairs for himself and his mother. While these movements went on, Mr. Witt picked up the paper again as though dissociating himself from the enterprise. The pack of cards and the bag of cowrie shells they used for counters lay on the green baize. It seemed to Philip that he was physically incapable of taking the proceedings further; and he lit a cigarette in slow pantomime to try to bridge the agonizing gap before the game should begin. His mother came to the table and sat with her hands in her lap: his father continued to read but Philip knew that he was perfectly well aware of how far the arrangements had gone.

There was a stupefying silence and immobility. Philip saw his hand that held the cigarette start to tremble and suddenly he could bear it no longer: he savagely emptied the shells out of their bag and ran through the pack to take out the club suit, that essential and lunatic preliminary to three-handed solo. Then he began to deal the cards, and at last his father folded his newspaper and let it drop to the floor. 'Count the shells out, Mother,' he said, taking up, as he always did, the cards one by one as they were dealt to him, so that the dealer was forced to concentrate on the task of not missing him.

'Solo,' said Mr. Witt, before the others had looked at their cards.

From below his half-lowered lids Philip watched his father's hands, covered with harsh skin that held the same blue tones as his face. Why do I hate you? he thought, and could find no better reasons than his father's habits and physique. And then, choking down his revulsion, he bent all his concentration on the play of the cards—the same wasteful, conscientious and self-destructive concentration that he brought to his work as a lawyer.

When the deal had passed once round, Philip began to set terms to his participation. One more round, he told himself, and he would go. But when the moment came his mother rose, brought from a cupboard a dish of liquorice allsorts and placed them in the centre of the card table, and the action forced for her a reprieve from his departure. Just another round—but then his father gathered the cards so eagerly and wilfully that the words necessary to excuse himself stuck in Philip's throat. His toes began to curl in his shoes with anxiety.

In the end—rudely, before a hand was quite over, like a boorish boy—he said: 'I must go after this.' His parents did not speak and for a moment he wondered if they had heard him. When the last card was played and the losers had paid out their shells, he rose, straightened his tie, feigned to stifle a yawn. His mother looked up and gave him a purposefully tremulous smile, but his father gathered the cards together as though to continue playing.

'Philip has to go out, dear,' said Mrs. Witt.

'Is that the finish, then?' asked Mr. Witt, but obviously not expecting a reply, and reaching out for a sweet and then for his newspaper.

It was now that he should go through the routine about the car, as he stood close to his father at the table, but the words would not come out. By an enormous effort of will he stopped before he got to the door, turned and said in a strangled voice: 'Can I take the car?' The request was a formality: his father used the car only at week-ends, but Philip felt like a child asking for a cherished but impossible indulgence.

Mr. Witt turned his head and looked at his son. 'Carry on,' he said.

'Good night,' Philip said. In the hall, alone, feeling his freedom stretch ahead like a beneficent change of season, he wondered whether it could possibly be that his father willingly or unconcernedly granted him the use of the car, whether the sanctions and taboos that surrounded it were creations only of his own mind. For a brief instant he saw life as an absurdly easy affair in which other people were infinitely simpler than himself, and then immediately he was drowned in the waves of contempt and selfish love that swept always through this house.

The Eastwoods lived on the other side of Saddleford. Philip, high on the soft leather of his father's pre-war Rolls-Royce, drove there almost automatically. The wiper made a clear segment in the beaded rectangle of windscreen across which passed the lighted shop windows, the neon signs, the cinema queues, the floodlit rain-shining public buildings of the town. At last he had to switch on his dipped headlights—and the road started to climb between mean houses with the yellow rectangles of factory windows showing through the interstices of vacant lots. He was thinking still of his father, more calmly now, even wondering why he regarded him incompletely, not as one normally regards other people but as a Siamese twin its sibling—undetached, too near, intimately involved. It made no difference that Philip could tell himself, as he had often done, that his father was ignorant, insensitive, of vulgar habits: nothing could break the spell of power he radiated.

Now Philip had reached Bellsgate, the fashionable suburb high above Saddleford. He passed the end of the road where Stuart Blackledge lived and a little farther on turned the Rolls into the drive of the Eastwoods' stone-built bungalow. Behind the leaded windows and the velvet curtains of the sitting-room he could discern the glow of the light, and he imagined Christine Eastwood sitting on a pouffe before the fire, alone, reading a book of poetry from her own shelves or a new book from Boots Library, a title which he would know but would never think to read himself.

He descended from the car, shut the door quietly as if even now he wished to preserve the possibility of returning without revealing his presence, and walked slowly to the porch over which hung a lantern in Tudor style. He rang the bell and in a few moments the light in the lantern went on: then Christine opened the door to him.

'Philip!' she said. But it was typical of their relationship that, though they had had no prior arrangement that he should call that evening, she was waiting for him and not really surprised at his appearance.

'Hello,' he said, and kissed her.

She opened the door of the cloakroom as he took off his coat. When he had hung it up he rubbed his face with both his hands, conscious of his pallor. 'It's cold,' he said.

Christine said: 'Come to the fire.'

'Are they in?' he asked, meaning her parents.

'They've gone to the Royalty.'

He had been right in imagining her alone, and on entering the sitting-room he saw the fringed shade of the standard lamp admitting an open book on the hearthrug to its circle of light. It occurred to him that she was the sort of person who could be disturbed at any moment of the day without having something secretive, untidy or disgraceful to hide. In the room was the odour of the perfume she used, light, almost antiseptic. He sat on the over-plump settee: she went to her pouffe and scrutinized him.

'You look tired, Philip,' she said. 'Have you been working tonight?'

'No. Playing cards. With my father and mother. More exhausting than work.' He rubbed his face again, thinking how his mother, too, had shown concern for his physical condition.

'Did you sleep badly?'

'Yes,' he had to say.

'Oh, Philip,' she said. 'You can't go on like this.'

'But I do go on like this.' He imagined her train of thought—his neurosis has led to the wreck of his physique, it is well known that marriage cures a bachelor's neurosis, it was time that he married her. And then immediately he doubted her ability to formulate even so innocently common a proposition. All the same, to avoid the point being reached he added quickly: 'From the age of sixteen—earlier—I've systematically denied my body all its mechanism demanded—exercise, sufficient food, early hours. I've never regarded it as being me. So you mustn't wonder at its looking cowed and pale after all those years as an unwanted visitor.'

'You work too hard,' Christine said. 'I worry about you.'

'But my trouble is just the opposite—I don't work hard enough. My work as a lawyer is simple and I neglect my writing. If I could work hard I should be a normal man—like Stuart Blackledge.'

'I wish you would be serious with me,' she said, turning her head from him. He saw her profile against the fire, the thin skin of the division between her nostrils which came down a little way below her short straight nose and glowed pinkly. He stretched out his legs, the warmth subconsciously relaxing him, and said: 'I'm more serious with you than with anyone.'

She was pleased and tried conscientiously not to show it. 'I wish that were true,' she said, and then immediately, as though she wanted to relish her pleasure alone or feared that what was between them might descend to some intenser level, rose to her feet and added: 'I'll make some chocolate. You'd like some, wouldn't you, Philip?'

Without waiting for his reply, for the drinking of chocolate was a ritual she had inaugurated for the good of his health, she walked in her brisk way out of the room, and he was left staring at the place she had vacated, remembering the first time his mother had, speaking of Christine, used the term 'your fiancée'. He had said, not irritably: 'She is not my fiancée, Mother,' thinking that his mother had placed upon the relationship deliberately, prematurely, the permanency she feared, so as to have the pleasure of his denial. That was at least a year ago; Christine was still not his fiancée but they were now paired in the minds of a larger circle, their relations had deepened a little, and both of them were settled, it seemed, in a routine of quite frequent meetings. And she was twenty-nine, a fastidious girl who during her long nubility had had several friends of the other sex but had never succeeded in becoming engaged—in fulfilling herself according to the canons (which Philip knew she almost certainly accepted) of her milieu. She had been rather too intellectual to be on easy terms with her compeers, and they had perhaps been awed by her sticking devotedly to the profession of teaching which—needlessly, in view of her father's money—she had assumed after her degree at her provincial university. Now, at the threshold of her spinsterhood, Philip had taken up with her: accidentally, it seemed to him, for looking back he could not remember when he had not known her, or known of her, nor how the odd meetings at public functions, at friends' houses, had merged into outings to concerts and the theatre and then to these evenings at her house.

They drank their chocolate sitting together on the settee, the tray in front of them on a hexagonal table of polished walnut. She said: 'It's bringing the colour to your cheeks.'

'I've never had any colour.'

'Your complexion is like your mother's,' she said.

'Is it?' he replied. 'Yes, I suppose it is. I've inherited everything from her—except my wish to write.'

'Where does that come from?' she asked.

He said: 'One of my father's brothers had a bass voice and sang in the Huddersfield Choral Society's choir. I've never heard of anything more creative in my family.'

She leaned over to put down her cup and saucer. A wisp of fair hair had become detached from the firm bun high in her neck. In this moment, he thought, the subdued light darkening her normally pale eyes, removing the angularities of her face, she looked pretty, and he bent across her, took her by the shoulders and kissed her. He felt against his lips the slight protrusion of her front teeth, and remembered vaguely how he had seen her at parties in his childhood, a thin girl with plaits and a brace in her mouth.

He raised his head and she spoke, as he knew she would, a few words as though to exculpate herself from the guilt and embarrassment of the first meaningful kiss of the evening: 'You make me lose my breath, Philip.'

'Foolish girl,' he said and, though she would never know, meaning it.

He looked into the eyes which regarded him and then kissed her again. When he drew away she gasped exaggeratedly.

'Darling,' he said, and with the next kiss sensed her response, the pressure of her own lips, and his hand slid down her back, its softness in one so slim surprising him as ever.

At last she was reclining with her head on an arm of the settee, her eyes bright, her hand pressing his head to hers for more kisses. And yet even then she said to him in an interval between their embraces, so as to retain in her conscience the idea that she was in reality detached from this compromising posture: 'Would you have liked some more chocolate?'

'No,' he said, beginning gently to unbutton her jersey and then the shirt underneath. She offered no objection when he eased her arms out of these garments. Her eyes were fixed on him virginally and confidently as her bosom was uncovered. To this point they had come months ago and had never passed it: like a nurse walking with an invalid they went again and again to the limit of what, in her estimation, was judicious—though the patient longed to try his strength in further explorations, the nurse through her superior moral and physical control was supreme.

As they lay there they heard voices suddenly outside the window. They rose in horror and Christine said: 'It's them.' He went to the door of the sitting-room with the desperate idea of holding it against her parents should they prematurely try to enter. By the fire, naked to the waist, she was feverishly pulling out the right way the sleeves of her shirt and jersey, and even in this moment the long view of her brought the blood to his throat.

'I never expected . . .' she whispered across at him.

'For God's sake hurry,' he breathed.

As the voices sounded in the hall she was fastening her jersey and he strode back from the door, snatching her brassière from the settee and cramming it into his pocket. When Mr. Eastwood entered they were in the not unexpected nor unbecoming state of almost imperceptibly dishevelled awkwardness usual in a couple left alone for the evening.

Mr. Eastwood was rubbing his hands. 'Hello, Philip,' he said. 'Saw your pantechnicon in the drive.'

As Philip greeted him he felt that the years had rolled away and he was back in his adolescence. It seemed to him that Christine's father, treating his daughter as a young girl still, adopted the same attitude to her friends, and Philip always found it impossible to assert his years, his position, his real self.

'I thought you were going back with Uncle George after the show,' Christine said, in the cold and complaining voice she often used with her parents.

'We were,' said Mr. Eastwood, 'but your mother had a splitting headache so we came straight home. How's the money-lending business, Philip?'

Philip made a suitable reply. Mr. Eastwood was a short, stout, well-scrubbed man, who wore a pearl pin in his tie and pointed highly-polished shoes on his small feet. He had settled himself comfortably in one of the armchairs: a man completely without embarrassment, undisconcertable, happy.

'What was the show like, Daddy?' asked Christine.

'Very good,' said Mr. Eastwood, promptly.

'*The Desert Song*, isn't it?' said Philip.

'Yes,' said Mr. Eastwood. 'Saddleford Amateurs. Very good show. Are you going?'

Philip was saved the necessity of a slightly disingenuous reply by the entry of Mrs. Eastwood, a lean, yellowish woman whom he feared. Before she spoke to him she said to Christine: 'You left the hot plate on.'

Christine said: 'It hasn't been on for long. I made some chocolate for us.'

'How is your headache, Mrs. Eastwood?' asked Philip.

'Splitting,' said Mrs. Eastwood. 'And our seats were

far too near the orchestra. Absolutely on top of the drums.'

'Well, you like to be near, you know,' said Mr. Eastwood cheerfully.

Mrs. Eastwood did not reply to this remark. 'Do you want tea?' she inquired of Christine, intending, but too irritable, to include her daughter's friend.

Christine looked at Philip.

'Not for me, thank you,' said Philip.

'I'll come and help,' said Christine, and the two women went out of the room.

Philip sat down tentatively and offered his cigarettes to Mr. Eastwood. 'Not before supper, thanks,' said Mr. Eastwood, and hummed a few bars from *The Desert Song*. Then he said: 'How are your mother and father keeping?'

While they talked Christine came in with sandwiches, and a cake on a silver cakestand. Philip rose nervously and said too eagerly: 'I think I had better be off.'

'You'll have something to eat before you go?' asked Mr. Eastwood.

'No, thank you,' said Philip, and made his adieus, conscious of his failure to impress or even get on any sort of terms with Mr. Eastwood. 'Say good night to your mother for me,' he instructed Christine in an audible voice as they walked out of the room together.

He got his coat from the closet and they went as they always did when her parents were in the house into the little space between the front and hall doors. Christine closed the hall door behind them.

'Oh, Philip,' she said, in the half light, 'wasn't it awful?' And she hid her head on his shoulder.

'No,' he said reassuringly. 'Not awful.'

'It was typical of them not to go to Uncle's. They never do what they say they will do. I should have known.'

'The aged are always changing their minds,' said Philip.

'It was awful,' she said again.

He kissed her and his hands, circling her beneath her jersey and loosened shirt, encountered no obstacle on their way to the deep division of her back and then across the perceptible ribs.

'I must go,' she said, and drew away from him.

He was reminded to pull the brassière out of his pocket and give it to her. 'I'll ring you, darling,' he said.

'Yes,' she said, her mind already back on her parents in the house. 'Good-bye, darling.'

He said, buttoning his overcoat: 'Toodleoo, said the elder Miss Fagin.' Before he reached the car he heard the door close and half turned to see the light go out in the Tudor lantern. Almost at once he reassumed his true identity. The rain had stopped: over a few yellow points of stars, thin but extensive clouds, whitened by the hidden moon, were moved by the wind. Briefly he thought of the inconclusiveness of his relations with Christine, when he might see her again, the monolithic stupidity of her domestic background; but as his desire for her died in the cold air he thought of his room, the desk light illuminating the sheets of paper, his father and mother asleep. Like a substantial coin found in the pocket of an old suit, a mysterious energy dissipated the last remnants of his weariness and he hastened the car towards the hours of invention that lay ahead.

In the early hours of the following morning Stuart Blackledge suddenly awoke. It was astonishing that he could open his eyes without effort and see the luminous dial of the alarm clock marking the unspeakable hour of four. Then he remembered the previous evening's drinking. Sometimes it made you sleep, sometimes it woke you up. He switched on the bedside lamp and went to the bathroom.

As he watched himself in the mirror drink a glass of water he was conscious of a seed of discomfort lodged in his feelings and tried, with a brain that seemed preternaturally clear, to work out what it was. He was still perhaps a trifle drunk, but only in his legs: his stomach was in perfect order. He thought of the office, but all that came to him was the little business about the garage spaces and he had now settled that satisfactorily. He imagined the future—Matheson's retirement, his own appointment, sitting in the General Manager's office at the centre of the web. It all seemed obvious and ordained. He ran his fingers through his hair: the dishevelled look was entirely uncharacteristic but not unbecoming.

Yet the seed remained. He remembered how last night he had driven from the office to the Queen's; looked in the men's snuggery for a quick one before going up to the cocktail bar, spoken to Mason, the solicitor; had said to him, with a curious satisfaction, putting down his empty glass, that he must move on to his missus. And how Rose, obeying his will, fulfilling the tenuous promise of her voice on the telephone, had soon come to him. They had had a good many Martinis, had met up by chance with young Kirby-Smith and his wife, dined with them in the Queen's grill room, had drunk three bottles between them of his favourite hock. Rose had driven the car home and, watching her gloved hands on the wheel, her nylon ankle on the clutch, he had hardly been able to wait to get to bed with her.

And yet it was not simple. Perhaps as one approached middle age it was not enough to gratify merely one's own desires. He had a gnawing sense that he had not measured up to the stature he wished to present to her—as though he had omitted to mark suitably an anniversary she regarded as of vast importance. He thought back, and wondered if their difference of the previous morning had never really healed for her and still smarted under the bandage of the drinks, the smoked salmon and fillet steak, the rather drunken embraces. And now he could not even recall the precipitating cause of that difference. That, too, was a sign of the maturity of their relationship; once, they would never have allowed a quarrel to disappear merely by lapse of time—it had to be violently exorcised, one side or the other, in the end, making an abject and loving concession.

He sighed and turned out the bathroom light. Sometimes Rose was a little hard, did not quite appreciate that after all a woman must give way to, must nourish and respect, a man who had to fight in the thickest part of the battle of the outside world. There were comparatively few men in England, certainly in the provinces, with the prospect, as he had, of earning a Cabinet Minister's salary in their early forties. All women loved luxury and security but some (and Rose was among them) were not quite willing to pay the full price for them.

In their bedroom the light over the bed illuminated the bed-head, quilted in an ivory, silky material, the crumpled pillows, Rose's dark hair. Stuart Blackledge climbed carefully into bed and switched out the light.

Rose did not stir and he felt a little stab of envy at hearing her calm, deep breathing. He settled his head on the pillow and deliberately set his mind to contemplate something pleasurable. He thought of his part in the agenda of tomorrow's Board Meeting and soon he drifted off to sleep.

III

Several lines of demarcation could be drawn among the members of the Board of the Saddleford Building Society, but the most obvious was that which separated the survivors of the old school of directors from those who had been appointed during and after the great growth of the society, which had corresponded to the great growth in speculative house-building in the nineteen-twenties and thirties. The old directors had been chapel men whose horizons were Saddleford and their own businesses and whose personal circumstances had been no more than modestly prosperous. The new directors were often businessmen with seats on the boards of commercial companies, and where they were professional men they had a sideline of politics or commercial interests or both. Some lived far out of Saddleford, were at home in Park Lane hotels, had been knighted. The new directors were polite to the old directors, ostentatiously paid respect to their long experience. The old directors had long since given up their struggle against the new directors, had accepted the inevitable, and took their fees as heroes of ancient wars take their pensions.

After the fortnightly Board Meeting the directors and

senior executives lunched together in their dining-room. It was a comparatively recent innovation that immediately before lunch gin and french and sherry were available in a corner of the dining-room, and one or two of the old directors, still disapproving, made it their practice to stay huddled in their seats at the Board Room table until these offensive beverages should have been consumed and the soup be ready to be served. The society's chairman, Ambrose Halford, was a chartered surveyor whose length of service put him among the old directors, but he had long ago circumspectly allied himself with the progressive forces, and his appointment to the chair just before the war had been a compromise acceptable to both sides. His conservatism showed itself in his rather too-large moustache and stiff collar: his radicalism in his slightly sporting tweeds and glass of sherry. Stuart Blackledge had followed him out of the Board Room, seen him supplied with sherry and now had him in a corner, cutting him off with his outward-turned back from any other suitors.

'I'm going to shock you, sir,' said Blackledge.

'Eh?' said the Chairman.

'I'm going to shock you in a month or two,' Blackledge repeated, grinning amiably, 'with a mortgage proposition. You won't like it.'

'Come on, Blackledge. Out with it.' The Chairman had a bluff manner and was known for putting a 'damn' or two into his public speeches.

'Flats,' said Blackledge, raising his glass and watching the Chairman over it.

The Chairman lowered the wrinkled lids of his eyes and his face took on an astute expression. He said: 'Whose are they? Your friend Hepworth's?'

'You know about them, sir?' said Blackledge, not very surprised but letting his voice ring with astonishment so that the Chairman would be flattered.

The Chairman smirked. 'Yes, I know about them. I still hear a few things.'

'Do you like the idea?' asked Blackledge, this time over-emphasizing his anxiety.

The Chairman grasped one side of his moustache and then ran his fingers along it. 'We've had this before, you know,' he said, wisely. 'Before the war. It's not a bit of good, Blackledge. From the legal angle.'

'Before the war was another era,' said Blackledge. 'For house building and for the society.'

'I agree,' said the Chairman. 'But saying that doesn't get round the legal snags.'

Blackledge became immediately serious. 'Suppose I told you, sir, that the legal question boiled down really to the valuation question—in other words, lend on well-built flats in a good district and the legal problems take care of themselves.'

'But you'll never get a lawyer to tell me that, Blackledge,' the Chairman said.

'Why don't you ask that lawyer, sir?' Blackledge, with a motion of his glass, indicated Philip Witt standing by himself at the window, looking out into the square.

'Mr. Witt,' boomed the Chairman, 'come over here a minute. I want to take Counsel's opinion.'

Stuart Blackledge waited with calm amusement for the obvious outcome of the Chairman and Witt's dialogue. There was no doubt that he had won the Chairman over and his eyes moved round the room almost involuntarily in search of other directors he could lobby. He went into a brief day-dream of meeting Cecil Hepworth in the

Queen's, telling him casually that he had as good as fulfilled his promise, that the finance for his flats was assured. Hepworth was an up and coming man, a man to please. Blackledge liked his association with Hepworth and he liked, too, to feel that he could match Hepworth's enterprise and freedom with the power of the society's great wealth.

In the Directors' and Senior Executives' lavatory two men were washing their hands. The younger was a blond man in his forties, wearing horn-rimmed spectacles with thick lenses which rested on a snub, insignificant nose and almost completely masked his expression. He spoke to the other man in deferential tones and even, out of deference, accommodated the tempo of his ablutions to his companion's, so that he reached out for a towel a moment after the other. This man was Arnold Gerson, the Accounts Manager of the society.

The other man was much older, though his hair, combed very close to his scalp like an extra skin, was still black. He had a sallow face, bilious brown eyes and a slight paunch. He was the society's vice-chairman, Harold Ashton. Both were chartered accountants.

'I quite agree, Sir Harold,' Gerson was saying.

'Admittedly there is full employment at the moment' —Sir Harold looked in the mirror and passed a brush over his skull to flatten a quite imaginary out-of-place hair—'but that is still a consequence of the aftermath of the war. No thanks to these Labour chaps.'

'I agree completely, Sir Harold,' said Gerson, watching the other intently as though learning from him the secret of successful grooming. After a short pause he said tentatively: 'Don't you think it might fairly be said that the Labour approach to economic problems is essentially a reckless one?'

Sir Harold continued with his own thoughts. 'Mark my words, there's another economic crisis round the corner. Fuel or balance of payments—you can take your choice.'

Gerson nodded and decided, because it might savour of presumption, not to use the hair brush himself. He followed Sir Harold to the door.

'But you know my views, Gerson. It's no part of a building society's function to indulge in speculation in any shape or form. Look at Daltons—how many realized that *those* were speculative when they were floated?'

'How wise you were to insist in the finance committee that we shouldn't touch them, Sir Harold!'

'I believe some societies have taken a nasty knock over Daltons,' said Sir Harold, with satisfaction.

'I've heard the same thing,' said Gerson.

Sir Harold stopped in his passage down the 'quarter-deck'. 'In confidence, Gerson, there is one thing I bitterly regret, and that is that I didn't oppose with more vigour those loans we made on commercial securities just after the war.'

'No one could have done more than you to point out the dangers in them, Sir Harold.'

'Possibly, possibly. But sometimes I feel I didn't emphasize sufficiently the principle of the thing—a moral principle almost. The duty of a building society is to encourage thrift and home-ownership. Now that is not a commonplace. It is something that goes to the root of our activities here and I'm afraid some of us rather forgot it in those days when we had large funds to lend and few houses to lend them on.'

'You never forgot it, Sir Harold.'

'It's nice of you to say so, Gerson.' Sir Harold resumed his walk towards the dining-room. 'You are still keeping a special eye on those commercial securities accounts, Gerson?'

'Yes, Sir Harold.'

Gerson reached out to open the door of the dining-room and then quickly stepped back to allow Sir Harold to enter first. There was a haze of cigarette smoke, the weak sunshine from the window gleamed on the men's white hair, the crystal and silver on the table: the background of good navy blue, black and dark grey cloth was rich and sombre. A slight oppression fell on the room when Sir Harold was seen, even among his equals, for he was feared by some and disliked by some, though all in the last analysis relied on his brain and righteousness. In the most important grouping of the Board he was the neo-conservative leader, carrying with him the old directors and usually all but the most recalcitrant of the new. Polite but fierce battles for his viewpoint lay behind him, and the extreme wing of the Board now realized, if they did not always admit, that the full operation of their policies would have to wait until his death.

Sir Harold's mere passage past the table of drinks condemned it adequately as the resource of lesser men, a solecism, to be pitied rather than pointed out. He went up to the Chairman, from whom Blackledge and Philip Witt immediately fell slightly away. Gerson had not followed Sir Harold, but had remained conveniently near the waitress in charge of the drinks so that he could ensure that at the proper moment the machinery for the serving of luncheon would be set in motion—a thoughtful but superfluous concern.

'How is Mrs. Halford, Chairman?' asked Sir Harold, meaning, it seemed to the Chairman, Let us begin lunch.

The Chairman supported one side of his moustache. 'Nicely, thank you,' he said, and disposed of the last of his sherry. 'Well,' he enunciated at large. 'Shall we sit down?' He had a strong ambivalence towards these fortnightly occasions: he liked sitting at the head of the Board and luncheon tables but disliked having to attempt to battle with the undercurrents of rivalry that he felt in both places; he liked the deference and presence of his fellow-men but disliked the forceful, impersonal presence of the Vice-Chairman always at his right hand.

On the Chairman's left at the head of the reproduction refectory table sat the society's General Manager, exercising unconsciously his talent for gracing an occasion yet in some essential way being abstracted from it, invulnerable to praise and blame alike. He took a spoonful of soup and said to the Chairman equably: 'They've hung old George Sutcliffe in your room, sir.'

The Chairman had been about to speak to Sir Harold and he turned to Matheson rather flustered: 'Eh? What's that?'

The General Manager carefully explained about the photograph.

'I hadn't noticed it,' said the Chairman.

'I don't suppose you remember the days when he used to come to work on a horse,' said the General Manager.

As the Chairman listened to this story he changed his mind about telling the Vice-Chairman of the proposition to lend on Hepworth's flats. The Vice-Chairman might have decided views about it difficult to receive except with oppressed assent and, after all, there were other topics of conversation.

At the bottom of the table Blackledge and Gerson were separated from one another by a gaunt director with bushy eyebrows called James Furness. This director said to Gerson in his loud voice: 'Managed any golf lately?'

'I don't play, sir.'

'Of course you don't, Gerson. I always forget.'

Blackledge could not resist rubbing in Gerson's deficiency. 'It's not that you dislike the game, is it, A.P.? Just that you haven't the necessary repertoire of language.' This was a veiled reference to the Accounts Manager's patronage of the Staff Christian Union which Furness showed he understood by emitting his grating laugh.

He took Gerson's upper arm between his thumb and index finger and squeezed hard. He said: 'You ought to build up a bit of muscle, you know, Gerson. All work and no play——'

Gerson smiled thinly and turned the obscure lenses of his glasses back to his plate. 'I walk a good deal, sir,' he said.

Blackledge leaned forward seriously: 'I had a couple of rounds at Newhall Park last Sunday, Mr. Furness. Have you ever played there?'

'A lot,' said Furness complacently. He was the managing director of a group of woollen mills who had risen from the looms: in middle age he had discovered in himself an aptitude for golf and a passion for the superior yet democratic social organization which went with it and in which he felt not at all his lack of a family background and an educated way of speech. 'Do you remember the long seventh—the dog-leg? I hadn't been playing the game six months when I had a bogey five there. . . .'

In the centre of the table Philip Witt carefully acted

the role of the society's solicitor. He had once heard that a director had said of him that he was very silent at these fortnightly luncheons: ever since he had struggled to avoid hiatuses in his conversations with his neighbours, for it hurt his conscience to fail in any particular of his behaviour as an officer of the society. On his right hand was the General Manager, for whom he had an affection which he believed was reciprocated, and who presented no difficulty, but since Matheson, in his turn, obviously felt a duty to talk to the Chairman, Philip was compelled to grapple with his other neighbour, a director called Dillon—a purple-faced estate agent who wore bow-ties. Out of the corner of his eye Philip saw Dillon drink his last spoonful of soup.

As he had planned he said: 'Mr. Dillon, can I reach you some beer?' Bottles of Bass were grouped in fours along the table.

'Thank you,' said Dillon. He was a man only animated by matters relating to his own sphere of business and normally sat with his lips tight and indrawn as though preventing an hæmorrhage from his engorged visage.

Witt poured the beer conscientiously on to his thumb and said: 'I hear that the Amateurs are putting on quite a decent show this week.'

'Are they?' replied Dillon.

'*The Desert Song*.'

'Oh, that.'

The soup plates were removed and the roast pork and dishes of vegetables began to appear: the menu reflected the society's roots in petty bourgeois life. In the momentary interval there were one or two efforts to broaden the several orbits of conversation. The Vice-Chairman, whose lust for detail was insatiable, spoke across the

Chairman and asked the General Manager about the health of the Branch Manager whose quite celebrated gallstones had been removed. James Furness leaned forward towards an ancient director called Eli Barlow, sitting silent on the opposite side of the table. 'I saw an old friend of yours in Leeds yesterday, Barlow,' he said in a voice even louder than usual. Barlow continued to munch on a piece of bread, hypnotized by a salt cellar.

'I say I saw an old friend of yours yesterday, Barlow,' repeated Furness. With his eye he followed the lead from the box at the side of Eli Barlow's plate to the plug in Eli Barlow's ear. Furness blew down his hairy nostrils, leaned back and said to Blackledge: 'He's forgotten to switch on his machine again.'

Philip Witt cut the fat off his pork and thought how in a biography the details which make a man so like other men are omitted. His own biographer would never know of this luncheon, of his kotowing to Dillon's oppressive and boring mind, of how he suffered a continence of urine when the Vice-Chairman stood in the porcelain compartment adjoining him—nor even of the absurd and degrading interruption of his and Christine's love-making. His devotion to, his identification with, the vulgar aims of the society, and his engagement to Christine that for his part was scarcely an engagement at all, could appear to posterity as significant symbols, purged of all that made them real to himself. Even his dyspepsia could leave its interesting mark divorced from the gross materials which gave it actual existence.

He said to Dillon: 'I hear you have a Joint Committee meeting this afternoon, sir.'

Dillon unclamped his lips, but only breath emerged.

'Yes,' he said. 'The first of the new committee this year.'

'With a mile-long agenda.'

'Yes.' Dillon took up his knife and fork at the end of arms that filled out the sleeves of his jacket like those of a guy.

'It's very good of you to take such an interest in it, sir. I know the staff appreciate it.' As he uttered this quite unfounded remark, Witt reminded himself of Gerson. Was it in fact possible to keep his society and his real self in two unconnected compartments? Or was it not already true that what he had so often denied to himself had already happened—that his real self was now a hopelessly debased alloy? Perhaps the mere fact of surviving in a world ruled by values to which he could not assent guaranteed his inevitable corruption.

'The Joint Committee is a very good thing,' said Dillon. 'I'm only too glad to serve on it.' He emphasized his words by drinking off his beer.

It was only in such moments when the flat conventional response impinged on his own seemingly limitless insight that Philip Witt felt a vast astonishment, terror almost, at the views of the majority of society. So the civilized anthropologist, visiting the savages he has known only through the books about them, sees for the first time their instruments of torture stained with indubitable and recent blood.

The Joint Committee of management and staff was an experiment only a year old, an application to white collar workers of a device used by industry which had impressed the Vice-Chairman when he had seen it at work in companies where he had a directorate. Naturally, since the society's employees were not members of a trade union, the Joint Committee's deliberations excluded the question of salary rates, but it was playing a useful part in the realm of paper drinking cups in the lavatories and ping-pong balls in the recreation room. The staff elected its six representatives on the committee, the management nominated its three, who this year were Dillon, Blackledge and Gerson. A young man who was one of the cashiers behind the counter in the banking hall acted as permanent secretary.

At two twenty-five the management representatives made their way to the canteen where the committee met. One of the trestle tables had been laid with a green baize cloth and pencils and paper, and chairs ranged round it. The staff representatives were already present but (as a man shown into a dentist's surgery in the absence of the dentist will refrain from sitting in the chair) had not taken their places at the table. On his entry Blackledge went straight up to the two female representatives, who were standing together in a rather oppressed way, and spoke a few words to them intended to put them at their ease. Then he turned and cracked a joke with a bald man with jowls, a clerk in the Insurance Department.

Blackledge prided himself that without sacrificing any of the dignity of his appearance he had the gift of approaching the staff on such occasions on terms of comradeship, and it was noticeable to him that Dillon and Gerson remained together, a little apart—no doubt through the former's stolidity and the latter's austerity and coldness. Though, Blackledge thought, an unfriendly commentator might fuse the austerity and coldness and call it misery. When Blackledge had finished his little tour of goodwill he glanced inquiringly at Dillon who nodded his purple face.

'It's half past two, ladies and gentlemen,' said Blackledge, 'shall we take our seats?'

There were a few moments of hesitancy, confusion and scraping chairs. When it was over it could be seen that the chair at the head of the table was vacant. To the right of it sat the secretary with his papers, on the left was Dillon, and next to him Gerson: Blackledge was democratically among the ruck towards the bottom. When everyone was settled there was a little silence, broken only by the sounds of washing up from the kitchen behind the canteen.

This silence was deliberately permitted by Blackledge, and when he had judged that it had made its effect he said: 'Well, ladies and gentlemen, we have to elect a new chairman, so perhaps you'll forgive me if I set the machinery in motion. Mr. Secretary, I expect you have the voting papers ready: will you please pass them round?'

The secretary rose and began to distribute slips of paper bearing the names of all the members of the committee. Blackledge went on: 'Before you record your votes, ladies and gentlemen, there is just one thing I have to say. Mr. Dillon does not wish you to consider him as a candidate for the chair. As the representative of the Board he thinks that his part will be played more appropriately as an ordinary member of the committee.' Blackledge smiled at Dillon and Dillon inclined his head in grave assent. 'Now,' continued Blackledge, 'if you will mark a cross against the candidate you wish to vote for, the secretary will come round in a few moments and collect your papers.'

Though it would have been an exaggeration to say that the election was rigged, Blackledge knew which way it would go. It had clearly been essential to make sure of a strong, personable chairman, capable of keeping the committee on the lines laid down for it. Some weeks ago, when the election for the staff representatives had been held and the Board of Directors had nominated the three management representatives, Blackledge had called the secretary into his room and asked him who was in the minds of the staff representatives as a possible chairman. The secretary, as Blackledge had anticipated, had not known. Blackledge had explained that Dillon would be a non-runner and how unfortunate it would be for the committee's efficiency if someone like Miss Hobson, a garrulous woman who always wore a mannish shirt and tie and was head of the Correspondence Department, were elected. 'I should be quite prepared to serve,' Blackledge said, 'and so, I dare say, would Mr. Gerson.' Two of the staff members of the committee were in Blackledge's own department. And Blackledge had also, when discussing Dillon's non-candidature, ensured that the director had understood that it was proper that Blackledge himself should be elected. A few days ago Blackledge had seen the secretary again and ascertained that now he was indeed enshrined in the staff representatives' minds as the fit person for the chair. Finally, Blackledge had told Gerson quite frankly that he had caused it to be indicated to the committee that it would be best for either he or Gerson to be elected chairman.

The secretary collected the papers and went back to his seat. There was a faintly embarrassed—it could hardly be called tense—interval while he unfolded the voting papers and arranged them in a pile. Then he began reading out the votes, pausing after each one while he recorded it in his rough minute book. Blackledge lit a cigarette.

'Mr. Blackledge,' said the secretary. 'Mr. Blackledge. Mr. Blackledge.'

It did not disturb him to hear his own name; indeed, it was something of a shock to him when the secretary said next: 'Mr. Gerson.' There was a puzzled split second before his reflexes told him that, of course, this was the vote he had himself recorded. Since his own vote would almost certainly be the only one not cast for himself it would be identifiable and therefore must go to Gerson: besides, A.P. was entitled to it as the next most senior member of the staff present.

'Mr. Blackledge,' said the secretary, and then, a moment or two after: 'Mr. Gerson.'

At first Blackledge thought that the wretched secretary had made a mistake, had counted Blackledge's voting paper twice, but a glance at the two piles quickly showed him that this was impossible. He felt a slight rise in the temperature of the skin under his jaw at the knowledge that one of these nine persons present had preferred Gerson to him. The bloody fool, he said to himself.

'Mr. Blackledge,' said the secretary. And again: 'Mr. Blackledge.'

Blackledge looked up with relief, realizing that momentarily he had been frightened that Gerson, after that totally unexpected vote might gain others, even all the rest and so secure the election. The office itself was unimportant: so far as Blackledge was concerned it could go to any member of the committee—except Gerson. Gerson, he at last admitted to himself, was too close beneath him in the hierarchy to be permitted any triumph over him. That was why, though the thing had been done almost unconsciously, he had taken the trouble to implant the seed of his own election in the minds of the committee members.

The secretary took up the last paper. 'Mr. Billington,' he read.

Blackledge was amazed: this time the warmth from his collar crept up his cheeks and he coughed to conceal this evidence of his emotion. Billington was the bloodhound-jawed man from Insurance Department: could he have voted for himself?

The secretary was reading out the result of the election. 'Mr. Billington, one vote. Mr. Gerson, two votes. Mr. Blackledge, six votes. Mr. Blackledge is elected.'

Blackledge rose and went to the chair at the head of the table. He heard himself say: 'Thank you very much, ladies and gentlemen. Now shall we start right away on the agenda: it's quite a formidable one. Item number one: minutes of the last meeting. Copies have been circulated. . . .' But his mind was still trying to work out the implications of the voting. If Billington had voted for himself, so could Gerson: that, with Blackledge's vote, would have given him two. But the thing was quite impossible: people on an occasion like this just didn't vote for themselves. Blackledge searched for the traitor who had preferred Gerson—Gerson—to himself. Almost immediately he lit upon the almost certainly guilty party: a young man with pimples and brilliantined but unruly hair called Crump. This Crump, Blackledge now recalled, worked in Gerson's department and was said to be bright. Too bloody bright, said Blackledge to himself: obviously Crump, too, had worked out the probable voting; realized that if he cast his vote for his master Gerson, Gerson would guess what had happened and be flattered. Blackledge made a mental note to have Crump transferred to another department; better still, to one of the branches.

But who on earth could have voted for Billington? Blackledge looked round the table. Not Billington himself, not the two men from his own Mortgage Department, certainly not the two women, not Dillon. Blackledge found himself gazing into Gerson's blind goggles, the great eyes of some prehistoric marine survival. By God, it was A.P.! A salt taste of rage rose into Blackledge's mouth.

He became conscious that the meeting was waiting for him and he looked quickly down at the agenda. 'Item number two: Report on the outing to Bolton Abbey,' he said. 'Mr. Secretary, are you going to make an oral report?'

The secretary started, but before he had got very far Blackledge said icily: 'Just a moment, Mr. Secretary. Will you go and ask the kitchen staff to make less noise with the crockery? There can be no reason for that quite intolerable clatter.' This was intended as a dig at Gerson, but was perhaps too subtle, for although his department was responsible for the canteen accounts it could scarcely be maintained that the injudicious conduct of the canteen staff redounded to its discredit.

Blackledge watched the secretary march across the canteen and thought: so Gerson dislikes me. He had never thought Gerson capable of any emotion at all. But there could be no other explanation for Gerson's extraordinary action. Blackledge asked himself if Gerson had realized that it would be possible to deduce the identity of the caster of the vote for Billington. The answer must certainly be yes: Gerson was not a complete fool. Was his action some sort of challenge? The first move of some planned and serious campaign?

The noise from the kitchen died suddenly away and the secretary marched back. 'Thank you, Mr. Secretary,' Blackledge said. 'Will you go on?'

Or was he, thought Blackledge, conscious of his own robust good looks and Gerson's weediness, attaching an unjustified significance to the incident? A boozy night, a fair hangover, a long board-meeting: it was easy to over-dramatize what might merely have been a sudden quirk on Gerson's part. Indeed, it was just possible that the vote for Billington had been cast not by Gerson but by some b.f. like Miss Hobson. Blackledge bent his gaze on this lady—on the frizzy grey hair, the masculine façade of the only too feminine chest—but she merely smiled back at him with the innocence of fifty years of spinsterhood.

Cecil Hepworth was tall, prematurely grey, with a Roman nose, and a chin that could not have been any smaller without being weak. Just before the war he had, on his father's death, become managing director of the building company his father had founded and immediately afterwards had built himself a house quite notorious in the Saddleford of its epoch for its advanced design. By now its concrete fascia had almost merged into the general Saddleford grime and time had made more commonplace its flat roof. Inside, some of the original décor still remained, the faded eyes and lips of a woman past her prime. In the sitting-room (to which Philip Witt was now shown by the maid) there was a black carpet stained by the infancy of Hepworth's children and a suite of sofa and easy chairs, similarly marked, as grey, and almost as massive, as elephants. The walls were painted beige and innocent of pictures; the curtains the green of a boiled sweet.

When Philip entered Hepworth came from his position by an elaborate cocktail cabinet to greet him. Hepworth's suit was expensive but unbrushed and his suède shoes were greasy.

'You know my wife,' he said, indicating a woman in slacks, with no eyebrows save for two asymmetrical painted ones, perched on one of the elephants' limbs. Philip nodded and murmured. Hepworth then introduced him to the two or three other guests, gave him a glass of sherry and took up the conversation where he had dropped it at Philip's entry. He was one of those ardent conversationalists with a complete indifference to another's interests.

Philip cautiously tasted his sherry, wondering whether he might not be able to make it last the whole of his stay. His stomach detested alcohol but he found it less embarrassing to suffer discomfort on these occasions than to refuse a drink. He gave Stuart Blackledge a black mark for not already being here: it was borne in upon him even more forcibly than when Stuart had persuaded him, over the post-luncheon coffee that very day, to come, that a cocktail party was a totally unsuitable venue for a discussion about the legal problems of flat-building. How typical it was of Stuart, once his mind and energies were bent upon some project, to bring in, 'put in the picture', as many supernumeraries as he could muster! For Stuart even the buying of a packet of cigarettes could involve his secretary, the society's telephone exchange, Ramsden and one of Ramsden's minions.

'He's a Jew, of course,' said Hepworth, finishing some

anecdote and walking over to Philip with the sherry bottle. Without Philip's leave he topped up the glass.

'What about little me?' asked Mrs. Hepworth.

'Are you drinking this stuff?' Hepworth inquired fondly.

'Yes,' said his wife. 'I had so much gin last night.'

Hepworth filled her glass, implanted a kiss on top of her bleached head, and took the bottle back to the cocktail cabinet.

'You have two children, haven't you, Mrs. Hepworth?' Philip asked.

She looked up at him through the bead curtains of her mascara'd lashes. 'Yes,' she said. 'Two little brats.' She was a woman in her late thirties with a long nose, who acted so completely the part of a demure girl of half unconscious and wholly charming impudence that it was impossible to discover whether in her true age she had assumed any real character at all.

'Boys?' pursued Philip dutifully.

Mrs. Hepworth nodded, her lower lip caught in her teeth.

Hearing this exchange, Hepworth strode keenly over. 'Where were you at school, Witt?' he demanded. Philip told him but he appeared not to hear. 'I've got my two down for Randells,' he said. 'I expect you've heard how good it has become under Gedge-Brown. It was always a fine school academically, and now it's got guts as well. And my God, a boy's got to have guts to make his way in this rat race of a modern world.'

Philip, his face cramped with false expression of interest as though Hepworth were breathing over him an arctic wind, not words, heard the faint sound of the door bell and hoped guiltily that it should be Blackledge so that they could reach the real business of the evening and he could depart. Like a member of some hopelessly oppressed and propertyless class in society, it seemed that he had insufficient insight into his plight to challenge the forces that drove him into situations like this so alien to his real self. He accepted the duties imposed by his office and his family not only as though they were fatal accidents of nationality or colour but also with a positive lust to execute them with the utmost conscientiousness of which he was capable.

'My boys have been thrashed,' Hepworth was saying, 'but we've never exerted any moral pressure on them for the sake of peace and quiet. The last thing we've wanted is to break their spirits and so we don't want to see them broken at boarding school. Do we, darling?'

'No, Cessie,' agreed Mrs. Hepworth.

'What about this talk of abolishing the Public Schools?' put in a man with a large horizontally-brushed moustache who was drinking beer out of a tankard at the other end of the room.

'They'll never do it,' said Hepworth. 'Half these Labour chaps are renegades from the Public Schools themselves. It's just window dressing—a sop to the working class.'

He was still speaking when the maid showed in Stuart and Rose Blackledge. After the reshuffling that this occasioned, Philip found himself standing next to Stuart.

'Could you do with an intelligent young man in your department, Philip?'

It was almost impossible to talk anything but shop with Blackledge. 'I might do, soon,' said Philip.

'Good,' said Stuart, pressing tobacco neatly into the bowl of his pipe. 'I've got the very man for you.'

'Who is it?'

'Crump. Ever come across him?'

'I don't think so.'

Stuart blew into his pipe to make sure he had not packed it too tightly. 'Works in Accounts Department. Bright boy. I'll get him transferred.'

'Won't A.P. have something to say? Bright boys are hard to come by these days.'

Stuart frowned at the flame of his match. 'We can't let Gerson's possessiveness stand in the way of a young man gaining valuable experience.'

Philip made as though to sip his sherry and then changed his mind in case Hepworth should fill up his glass again. He said: 'When are we going to talk about the flats problem?'

'You're not in a hurry to get away, are you, Philip?'

'Well,' Philip said, weakly.

'I want Hepworth to know we're interested. You being here is good propaganda. I know he appreciates it. We'll have a little chat later on.' Blackledge clapped Philip lightly on the shoulder, smiled at him round the stem of his pipe and walked away to join Hepworth who was leaning against the mantelpiece under a frameless mirror of curious geometrical shape.

There could be a story, Philip thought, of a father deeply in love with his infant child. But as the child grows in strength it also grows in ferocity—like the cub of a wild beast, and the father moves rapidly through the stage of admiration for his little son's health and power to a state of disquiet at the problems of management the baby presents. The cot is roofed in with stout cord, but soon even this is insufficient and the distracted father is driven to ask at the city's zoo if there is a possibility of his buying a steel cage. . . .

Below him and to his left Mrs. Blackledge presented the back of her head to him as she talked with Mrs. Hepworth on the sofa. He saw how her hair, cut quite short, fell gently into the hollow of her neck formed by the two muscles rising from her shoulders. Though he had met her a number of times, at functions held by the society, and less frequently on such occasions as the present, this view of her presented her to him for the first time as a person divorced from her official status as the Mortgage Manager's wife. He chose to remove the conspicuousness of his isolation by moving round, sitting on the arm of the sofa and bending a feignedly interested ear to the conversation of the two women.

'I go into slacks in November and never come out of them until April,' said Mrs. Hepworth. 'I'm such a cold creature.' She observed Philip's nearer presence and smiled up at him. 'Oh, you awful man, eavesdropping on a feminine tête-à-tête!'

Always helpless before such remarks, all Philip could find to say was: 'I'm sorry.'

'Do you know Mrs. Blackledge?' Mrs. Hepworth asked, and added immediately: 'Of course you must do. Foolish me.'

'All the S.B.S. wives know more about their husbands' colleagues than they do about their husbands,' said Rose Blackledge. 'They get all the office scandal—all of it that isn't to their own husbands' disadvantage.'

'Do they?' said Mrs. Hepworth. 'Tell me something about Mr. Witt.'

Rose Blackledge laughed. Philip revolved the stem of his glass and said: 'I hadn't realized that I might be an object of interest outside the office.'

Mrs. Hepworth was not one to let a feeble joke die.

'Come along, Mrs. Blackledge. What's the latest scandal about our friend here?'

Rose laughed again, less spontaneously, and Philip tried to think of something to say to hide his discomfort. Happily at this moment Cecil Hepworth called from the other end of the room: 'Darling! Come here, darling!'

Mrs. Hepworth uncoiled her trousered legs and tossed her bleached curls. 'What do you want, Cessie?' she demanded but trotted obediently over. There was a little silence between the pair left alone on the sofa in which Philip reviewed and rejected several observations he might make about the society and its people. He tried in vain to recall anything he had heard about Mrs. Blackledge which might give him a clue to her interests. She lived in Bellsgate, had no children: unpromising topics.

'Did you know the Hepworths before tonight, Mr. Witt?' she asked, and he realized that she, too, had been scraping the bottom of the conversational barrel.

'Him, not her,' he said.

She looked at him as at a strange dog one passes in the street that a moment before has been barking and then, apparently reassured, said: 'She has a trick of making you say things you don't want to—do things, too.'

'That's not uncommon,' he said.

She considered, and agreed doubtfully.

'Perhaps I mean that the weak or amiable person finds it not uncommon,' he went on.

'I must try to work out which I am,' she said.

'Only *vis-à-vis* Mrs. Hepworth, I'm sure,' he said.

She let this drop and said: 'It's strange since you and Stuart have worked together so long that we haven't met like this before.'

He felt a slight uneasiness at these words as though

they might be followed by some formidably boring invitation—a bridge evening, a poetry reading. He replied, avoiding her eyes: 'I think most of us at the society feel the dangers of mixing our social and business lives.' When he heard her laugh, he smiled and added: 'I'm sorry, Mrs. Blackledge, that wasn't very polite.'

'I meant,' she said, 'that although we've met before we've never talked to each other.'

'No,' he said, looking into her face for the first time and seeing that though her eyes were clear, light blue, her skin preternaturally clear and pale, her nose prevented her from being beautiful; and his feeling of apprehension was replaced by a stirring of interest.

'I used to know a friend of yours,' she said. 'Charles Tillyard.'

He was astonished. 'You knew Charles?'

She confirmed it.

'When?' he asked, as though cross-examining her.

'The middle part of the war.'

'Oh, I see,' he said. 'I couldn't understand how you knew him and yet I didn't know you—I mean know you apart from Stuart.'

'When I knew Charles you were in the Army,' she said.

'Yes, of course.' He fell silent. Then he said: 'You can't imagine how the mere mention of him brings back that time—the life before the war—that in one way seems impossibly remote and in another only the other day. He talked to you about me, then?'

'Yes,' she said.

'I met Charles in 1936 when I was nineteen. I was articled to Mason & Mason but law—the idea that I had to make my life out of it—had hardly touched me. I was living in a dream world of literature—the most pernicious kind of literature for me: Francis Thompson and Maeterlinck and—and worse writers I can't remember now. Then in a few months my whole outlook was changed. I'd always thought of myself as a poet and always tried to write "beautiful" poems. I never wrote a line of verse after I knew Charles.'

'I didn't know he was interested in literature,' she said.

'He wasn't. He was interested in politics, as you know. And interested in a curious way. As far as I know he was never a member of a party. In fact it was a shock to me when I found that he was acting as assistant to the Labour Agent in the 1937 election. Because the point about him was that he was almost entirely ineffectual. I never really knew why he came to Saddleford. He had some sort of interest in that pie shop in Sheffield Street but I haven't the faintest notion whether he acquired it after he came or whether it was the cause of his coming. He was separated from his wife and there were proceedings of some kind, but they never made any progress while I knew him.'

She said: 'And yet he had this influence on you.'

'I was ripe—over-ripe—to be influenced: the most repulsive kind of provincial adolescent intellectual. He showed me a world that I never knew existed. The first night I was alone with him we called on a friend of his who was an electrician employed by the Saddleford Corporation—a working class intellectual. Linoleum on the floor; old, badly-printed editions of Labriola and Engels at the back of the dresser. I was bewildered and excited. The two of them argued: "A man earns ten dinners a week . . ." Charles leaning forward, as he did, elbows on his thighs, and then the friend's wife coming home, after a rehearsal of *Elijah*, and making tea for us, with a doily under the plate of biscuits.' Philip smiled. 'It doesn't sound much of an intellectual revolution to you, I'm sure,' he said. 'It was the times, perhaps, as much as Charles, which changed my outlook on creative activity and my ideas about people—Spain, the unemployed, the flood of books and pamphlets and periodicals about theories which were no longer theories but practical politics. Though all this did not really involve me—I was never more interested in politics than Charles was in literature. Looking back from this distance it's hard to see just what happened to me.' A burst of laughter from the group round the fireplace caused Philip to turn his head and the interruption made him wonder, as he paused before saying what he was going to say, if he was being boring or incomprehensible. 'I suppose it was the realization that the writer—all artists—in our society must be dissident.'

She took him up on an earlier statement. 'He did have money in the pie shop,' she said.

'Dear Charles.'

She added: 'He was working there when I knew him.'

'The assistants must have been called up.'

'Did you ever——?' she began and got no further because Stuart Blackledge leaned across her and said: 'Sorry, darling—I'm going to take Philip away for a little chat with Cecil in the next room.'

Philip excused himself and got up.

'Try not to be long,' said Rose Blackledge to her husband.

'Darling,' said Blackledge, on the edge of irritability, 'we really have to have this discussion.'

Witt, marvelling at the gratuitous mutual exacerbation

displayed by all married couples, said to Blackledge as they walked away: 'I think your wife rather dreads being left with Mrs. Hepworth.'

'Oh, Bobby Hepworth's not a bad sort,' said Blackledge, dismissing the subject and leading the way into what was known in the Hepworth household as 'the den'. Hepworth himself was already there, switching on an enormous chromium electric fire which emitted a red glow through an ingenious simulation of coal. Too late Witt realized how incurious he had been about Rose Blackledge's own relations with Charles Tillyard and wondered, as one wonders if a plate of cakes will come round again to enable one to make a second and better choice, if he would have the opportunity of speaking to her later.

The walls of the den were half-panelled in urine-coloured wood. Above the desk at which Hepworth now seated himself was a framed certificate of his attainment of some position in the hierarchy of Masonry. He leaned forward, pushed aside a coloured photograph of his children so as to see Witt better, and said: 'Now, gentlemen.'

As Blackledge drove his car away from the Hepworths', he said to his wife: 'We weren't very long away from you, you see.' This was disingenuous of him because he had sensed in the brief time he and Rose had been alone since the party—standing on the step, walking down the path, entering the car—that she was displeased with him.

'No,' she said, dropping the match she had just used to light a cigarette in the ash tray on the dashboard. Even this innocent-seeming gesture contrived to show him that in her estimation his behaviour had been inadequate. A little patch of injustice ached in his chest. My God, he thought, there had really been nothing for her to take offence about. His voice, his words, had perhaps been a little sharp, even domineering, but wives shouldn't say 'try not to be long'—shouldn't, in fact, try to exert any influence in the sphere of their husbands' affairs. He decided to ignore the fact of her displeasure, let time wear it out.

In consciously even tones he said: 'I saw you having a long talk with Philip. How did you get on with him?'

'All right,' she said.

'He's a queer fish, you know—highbrow and so on. But quite easy to handle if you go about it the right way. He's been good on this flats question—there'll be no objection from him when I put it up to the Board.' Rain started to flaw the windscreen and Blackledge switched on the wipers. 'As a matter of fact I planted the seed of the scheme in Ambrose Halford's mind at lunch. Of course, Cecil has still got to get the licences, but he knows the right people. It will be good business.'

Rose deposited some ash in the ash tray and he gave her a quick glance. In spite of himself, he said with feeling: 'Aren't you interested in what I'm trying to do?'

'Yes,' she said.

'You don't sound to be.'

'Why are you doing this for Cecil?'

'I'm not doing it for Cecil: I'm doing it for the society.'

'Why do you do it for the society?'

'My dear girl,' he said, 'it's my job.'

'But what do you get out of it?'

'Well, the society grows and prospers,' he said, and thought of himself as the General Manager with a stab to his vitals half apprehensive, half happily anticipatory. 'You're rather wrong side out tonight, darling,' he added.

'Am I?'

He halted the car at a red traffic light and turned to her. He could not bear it, after all, that she had shut to him her loving and sympathetic self. 'What *is* the matter, darling? Are you vexed because I left you alone at Cecil and Bobby's?'

'Of course not.'

'Because of what I said?'

'You are always saying things like that to me and in that manner.'

'Nonsense,' he said. 'It's you who takes——'

'They're green,' she interrupted.

He threw the car bad temperedly into gear and drove in silence for a few minutes. He wanted to tell her that perhaps his nerves were on edge these days and that it was because of his age and Matheson's imminent retirement, and he was sorry. But some maggot drove him to try to hurt her, to prolong and worsen the chasm between them. He said: 'You don't help me very much, do you?'

She did not reply.

'I used to look to you to support me in my life. Now you seem to take offence at nothing. And show less and less interest in the society's business. It's unfair.' He thought of the voting at the meeting of the Joint Committee: from this distance he realized, almost with fear, that he had two enemies in the society. No one could have been fairer with his subordinates, more amiable with his equals, than he—and yet Gerson and his toady, underhanded and jealous, had wilfully blinded themselves to his virtues. Luckily they were freaks: among the great majority of men of goodwill with whom he had to deal they could do him no serious harm. But one could not help being a little shaken at the startling evidence of man's duplicity. He wanted, suddenly, more than anything else in the world, to tell Rose about the voting, to share with her the tiny, ridiculous, but very real burden, to hear her reassurances. But sensing the integument of disapproval which enclosed her, the words stuck in his mouth, and he found he could not confide in her. Instead, he said: 'Can you tell me why you should take offence at my merely saying that I'd got to have that private talk with Cecil and Philip?'

'You know that it wasn't that,' Rose said, wearily.

'It wasn't that,' he repeated. 'Then what on earth was it?' But his innocence was only partially genuine. 'What was it? Tell me.'

'I hate these scenes,' she said.

'Well, you make them, darling,' he said. 'Now what was this thing that upset you?' But really he knew and at last had to bring it out. 'Do you mean you were offended at my saying to Bobby that you weren't interested in the look of our house—or whatever I said?'

Again she did not reply.

'Well, my God, Rose, it was only the truth. You *aren't* interested. Are you?'

She was as unresponsive, as remote, as a cat. He was still wearing the almost-new black homberg that he wore on Board days: it hurt his forehead and he eased it back a little. Almost automatically he had taken the route for home. He had intended to suggest that they went to the Queen's Grill for supper, but Rose's conduct had knocked that idea on the head. He visualized the wastes of the evening that lay before him. Probably she would not eat any supper herself. They would read in their chairs and then go upstairs, silently undress and lie apart in their bed. He thought of the familiar moment when she unhooked her stockings and they fell, their flimsiness not quite responsive to gravity, half-way down her legs, and he marvelled that a few cold words between them could take the image so far from his possession—as though he had never in the past gone to her in that moment and never would again.

IV

As the spring matured into summer Philip Witt discovered in his mother a fresh and irritating habit—that of prefacing her observations with the words 'of course'; using the phrase particularly when imparting information of an unusual or controversial nature. It was with such habits—tricks of speech or little domestic innovations, like the substitution of mats for table cloth—that Mrs. Witt tried to get on terms with her son's intellectualism. These efforts to improve herself and keep pace with the new generation were to her considerable and satisfying but passed unremarked by her family and circle of friends—except by Philip, to whom it always seemed that his mother's conduct was notoriously ridiculous in its small variations from the commonplace.

Retreating to his room from these nagging characteristics of his mother, from his father's aged but still overpowering presence, he would often be unable to write until he had worked out in his imagination some practical gesture of protest against them—an effective gesture which would yet involve him only at second-hand. So in his office, shrinking from the naked contact with another personality, he would often deal with a situation which demanded a telephone call or an interview by deliberately procrastinating or writing a memorandum. Often, not entirely seriously, he had sat down and started to compose a letter to his parents about their intolerable family situation. 'My dear Mother and Father, At first you will be surprised to receive a letter from one you see every day—indeed, to whom you may have spoken a few moments before you read these words—but on reflection you will quickly understand that among husband and wife, parents and children, the intimacy that once existed—which may still exist—precludes the true, the greater intimacy which permits the real characters of the protagonists to speak their minds, exert their proper force, fulfil their dearest wishes . . .' But what could follow? After all, it was impossible to write: 'I hate your clichés of speech: I cannot bear your eating toast with open lips.' Or, rather, not impossible to write, but futile, mad even, to communicate formally.

In the family every emotion has its score of trivial counterparts. Soon after the war, Philip had let fall the suggestion that he should, for several false reasons, find a flat for himself in Saddleford. His mother had taken up the idea with an interest which had astonished him until he saw that her plans for him were like those of a man who, turning the Pacific and Tibetan pages of the atlas, proposes for himself specific but quite illusory itineraries. It was left to his father to voice the insuperable practical objections to his having a separate establishment and again he marvelled at the practical fertility of his father's mind until he saw that the notions had been planted there by his mother. And the objections, Philip saw only too clearly, were formidably well-founded. It was true that he had had a 'patch' on the lung; that he needed coddling; that it would be impossible to explain to his parents' friends that his secession was not the result of a quarrel between parents and son; that his parents were ageing, loved their only child and wanted him always with them. The breaking down of the vast barriers between himself and a free life demanded no less than his parents' death.

His imagination calmly anticipated this event because of its utter impossibility. For it was his love that had caused his mother and father to assume their gigantic shapes; and though his reason might see a future without them, emotion had shaped his life to accommodate them permanently. This settled state—settled yet tense—ruled, so far as he was concerned, his relationship with Christine Eastwood. He was content for it to continue in its ambiguous, frozen condition, just as when, in his profession he was occasionally engaged in litigation, he wished that the uncommitted, unurgent preliminaries of the action could go on for ever. He feared the decision of the trial.

He feared, too, as the weeks passed, the more rational attitude of Christine's parents, especially Mrs. Eastwood's. Though nothing of reproach was uttered, he sensed that they had decided that the time was approaching when the relationship should reach the conventional climax of a formal engagement and a tentative marriage date. Neither age nor money prevented it; indeed, had he not appeared to Mrs. Eastwood as the providential rescuer of their daughter from a threatened permanent spinsterhood, she would no doubt already have taxed him openly as to his 'intentions', as though he had been a philanderer or adventurer instead of one of the town's ostensibly most eligible bachelors. But already she was beginning to forget the inconveniences of her daughter's former unattached state and now that Christine had proved that she was still marriageable Mrs. Eastwood saw more clearly Philip's disadvantages. He had strange interests, he had reserves she could not plumb, she suspected his morals, he did not belong to any recognizable social set. These, perhaps, were all things that marriage could rectify, but marriage seemed as far off as ever. When Mrs. Eastwood hinted that everyone was awaiting the announcement, Christine became silent and uninterested, as though she had caught from Philip the vicious virus of unpracticality or bohemianism. Mrs. Eastwood continued to tell herself that she could, after all Christine's virginal years, trust her daughter, but she also continued to worry about her. The atmosphere in the Eastwood house had sometimes an alien electricity.

So it was that the three sides of his life he had created for himself (or, it often appeared to him, had been created for him, as though his existence were fictional, not real)—his ambiguous love for his parents and for Christine, and his profession, went on, like a symphonic climax too prolonged, in a tension that had become boring and ungraspable.

At the office his brain continued easily to deal with the problems that were presented to him. Because of his special position he stood outside the personal forces that played among directors and executives, nor were his affections much engaged by any of his colleagues. Sitting in his dark ground-floor room he would sometimes think that he was completely and paradoxically separate from the complicated activities around and above him: he might even push aside the lease or statute on which he was working, take a clean sheet of paper and write: 'At the demonstration of the torture machine it became, by a series of small accidents and ill-arranged appointments, necessary for the inventor himself to squeeze between the plastic straps or straddle over the chromium plated bars. In this unfamiliar position he was at first unable to direct the onlookers as to the order of pressure of the levers and for a moment his pulses thudded with anxiety at the thought that so many years of experiment were in danger of being wasted. . . .'

And then his internal telephone would buzz and he would guiltily lift the receiver, hearing at the other end the General Manager's mild voice—the deceptive mildness, it seemed to him, of a father which at any time might change to a righteous indignation against which his inferior status afforded him no defence. That no one in Saddleford House ever directed anger against him gave no reassurance of the comfort and dignity of his position. With his nominal superiors—the directors and the General Manager—he exerted all his concern to assure them of his conscientiousness, and not the least element of acting in this was his private knowledge that really he was not conscientious. His relationship with men like Blackledge held uneasily within itself the seeds of their possible future power. Nor were his feelings in all these connexions altered in the slightest by his clear realization that he despised his work and fundamentally despised all those who had surrendered to it more than superficial allegiance. Years ago he had thought that the sanctions and coercions of his professional life could never touch the realities of his existence—his writing, his reading, his private morality. Now he knew, though in a fashion he continued to struggle against the knowledge, that merely to get one's bread in the world of Hepworths and Gersons, let alone achieve butter on it, meant a life of such compromise as to make it indistinguishable from lives too ignorant and ignoble to know that the problem of compromise could exist.

With all his insight into his own predicament it was impossible for him to see himself as many at Saddleford House saw him—aloof, handsome, formidably intelligent, slightly alien in dress and appearance, impressive even on closer acquaintance because of his courtesy and infinite consideration for others. So the ordinary reader handles with respect and awe the finely produced book, incapable of realizing the author's fearful depression and hesitancy, the publisher's tight-rope solvency, the printer's and binder's illness and insecurity. The scandals and intrigues at Saddleford House, paramount among which was now the situation of the aged king and powerful barons—the question of Matheson's retirement and successor—were never communicated to Philip Witt: he moved among them with the ignorant purity of a fabled youngest son.

The Blackledges' house, one of the first to be built in what had now become the suburb of Bellsgate, was made of the local basket-coloured stone and its gothic windows looked out from an eminence of lawn and rock-garden on the reasonably distant chimneys of Saddleford's mills. At the side was a conservatory and above it sparrows nested under the eaves and in the aperture where the waste pipes left the bathroom. A mechanism existed for opening the conservatory's skylights and in summer they were left permanently ajar. One morning Rose Blackledge got up to find that a fledgling sparrow had fallen or inadvertently flown through the gap and now crouched pulsing among the pots of evergreens ranged along the conservatory shelf. It was the unnaturally loud chattering and fluttering from the other birds above the conservatory roof which had caused her to look for something unusual and so find the intruder. Cautiously she opened the glass door to the conservatory from the passage, tiptoed across the tiles, and opened the other door to the garden. Turning back, she saw their cat, Ludo, standing interestedly at the entrance to the conservatory. She rushed in a panic to bar its way and the suddenly-startled fledgling fluttered off the shelf and disappeared in a hole at the bottom of the rockery that lined one wall of the conservatory. Rose picked up the cat, shut the passage door and watched through the glass for the bird to appear and fly through the door opposite to freedom. It did not appear. The chirping from the birds above the conservatory roof grew very loud and urgent.

Rose shut Ludo in the dining-room, went along to the bathroom and told Stuart about the bird.

'Poor thing,' he said.

'Will you get it out, Stuart?'

'My dear girl, I'm in the middle of shaving.' He flourished his razor. 'You get it out.'

'I don't think I could dare to put my hand in the hole.'

'Dare,' he repeated, his voice rather choked because his head was thrown back as he shaved under his chin. 'It's a bird, not a scorpion.'

'I know,' she said doggedly. 'All the same, I simply couldn't put my hand in and suddenly feel it there.'

'All right,' he said. 'I'll come when I've finished.'

'Now,' she asked. 'It might go further in.'

He sighed, put down his razor, put on his dressing-gown and went to the conservatory. 'Where did it go?'

'There,' she pointed, keeping a safe distance. 'Don't hurt it, Stuart.'

'Of course I won't hurt it.' He got down on his knees. 'I can't feel anything. Are you sure this is where it went?'

'Yes. Feel all round, Stuart. Very gently.'

'I am feeling, darling. The bloody thing curves at the end and I can't get my hand round.'

'Try your other hand.'

'Wouldn't be any use.' He stood up. 'You'll have to wait till it comes out of its own accord. Look at my hand—it's filthy in there.'

'It will never come out by itself. It's too frightened.'

'It won't come out while we're standing here talking,' he said.

'It must be absolutely terrified.'

'Darling, it's nothing to get worked up about.'

'I should have seen that Ludo was shut up before I opened the door,' she said, miserably.

'Look,' he said, 'I must finish shaving.' He marched off, leaving her wondering whether she might not, after all, conquer her repugnancy, and try herself to reach in, feel the living, alien being and release it without injuring its alarming frailty.

Stuart, at length emerging from the bathroom, saw her still standing at the conservatory door. 'Darling,' he called, 'what on earth are you doing? What about breakfast?'

Reluctantly she shut the door and went along to the kitchen. When she took his bacon and egg to the dining-room his empty grape fruit hemisphere was pushed meaningly far away from him and his face was hidden in the *Daily Telegraph.* He let the bacon and egg rest before him for a few moments before he lowered the newspaper.

'You know I hate to be late,' he said.

'Sorry,' she said.

He sighed and took up his knife and fork. She poured coffee for herself and seeing this he said: 'Aren't you having any breakfast?'

'No.'

'Why?'

'I'm worried about that bird.'

'My God, Rosie, that's no reason why you should starve yourself.' He was a man convinced of the disaster of under-eating.

'The bird will starve in that hole.'

He ate a mouthful of bacon and then suggested: 'Why don't you put some bread down for it near the hole? It will come out for it, see the open door, and fly away.'

'Yes,' she said, putting down her cup and getting up.

'Finish your coffee first, darling,' he said.

'Later.' She paused by the door and looked at the cat lying on the rug with paws tucked in and a false expression of uninterest. 'Don't let Ludo out whatever you do.'

'No, darling,' he said, his eyes on the newspaper.

When he was ready to get the car out she was still at the end of the passage, watching through the glass doors.

'Good-bye, darling,' he said and kissed her.

'Nothing's happened,' she said. 'Could you have another try?'

He shifted his brief case to his other hand and looked

superfluously at his wrist watch. 'I'm terribly late already. And I'm sure I couldn't reach it. Get Mrs. Horrocks to help you when she comes.' Mrs. Horrocks was the daily woman.

'She isn't coming today. It's her sister's funeral.'

'Oh,' he said, and swung his brief case rather helplessly. 'Well, I simply must go, darling.'

'Good-bye,' she said.

As, with excessive vigour, he pulled up the garage door, he thought how unjust it was that he should be compelled to leave the house as though guilty of some inadequacy or even some positive offence. Women did not realize that the trivia of domesticity must give way before the demands of the more important and exclusively masculine world of affairs. All the same, the fact that it was possible for him to escape from even so foolish a concern as the trapped bird—that for Rose it remained, like a sick relation or a smoking chimney, something that she had to see through—gave him an uneasiness which was dispersed neither by his feeling of being badly done to nor by his slight display of temper with the garage door, the starter and a slow middle-of-the-road driver he encountered on the main road to Saddleford.

But by the time he had reached the first traffic lights and could see the blackened buildings, the bright shop fronts and the hurrying office workers of the town, glance down at the brief case and newspaper on the seat beside him, dwell a moment on his smooth face, tightly-knotted tie, brushed-back wings of hair in the driving mirror, he had forgotten the little drama of his home and looked forward to his day at the office—his mind unspecific but alert and full, like that of a well-prepared examinee.

At Saddleford House the Correspondence Department staff came half an hour earlier in the morning than the rest so that the post was already sorted at the start of the working day. Blackledge's letters, like those of all the senior executives, were delivered to his secretary. By the time he arrived they were on his desk with their relevant files.

He was not the first of the senior executives to arrive: Gerson was always there before him. Once this had quite perturbed him, as though in some ill-defined way it gave Gerson an advantage over him. But it was really utterly inappropriate for him to arrive before the post was on his desk, to make his way through the crowded and noisy corridors which marked the arrival of the ordinary staff, and soon he had come to regard Gerson's unnecessary punctuality as a disadvantage to Gerson, denoting a barren home life, an insecurity of position, a character he had once seen described in a magazine as anal-erotic, whatever that obviously derogatory term might mean. There was a sane and balanced practice in these matters: one ought to demonstrate that one was not the slave of the clock, at the same time making sure that Matheson did not inquire for one in vain.

Blackledge put his hat and gloves in the wardrobe in his office and ran the brush he kept there over his hair. Then he sat at his desk, filled his pipe and got it thoroughly going. The files and their relevant letters were piled at his right hand. On the heavy leather-bound blotter in front of him were the circulars, the memoranda, the letters, which were new or had no file to be assigned to. He took the well-sharpened red pencil he always used for annotating and for which he knew he was famous, and read rapidly through an information sheet from the Building Societies' Alliance about income tax, and a cyclostyled memorandum from the Premises Manager about the change of address of the society's branch office in Birmingham. Underneath the latter was another cyclostyled memorandum from the Premises Manager headed 'Garage Spaces'. It said that the enlarged garage would be available for use as from the following Monday and then gave, opposite their respective numbers, the names of the twelve executives who had been allocated spaces. Number 1 was Matheson, 2 Gerson, 3 Blackledge.

Blackledge was stunned. He had read the first few places at a glance and now tried to read them slowly and separately in the hope that his eyes had deceived him. A great rage filled his chest and throat and he snatched off the receiver of his internal telephone and dialled the Premises Manager.

'Blackledge here,' he said. 'I've just got your memo. about the garage spaces.'

'Oh yes,' said the Premises Manager. He seemed unaware of the emotion which Blackledge himself heard modulating and strangling his voice.

'Didn't Ramsden pass on to you the note I made allocating the spaces?'

'Was that some weeks ago, Mr. Blackledge?' The Premises Manager was large, without guile and slow-speaking.

'Yes, of course,' said Blackledge.

'Well, Mr. Blackledge, there was a lot of argument about who should have the new spaces. I couldn't get the chaps concerned to agree so I had a word with the General Manager and he took the whole thing out of my hands.'

'But this is your memo.'

'It's the G.M.'s numbers, Mr. Blackledge.'

'Didn't you compare them with my list?'

'No. Naturally not, Mr. Blackledge, after the G.M.—'

'It should never have been a matter for Mr. Matheson,' interrupted Blackledge. 'Far too trivial.'

'Well, Mr. Blackledge, in the ordinary way I shouldn't have dreamt of going to see Mr. Matheson, naturally, but there seemed to be a deadlock about these new spaces——'

Blackledge put down his receiver and sat for a moment staring into a chasm that yawned just beyond his desk. Then he took up the offending memorandum, walked rapidly out of the room and along the corridor, and burst into the General Manager's room almost without knocking.

It was empty. The desk and its fittings were as uncluttered as though Matheson were on a long holiday, except that in his 'In' tray there was a copy of *Illustrated*. Of course, he had not yet arrived, and when he did all he would do would be to interfere in trivia—and trivia which did not really concern him. Blackledge turned on his heel and went back to his own room.

Half-past nine: there was probably another quarter of an hour to wait. Blackledge could not face the papers on his desk: he looked out into the square, chalky-grey in the morning sunshine, his fingers in his trousers pocket automatically counting his change. The first shock of his anger began to recede and he thought how the others who would receive the memorandum—who at this moment were probably reading it—would at first be surprised and then gleeful at the vital numbers, as one is always gleeful at the catastrophe which does not involve oneself. Not that they wanted to see him discomfited, Blackledge thought, for he had always taken pains, where pains were necessary, to make himself popular with the staff—except Gerson. He was certainly not liked by Gerson and Gerson would desire more than anything to see him done down—provided that did not involve Gerson himself in any risky action. Had Gerson had anything to do with the memorandum, or was it entirely Matheson's thoughtlessness?

Blackledge tried to imagine Gerson working on the General Manager to obtain for himself the second garage space, but the picture failed to focus. And it surely could not be that all these years he had been underestimating, misconceiving, Gerson's character. He heard the door open and whirled round from the window, his pulses throbbing, thinking, confusedly, that it must be the General Manager, his mind as full of the memorandum as Blackledge's own. But it was his secretary, and quickly he said to her: 'I'm not ready for you yet, Maureen.'

'Will you ring, Mr. Blackledge?' she asked.

He said he would, remembering even in this hateful instant to bestow upon her what he knew was his charming smile, and she went out. He gave her a few moments to get away from the 'quarter deck' and then went out himself. But now he had lost the impetus of rage and by the time he had reached the General Manager's door he was halted by the thought that perhaps it would be quite impossible to change the offending numbers. And if it were impossible, protest was more than useless—it was damaging. Was the thing, after all, of no real importance to the rest of the society—a not uncharacteristic product of Matheson's dream world, scarcely remarked on, quickly forgotten?

He stood for a second in front of the General Manager's door, paralysed by the choice of the two courses before him. Then, after glancing round to make sure he was not observed, he strode back to his own room. As soon as he had made this decision he felt a regret that hurt him physically, a gnawing sense of permanently-missed opportunity, a consciousness of defeat that he could not remember experiencing since the weakness of his childhood. He picked up his red pencil and found that his hand was sweating.

The ringing of the external telephone broke in on his uncomprehending reading of a staff surveyor's report. His mind automatically framed what his response should be to some demand for an explanation of how Gerson appeared to be his senior, in immediate succession to Matheson. He lifted the receiver and said: 'Mortgage Manager.'

'Stuart, a terrible thing's happened,' said Rose. Her voice was unfamiliarly deep and broken.

'Rosie, what on earth's the matter?' he said, fearful.

'The bird's been killed.'

His mind returned immediately to the memorandum. 'What a shame!' he said.

'It was my fault.'

'I'm sure it wasn't, darling,' he said.

'After you left, the mother bird got in the conservatory through the top window. It made a terrific noise, chirping. And in the end the little bird came out of the rockery. It couldn't really fly, but the mother bird fluttered over it and encouraged it. In fact, showed it the way out through the garden door. And at last it got out, on the step outside the door, and crouched there, you know, looking round.'

Blackledge found that his pencil was making a nervous, heavy design on his scribbling pad: while Rose had been speaking he had completely changed his mind about the memorandum. He had decided that he could not let it rest, that he must see Matheson, and soon.

'I watched it through the side window,' Rose said. 'The other birds were on the conservatory gutter, very noisy, and the mother had come out and kept flying down to it. Then just for a moment I went away, only for a cigarette. I came straight back and saw Ludo with the bird in his mouth. I banged on the window but he ran off with it into the bushes. I couldn't find him—he must have gone through the fence.'

'Well, darling,' he said, trying tactfully to cut her short, 'how can you say it was your fault? Cats do go after birds.'

'Ludo got into the garden through the sitting-room window—I'd forgotten it was open. And then going for a cigarette . . .'

'Rosie, don't upset yourself like this about it.'

'It's so pathetic, Stuart. When Ludo had it all the others were making a tremendous chirping and two of them even fluttered over him trying to drive him away. And now the mother keeps coming down to the step, looking, and there's still that noise going on.'

'Rosie, please. It's only a bird.' But in his mind was the uneasy thought that perhaps it was not only a bird: in the year after their marriage she had had a child that had only survived three days and she had never wanted another.

'. . . so helpless,' she was saying, 'just crouching there. . . . And then how terrible for it to see Ludo and——'

'Darling, you must try to forget it,' he interrupted.

'I'll never forget it,' she said.

Matheson must certainly be in now, he thought, and soon he would be having his stream of callers. 'Look, darling,' he said, 'I'm frightfully busy. I'll ring you up when I get back from lunch, shall I?'

She said: 'You don't realize how terrible it was.'

'I do,' he said, shifting round in anticipation of returning the receiver to its cradle. 'Keep your pecker up, darling. I must go now. Good-bye.' He waited for a moment or two, but she said nothing. Half guiltily, half exasperatedly, he put the receiver down. What a time for her to telephone him, he thought: as though he had nothing better to do than talk about the phenomenon of cats eating birds!

At that moment there was a loud knock on the door: after a discreet pause it opened to admit Ramsden. He coughed and said: 'Is it convenient for me to have a word with you, sir?'

'No, Ramsden,' Blackledge said.

'I'm sorry, sir,' said the House Manager. In the manner of a courtier leaving royalty, he began to make his exit.

Once again, in an instant, Blackledge changed his mind about the memorandum. Obviously, it came to him, he must ignore it: he thought of his ability, his position, the goodwill he had earned with the overwhelming majority of directors and staff, and knew that pin pricks could not harm him.

'All right, Ramsden.' Blackledge smiled warmly. 'Five minutes, then.'

'Thank you very much, sir. It's very good of you.'

Blackledge held the hand with the signet ring over his

great ash tray and knocked out his pipe. 'What's your worry, Ramsden?'

'It's about my quarters in the basement, sir. The Premises Manager doesn't seem to be able to do much for me and so I thought I ought to see you, sir.'

'Sit down, Ramsden,' said Blackledge, sitting down himself and feeling for his tobacco pouch. 'Let's hear your grouch.'

'Well, sir, what I think is, my office is no advert for the society. . . .'

As the House Manager talked, Blackledge suddenly wondered whether he knew about the numbers of the garage spaces. Ramsden's face wore that expression of mixed innocence and guile which the faces of mature regular servicemen so often assume: it was impossible to read behind it. Despite the incongruity of his betraying his feeling before so minor a personage, Blackledge felt the heat rising below his ears. Could it possibly be that Ramsden's appeal to him over the head of the Premises Manager was a deliberate—even derisory—test of his power?

'Now yesterday,' Ramsden was saying, 'the traveller for "Shift" actually got lost on his way to my office. One of my assistants found him in the waste-paper store. . . .' The two knobs on the House Manager's forehead shone with the effort of his advocacy: the man was surely as honest as the day. Blackledge warmed to him, to his boring complaints, to the idea that to such men he was the powerful *paterfamilias*. By God, he would show that he was the man to get things done in this society: he would have Ramsden moved if it were the last thing he did.

The morning sun came round and struck through the window of Arnold Gerson's office. He put his pen down, rose, and carefully adjusted the blind so that his desk was shielded from the glare. Then he sat down again in his unupholstered swivel chair—the sort of chair that even those with the smallest pretensions in the society possessed. The walls of the room were distempered cream, and, except for a calendar from some missionary organization, completely bare. Gerson took up his pen and dipped it in the ink—he had never used a fountain pen.

It was quite unconsciously that he exercised the same parsimony with the society's money as with his own. A universal principle governed his life—that of provident management. It was axiomatic that a substantial part of both his own and the society's income should be put to reserve. He had taught his children likewise to save a fixed proportion of their Saturday allowances. Family outings were budgeted for and planned long in advance. He took the *Daily Mail* at home and read at the office the society's copy of *The Times*.

He had not, as he knew, a very good brain, and so he had trained himself to a pitch of almost terrifying scrupulousness. With the patience of Job he checked and double checked all his figures, wrote several drafts of important letters and memoranda, scrutinized and signed every communication that went out of his large department, kept an elaborate diary of reminders and anniversaries, saw that he had authority for any action that had the least likelihood of being questioned. His working day merged almost imperceptibly into his evening's leisure. He was always the last of the executives to leave the office and before he put on his hat and coat he would walk to the General Manager's room, knock on the door and open it discreetly to make sure that Matheson had really gone and would not require him again. Gerson loved the quiet, dimly-lit corridors of Saddleford House at that moment of the day: he permitted himself to relax, walk rather slowly, hum a little tune. Then he would pack some work into his brief case, walk down to the garage, start his pre-war Morris on the handle to save the battery, and drive cautiously home. The evening meal was high tea, which his children shared: over it he questioned them about their day's work and told them and his wife something of his own. Afterwards he took his brief case to the quiet of the breakfast room.

He had married his wife in the humble days of his career, when he was a junior clerk in a chartered accountant's office. His progress had filled her with awe and she completely accepted his domination of the family's life—a domination, however, which was exercised by a code of conduct so ancient and so natural to him that as a husband and father he exuded only mildness and reason. Very occasionally Mrs. Gerson was shocked by what she initially regarded as an outburst of daring extravagance in her husband, but which she grew to see as a far-sighted economy or tactical or social advantage: such was his first purchase of a car and, at the time the eldest child won a scholarship to a grammar school, of the *Encyclopædia Britannica*. These things were a mark of Arnold's superiority.

On this morning Gerson was analysing the last accounts of a company called West End House Limited, and preparing a chronological resumé of the contents of the society's relevant file. He worked slowly and thoughtfully so that he should be able to answer any factual question which the General Manager might ask when he put the matter before him. Earlier in the morning he had read the Premises Manager's memorandum giving the revised numbers of the garage spaces. He had not permitted himself to take any pleasure in or attach any significance to the fact that this was the first list in which he had appeared as second name in the hierarchy of the society. He knew from long experience that promotion came not through omens or accidents but by conscientious work and the assiduous service of truly important superiors.

The Saddleford Building Society's sports ground was on a hill to the north of the town where the new houses were beginning to straggle and give way to moorland quilted with dark, dry-stone walls. The annual Flannel Dance organized by the S.B.S. Sports Club was held in the large pavilion overlooking the cricket pitch. It was an event which the society's senior executives and even a few of the directors made a point of attending.

As Philip Witt and Christine walked from the car park towards the pavilion, the melancholy tones of the saxophone, dominating the little band, floated towards them through the still-bright evening air. She was wearing a camel-hair coat slung round her shoulders: since she slightly preceded him he saw that it was slipping off and he stopped her so that he could adjust it.

'You don't really love me,' she said. She spoke with her face averted and so quietly that he was not sure that he had heard aright. In the car she had been talking of her headmistress' views on the origin of the universe.

'You don't really love me,' she repeated for him.

Half a dozen replies sprang to his mind. 'Why should you say that?' he temporized.

'You know why,' she said.

But, he thought, he could conjure up several reasons. These moments were not unusual in their relationship, but some demon of weariness or contention drove the compromising answer from his lips. 'I don't think I'm capable of loving anyone,' he said.

'Why do you keep on seeing me?' she asked.

'I mean capable of loving in the way you want to be loved,' he added.

'I'm so unhappy,' she said, and looking at her face, transfigured for once with real emotion, he saw that she was.

'I didn't know you felt like that,' he said, compassionately.

'We get further apart instead of closer.' She anticipated his slight movement of dissent and added: 'No, that's not right: we just stay at the same distance. I can't get to know you any better, mean anything more to you. I know you're far above me in so many things, but if you loved me——'

He suddenly saw the future as a treacly atmosphere of inferior intellectual exchanges with a partner of declining sexual attractiveness. 'I'm ready to be known,' he interrupted coldly.

'No, it's hopeless,' she said and automatically began to open her handbag to find the materials to repair whatever ravages emotion had made in her make-up.

'Well, if you think that——' He checked the irrevocable words, as a prisoner perceives, considers and rejects the opportunity of escape. And doing so he was seized with the clearest conception of her character and situation: her carefully arranged hair, her pretty but no longer girlish face, even her clothes—the little pink sprig on her dress, the double straps to each black shoe—seemed to him steeped in pathos, and once again he knew why he had allowed this relationship to grow up. 'Christine,' he said, 'we can't possibly end it, can we?'

'I don't want to,' she said, in a voice she had never used with him. 'I don't.'

He stepped closer to her, grasping her bare forearm, sensing acutely as he always did the utter unreality—the concocted, fictitious, yet desperate nature—of all scenes in which emotion causes the protagonists to transcend the canons of ordinary behaviour.

'No, Philip,' she whispered, reassuming in an instant her public persona. He half turned and saw Stuart and Rose Blackledge coming towards them along the path from the car park. Blackledge waved at them genially: he was dressed almost too appropriately for the occasion in grey flannel trousers, the tie of his Old Boys' organization, and a navy blue blazer which revealed something of the white woollen pullover underneath.

'We're desperately late,' he said, as he came up. 'I'm relieved to find other miscreants.'

'You know Miss Eastwood, don't you, Stuart?' said Philip.

The necessary introductions made, they moved towards the pavilion. Philip, finding himself with Rose Blackledge, marvelled at the ease with which Blackledge had borne off Christine, his distinguished head bent to her in some fluent conversation, without doubt about himself. 'Did you come to this affair last year, Mrs. Blackledge?' he forced himself to remark.

'Don't you remember?' she asked.

The slight freshness of her reply made him recall what he had completely forgotten—that at the Hepworths' horrible party they had progressed beyond the small talk of the social encounters of business associates. He grinned and said: 'Yes, I do. It wasn't even a decent conventional conversational gambit, was it?'

'No,' she said. 'Do you hate these things so much?'

'Not so much. I'm just no good at them. I mean I'm only bored when I feel I'm not acting my part very well.'

'You've got to act?' she said, shocked.

At this moment they passed through the pavilion door into an envelope of music that ended with a cymbal clash, a burst of applause and then a sudden chatter of voices from the dancing floor that lay beyond a farther door. Stuart and Christine were waiting for them. Stuart said: 'Come along. You girls can leave your coats in the committee room.' He led the way briskly to a room on the right which had been labelled for the evening 'Private'. In this room a table had been covered with a white cloth and arranged with drinks, food and flowers: behind it stood one of the canteen waitresses. The room was reserved for the comfort of the directors and senior executives. In front of the table the Vice-Chairman was sipping a glass of orangeade: the General Manager stood by him, but their lives appeared to be running in different worlds.

Stuart Blackledge walked up to the Vice-Chairman and said warmly: 'How nice of you to come, Sir Harold!'

'Good evening, Blackledge,' said Ashton, and added immediately: 'The path from the car park was rather slippery after the rain. Do we insure against third party risks on these occasions?'

'I'm not sure, Sir Harold,' said Stuart. 'I'll find out and see that it's done in the future. We ought to be covered.'

'Of course we ought,' said Ashton.

Christine and Rose came up to the table and Philip, deliberately but characteristically on the perimeter, saw Stuart introduce Christine to the Vice-Chairman who immediately assumed the air a ferocious headmaster assumes on the school's sports day.

'Is Lady Ashton here, Sir Harold?' asked Rose.

'No. Her arthritis has immobilized her,' said Ashton, as though he were speaking of his motor car.

'I'm sorry to hear that,' said Stuart. He allowed a decent pause for his sympathy to sink in and then asked Christine and Rose what they would have to drink.

Gerson and his wife came in through the door which led directly to the dance floor. Gerson's pale forehead glistened with his exertions. By the side of his blond neatness, Mrs. Gerson—dumpy, mottled, dowdy, and looking all of her forty-three years—had an ambiguous air; not young enough, it seemed, to be his wife, not old enough to be his mother. They joined the group at the table, Gerson slipping unobtrusively to a strategic post at Sir Harold Ashton's elbow.

Philip found himself looking along the pink straight parting of the General Manager's smooth silver hair. Matheson said, pressing gently with his foot on the floor: 'It's done very well.'

'The pavilion?' questioned Philip.

'I must say I was rather against a wooden structure, but it was that or something very much smaller. Bloodworths built it for us, you remember.'

'It was before my time, sir.'

'Was it?' The General Manager betrayed mild astonishment. 'Was it? '32? Well, well.'

In the next room the band sent out again its hollow tone. Stuart asked Christine to dance and they went out: there was what Philip felt to be an embarrassing pause. It seemed absurd mimetic behaviour in him immediately to follow suit: on the other hand one could not delay too long or the music would stop. Gerson, taking an example from Sir Harold, was ordering a glass of orange squash for himself. The pause lengthened intolerably and Philip felt Sir Harold's eyes, like sucked brown sweets, fixed accusingly upon him, as though the Vice-Chairman had expected nothing but this anti-social behaviour from one whom he had long regarded as a social oddity.

'Would you like to dance?' Philip asked Mrs. Gerson.

Mrs. Gerson said she would, and as soon as he was ushering her through the door he knew that this duty had been chosen by the masochistic instinct that ruled his life, for quite as easily and more appropriately he could have danced with Mrs. Blackledge: the thought of that lost possibility was enough to make him realize that he desired to dance with her. He put his arm round Mrs. Gerson's hard waist and steered her into the slowly moving circle.

When he was not exchanging with her the brief inanities usual with those who merely dance dutifully, he was compelled to nod and smile to the passing faces he knew so well behind the desks, counters and machines of Saddleford House. There was a sprinkling of bald and grey, iron-waved heads, but the dancers were predominantly youthful—the filing, mailing and addressograph girls and their boy friends, the junior clerks from the accounting departments. Most were seedy or plain, but occasionally a girl swam past with her face and figure a passable imitation of the current cinematic conception of beauty, piloted with excessive skill by a young man with hair too short and jacket too long.

Philip began to go over in his mind the scene with Christine as they had walked from the car park and, as though this strange activity of holding Gerson's wife in his arms had broken down the channels of his familiar thoughts, he assumed what he had never before assumed —that he could marry Christine. And from that he was led to a consideration of the startling proposition that Christine would not consent to live with him in his parents' house and that they would have to set up an establishment of their own in which, except for the exertion of Christine's personality and desires, he would be absolute king.

'Have you got the television, Mr. Witt?' asked Mrs. Gerson.

He looked down at the upturned face (in which the spectacles rested on little pads of veined cheeks which powder had turned purplish) and with an effort of concentration made a suitable reply. He thought how utterly astonishing it was that this reason for the desirability of marriage had never, among the dozen reasons which in the past he had advanced for its impossibility, occurred to him; and his speculations, like those of one who starts with the assumption that he has won an enormous sum in a lottery, ran on in extravagant and complicated combinations.

When at last he returned Mrs. Gerson to the Committee Room he looked round immediately for Christine, as though, like his thoughts, she too might have taken on new potentialities and, changing from the ordinary woman she was, become a creature designed, as it were, by himself to fit, to heal, the raw edges of his deficiencies. He saw that she was talking to Sir Harold and that she wore what he had once privately characterized as her 'telephone face'—the expression that corresponded to the slightly more refined, more interested, more animated voice that he heard when he rang her up. If only she were simple how much easier his life would be! And by simple he meant freed from the passions and behaviour not natural, it seemed to him, to the human animal but imposed by the conditioning of a society which now corresponded to, served the wishes of, freaks and imbeciles. For it was an axiom of his belief that the generality of men and women were not in those categories, however plainly tagged with the ostensible evidence of belonging there.

He asked Mrs. Gerson if she would have a drink: she assented and he found himself at the table standing by the Chairman, who turned from a conversation with the Assistant Secretary to greet him.

'You're surely not drinking gin and lime, Mr. Witt,' remarked the Chairman.

Philip explained that his order was for Mrs. Gerson.

'Ah,' said the Chairman, 'I thought it was funny. When you get over your little tummy trouble you want to keep off gin. Some years ago'—the Chairman half turned so as to bring the Assistant Secretary into his audience—'I 'ad a very bad cold in the 'ead'—the proximity of the two aspirates defeated him. 'Now I always take a glass of whisky and eat a boiled onion last thing at night when I have a bad cold, but on this occasion Mrs. Halford was at Scarborough and so she wasn't able to do the onion for me and for some reason we hadn't a drop of whisky in the house. So I looked in the kitchen and found some scallions—spring onions, you know—and I ate about a dozen of these in bed, with a very big gin and hot water. When I laid down the bottom of the bed reared up a mile high and I came out in such a terrible sweat I thought my last moments had come. But, by gum, in the morning I hadn't a trace of that cold!'

The Assistant Secretary laughed politely and sympathetically: he was a youngish man who sometimes wore fancy waistcoats and said he had flown fighter aircraft during the war. 'But that sounds like a recommendation for gin, sir.'

Philip smilingly edged away bearing the gin and lime. Mrs. Gerson was in a group that included the Vice-Chairman: as Philip handed her the glass the band in the room beyond could be heard to strike up a martial air. 'Isn't that a Paul Jones?' inquired Sir Harold sharply. 'Come along, you young men. Do your duty.' Sir Harold let his eye linger particularly on Philip who, with the other men within the orbit of the Vice-Chairman's power, trooped obediently into the next room.

Philip danced a quick-step with Miss Hobson, the senior lady who sat on the Joint Committee, and then a waltz with a ginger girl in green taffeta who, when he asked her, said she had come with a young man who worked for the Saddleford but that she herself worked in Marks and Spencer's. As the music changed its tune to indicate once more that the couples must split up, the men to circle round the opposing circle of women, Philip felt that the proceedings were really too primitively anthropological for him to participate in them further, and, finding himself near the main double doors leading from the dance floor, he slipped (he hoped unobtrusively) through them, across the entrance hall, and into the cool open air. A man and girl were leaning close together against the rail of the veranda which ran along the front of the pavilion so Philip moved leisurely to the end of the building. The sky was now a graduated dark blue and in its lightest part a bright star had come out over the yellow slots of factory windows far below where the town lay in its valley.

As he struck a light for his cigarette, he saw that a near-by deck-chair facing the tennis courts at the side of the pavilion was occupied by a female figure who rose at the scratch of the match, made momentarily as if to move off, and then approached him.

'I was getting some air,' said Rose Blackledge, obviously feeling that her presence needed an explanation.

'It always does get stuffy in the pavilion,' he answered readily, and immediately remembered her implied denigration of his admission that he played whatever part was required by the situation in which he found himself. She took the cigarette he offered her: the flame lit for an instant her pale face, and then there fell once more between them the gloom that seemed to him not to separate them but, like some slightly unusual common predicament, to put them in quick sympathy. 'I was hoping we'd have the chance to speak again,' he said, hardly acting at all.

'Were you?'

'I should have asked you to dance right at the beginning of the evening.'

'Should have?'

He laughed. 'I mean I wanted to but I was too shy and chose Mrs. Gerson instead.'

'Are you really shy?' she questioned again.

'Perhaps when one grows out of one's adolescence and is still shy, the shyness becomes something else—some other trait, like cowardice or self-pity.' He saw, when she pulled on her cigarette and the glow illuminated her face, that a jewel of moisture glittered in the corner of her eye, and his first impression was confirmed that her presence alone in the deck-chair had been dictated by emotion. It was, he supposed, the hangover of some marital crisis, for he remembered feeling, when she and Stuart had first arrived, a sense of the constrained atmosphere engendered by a temporarily estranged couple. He thought, and jeered at himself for thinking, of himself in Stuart Blackledge's place—a more sensitive, a more considerate, husband for her.

'Isn't it funny that we haven't met since that night at the Hepworths'?' she said.

'Funny?' he repeated and then immediately added: 'It nagged me afterwards that I'd talked all about myself—that I'd come away without knowing how you'd met Charles Tillyard, for example.'

'At the chamber concerts.'

'Chamber concerts in Saddleford!'

'You must have been in the Army when Saddleford had its era of culture.'

Again he was rather astonished at the way she spoke, as though she were not the wife of the Mortgage Manager, did not live at Bellsgate, but were someone for whom miraculously he might feel an affection. 'You lived in London before the war,' he said, remembering casual office conversations.

'Yes. I was posted to Saddleford—the maintenance unit at Furleigh—when I was in the W.A.A.F. That was 1941. And I've been here ever since.'

How young she must have been in 1941, he thought, remembering the impact on his own youth of his calling-up. He tried in his imagination to bridge the gulf between her arrival at the bleak collection of huts at Furleigh, her concert-going, her acquaintance with Tillyard and no doubt some others of the shabby Saddleford intellectuals of those days, and—the gulf seemed staggering—her marriage (in 1944, was it?) to Stuart Blackledge, who even then had a commanding position in the society and in the town. 'Are you sorry?' he asked.

'That I was posted to Saddleford?'

'That you've been here ever since.'

'No,' she said. 'Of course not.'

Of course not: he was reading into her desires and subtleties that could not be there. Even girls who go to concerts at length marry ambitious and worldly men.

'That sounds as though I were defending myself, doesn't it?' she added. 'I mean the emphasis. But when at first I used to shop at Woolworth's, and have some coffee in Beard's and go to the film at the Regal because it seemed a bit more promising than the one at the Odeon I should have been appalled if anyone had told me I should live my life here. Now I see everything differently—as though before I'd been seeing the set from the back of the stage.'

'I've never sat in the stalls,' he said.

She flicked her cigarette away in a little glowing arc. 'The strange thing was I'd read *The Journal of Private Fall* before I knew Charles and found that you weren't a legend but lived here.'

'My only book,' he said.

She turned to him eagerly and said, 'Why have you stopped writing? Is that a—an impertinent question?'

He tried to answer seriously but could find no beginning to the sequence of cause and effect. 'No,' he said at length. 'Not impertinent.'

'One day I saw an airman reading it in the Saddleford Arms.'

'I haven't stopped writing,' he corrected her. 'Just stopped writing things that can be finished. That's the wrong way to put it: I was always that kind of writer—*Private Fall* was a freak fathered by the war. But I don't like talking about my work.'

'I'm sorry.'

'That was rude and untrue. No writer dislikes talking about his work. But I'm unused to talking about mine, and in any case I'm guilty about it.'

'Stuart says you're a good lawyer.'

'Stuart likes to believe what it makes him happy to believe.'

'Is it impossible to be successful in the world of'—again she searched for a word—'in *that* world and also be an artist?'

'No. But this world'—and he indicated the parabolas of the slack tennis nets, the crude mass of the pavilion which faintly exuded the chatter of voices and a persistent drum throb, the faintly gleaming chassis in the car park—'this world has a moral content which makes it useless as the material for art. Unless the artist criticizes it from a standpoint outside art. So that my work must eschew reality—at any rate the reality of my ordinary life. And that's why it stays unfinished.'

'That's too difficult for me,' she said.

'Imagine the Chairman trying to write a work of art out of the life of the Vice-Chairman.'

'But you're not the Chairman,' she objected.

'Only when I'm away from the office, from the people of the office, from the tentacles the office sends out into my so-called free hours. Otherwise, because I serve the Chairman and his aims and ideals, I am the Chairman.'

She was silent for a moment, and then said: 'All the same, you're not.'

He laughed, and perhaps because he felt suddenly that he could talk to her inexhaustibly, he said: 'I think I must go and find my secretary and dance with her or I shall be in her bad books.'

'I'll go back too.'

And as they took the few paces to the pavilion door he realized that he had become sufficiently intimate with her to have asked, if there had been time and he could have weighed the consequence quickly enough, why she had come out here alone to drop a tear.

'Let's stop at the Queen's for a nightcap,' Stuart Blackledge said.

'All right,' said Rose.

'It's very hard to get the right number of drinks in Ashton's company. He's one of those teetotallers who propagates his principles with silent disapproval.'

'You talk a lot about drinking these days,' said Rose.

'Do I?' Stuart wondered whether he would have a better chance of a parking space at the back of the Queen's, decided he wouldn't, changed his mind at the last moment and turned the car in with a squeal of wheels, a piece of driving he knew Rose would detest and which he regretted but saw as inevitable. So many things were really inevitable which others saw as avoidable.

The cocktail bar was full of smoke and of people who had had more to drink than they had.

'Good evening, Mr. Blackledge,' said the waiter.

'Good evening, George. Scotch for me. Darling?'

'Gin and tonic.'

'We shan't have time for another, George, shall we? Better make them doubles.'

Stuart was interested to see at the next table a member of the Saddleford Council, an old man with a large pale pitted nose, drinking with a middle-aged lady in a fox fur who was not his wife.

The waiter came with the drinks. 'The Frenchman won the big fight, Mr. Blackledge.'

'Did he?' said Stuart. 'I'm not surprised.'

'Water, Mr. Blackledge?'

'Just a spot. How's the family, George?'

'Nicely, thanks.'

When the waiter had gone away, Stuart said: 'George is an S.B.S. borrowing member. They tell me he pays his subscriptions every month in shillings and sixpences. Does pretty well, does George.' He leaned nearer to his wife's ear. 'Do you know the lady with Councillor Briggs?'

'Behind us? No.'

Stuart took his glass. 'Cheers.'

'Cheers.'

When he had put the glass down, he looked at Rose carefully, and said, in a voice he meant to be sympathetic but which came out with an edge of irritation: 'You're not still thinking about that bird, are you?'

'Yes.'

'But what's the use, darling? What's the use?'

'I can't help it.'

'You're being morbid.'

'You didn't see it crouching on the step.'

'Oh come, Rose. Cats eat birds every day.'

She did not reply and she was not looking at him. A young man wearing a check jacket slashed with leather and a girl with a horse's tail of hair were laughing together at the bar. Stuart felt a savage pang of envy at their easy and happy relationship, and a sudden lust for the girl. As so often lately, his relations with Rose seemed to stretch ahead humourless, sexless and difficult. And with this depressing conception came another: he remembered the fatal memorandum of the morning that had relegated his car to the third space in the garage. That was a thing about which he should be able to confide in Rose, get her confirmation of his view that it was accidental and unimportant and of his decision to take no action. But in her present mood it was impossible to engage her sympathy.

He said, with a passable air of reasonableness: 'You know, darling, you really must stop taking these trivial things to heart. It's not healthy. You brood and brood, and it doesn't do a bit of good. You've just got to forget that blessed bird. Haven't you?'

'Yes,' she said.

It was late by the time Philip had taken Christine home. He put the car away and let himself in quietly. As he approached the door of his parents' room on his way to his own he saw that it was ajar, and then he heard his mother whisper: 'Is that you, Philip?'

'Yes, Mother.'

The head and shoulders of Mrs. Witt, illuminated by the dim light in the landing, appeared round the door; the head in curling pins, the shoulders in a white nightdress. 'I left you some sandwiches and milk,' she said. 'Did you see them?'

'I don't want anything, Mother.'

'Oh, Philip,' she said.

'I've been eating and drinking the whole evening.'

'It's so late, Philip.'

'Quarter to twelve.'

'You'll be hungry in the night, dear. They're home-boiled ham, the sandwiches.'

'I couldn't eat a thing.'

Mr. Witt's muffled voice said: 'What's that, Mother?'

Mrs. Witt took her head back in the bedroom and Philip heard her say: 'It's only Philip.'

'What time is it?' Mr. Witt inquired.

'Going up to twelve.' Mrs. Witt's face appeared again, smiling conspiratorially. 'Just have a little something for me, dear,' she said in her quietest tones.

'I'll have the milk.' Philip turned back. 'Good night, Mother.'

'It will be nice and creamy, dear: it's been standing all evening.'

'Good night, Mother,' he said again, over his shoulder, guilty that he hadn't kissed her.

'Good night, Philip,' she called, wistfully.

When he returned with the milk the door was shut, and he went on to his own room. He found that his hands were trembling: it was not only because of the ridiculous dialogue with his mother but also the criticism and contempt behind his father's fragmentary intervention. He put the glass down on his desk next to an open notebook. Some time ago he would have locked it away against his parents' eyes, but now he did not bother: he could not tell whether this was a victory or defeat for him. He read the last entry in the notebook:

'A sensitive man, faced with the problem of transporting a pair of goloshes from his office to his home, conceives and has to reject as impracticable a number of methods—such as putting them in his overcoat pockets or brief case, or under his arms below his overcoat—consonant with his morbid hatred of assuming an unusual appearance. It does not occur to him to wear them.'

He closed the notebook, seized with a paralysing depression that he felt physically, as though it were a stroke, to his very fingertips. He could not work tonight: nor any night. He began to undress and soon saw in the mirror on the door of the Victorian wardrobe the familiar thin body that accorded so ill with the generously-modelled head, the calm, moustached face. He put his pyjamas on and drank the milk. It seemed to him that the whole house vibrated subtly with his father's snoring, but this could scarcely be so.

In bed he opened a book but gazed at it unseeing, thinking of the events of the evening which in retrospect took on a farcical vapidity. It was inconceivable that the intelligence contained in his skull should know how to accommodate itself to his life. He switched out the light and lay back on the pillows. A late tram ground past and then a far-off dog uttered a long series of carefully-timed barks. At dawn he awoke out of a dream, remembering vividly Rose Blackledge's face; and he realized with an intensity that brought an actual pain to his heart that he wanted to see her again. Through all his routine for combating early morning insomnia—the naked walk round the room, the visit to the lavatory, the sucked magnesia tablet, the conscious relaxing—the pain persisted, like a pain felt by an inexperienced boy after a meeting with a girl far beyond his reach in beauty and age.

V

When Arnold Gerson had transferred the contents of the West End House file to his little skull he made an appointment with the General Manager through the latter's secretary. Had he been closely examined he would have had to admit that it was not really necessary for him to go through this formula to see Matheson, but on matters of ceremony and decorum he held certain dogmas and one of them was that Matheson was a busy man on whom even his lieutenants should not impinge without warning. At the precise time of the appointment he knocked on and opened the General Manager's door to find Matheson with one foot on the window ledge adjusting his suspender.

'I'm sorry, sir,' he said, making as though to back out.

'Come in, Gerson,' said the General Manager. 'I'd forgotten you were seeing me this morning.'

'Isn't it convenient, sir? I can come back later.'

'No. Sit down.' Matheson pushed his copy of the *Daily Mail* off his blotter, indicating his eagerness to consider the society's affairs, and said: 'I can never find a make of suspender with really good elastic. It always seems to perish quickly.'

'It is apt to do that,' Gerson replied. He had been

about to rest the bulky West End House file on the edge of Matheson's desk, but this seemed to him a rather too pointed gesture in view of the lightness of the conversation, so he kept it on his knees.

Matheson said: 'I believe some men don't wear suspenders at all.'

'That's true, sir.'

'I couldn't do that. I'd feel untidy with my socks round my ankles.' The General Manager gazed towards the ceiling in contemplation of the idea, elbows resting on the fine quality hide of the chair arms, his well-manicured hands lightly touching each other, his white hair catching the morning light—the image of a spiritual but kindly and not remote ecclesiastic. Gerson breathed quietly and kept very still, waiting with patient deference for the General Manager to come round to the point of his visit. Matheson leaned forward and took a cigarette from the enormous silver box the staff had presented to him last year to mark his jubilee of service with the society. 'Lovely box, isn't it?' remarked the General Manager.

'It is lovely.'

Matheson lit his cigarette and sighed gently: he had got through life by an attitude of diplomatic procrastination, having learnt early that most problems solve themselves in time and that longevity feeds even the most idle ambition. 'Well, lad,' he said, 'what's in that nasty looking file you've got there?'

Gerson at last put the file on the desk. 'West End House Limited,' he said. 'Do you remember the case, sir? We advanced £52,000 in 1946. The security was a block of shops and furnished flatlets with a restaurant in Abercrombie Street, London, W.1. It had been requisitioned by the Ministry of Aircraft Production during the war and on derequisitioning it was sold by the former owners to West End House Limited, a new company formed for the purpose of acquiring it.'

'I remember,' said Matheson. '1946 was it? Doesn't the time flash by?'

'Yes, sir.' Gerson paused a moment to allow this philosophical reflection of the General Manager's to sink in, then coughed discreetly and continued. 'The mortgage provided for the advance to be repaid at the rate of £2,500 per annum, by quarterly instalments—after the first two years at interest only. We've had a little trouble with the last few instalments and now'—Gerson opened the file suddenly for his little effect of drama—'the company has written asking us to suspend capital repayments.'

'Hm,' said Matheson, non-committally.

'Of course, I asked them for their latest accounts and details of the letting of the building. They're not too good, I'm afraid. Taking the lettings first; it seems that the restaurant is vacant——'

'Vacant!' said the General Manager, actually leaning forward a little in his chair.

'The company that was running it has gone into liquidation and the liquidator is expected to disclaim the lease. And then some of the shops are empty.'

'This sounds like rank bad management,' said the General Manager.

'Yes, sir. The residential accommodation seems to be fairly fully occupied, but there are a number of tenants in arrears. And that brings me to the company's accounts. It's grossly over-capitalized, so that without the restaurant rent and some of the shop rents it couldn't possibly continue trading. It would barely tick over if the premises were fully let: originally there was clearly too optimistic an estimate made of the rental value of the non-residential units. The company issued a debenture in——'

'Wait a bit,' said Matheson, detesting this flood of what he called technicalities. 'Just let's look at the society's position. What's the present mortgage debt?'

'£45,750 plus interest.'

'And what was the purchase price when the company bought?'

'£72,000 for the freehold. And they paid £7,500 for the furniture, fittings and so forth.'

'And the society's valuation at the time?'

'£70,000, excluding the contents.'

Matheson smiled: 'Well, it doesn't look too bad, Gerson.'

Gerson felt that the position he had taken up was under assault. 'I wanted particularly to draw your attention to the schedule of lettings. On that basis——'

'Suppose at the worst,' interrupted the General Manager, 'that the society has to sell. There's a margin between mortgage debt and valuation of—um—£25,000 in our favour.'

'£24,250,' said Gerson.

'Yes,' said Matheson. 'Well, that's a decent bit of slack, lad.'

The Accounts Manager determinedly drove his spectacles against the bridge of his thin nose. 'No, sir. I'm afraid I have to disagree there. I don't see how a valuation of £70,000 could possibly be justified on that schedule of lettings. I know I'm only an accountant, not a surveyor, but those figures speak for themselves, sir.'

'Do you mean the society over-valued?'

Gerson became cautious. 'I don't know how the revenue position of that building was presented to us in 1946.'

'Damn it, lad, even if we over-valued by £10,000 there's still a margin of——' The General Manager looked up at the ceiling and moved his lips silently.

'£14,250,' supplied Gerson.

'That should take care of any accidents.' Matheson passed his hand over his sleek silver head. 'You still don't look very happy.'

'I'm not, sir,' said Gerson.

'Come along, then: what do *you* think the present value of the place is?'

Gerson shifted the file a little. '£35,000?' he said, questioningly.

'£35,000! With a mortgage debt of £45,000!' Matheson was shaken.

'£45,750 and the current interest,' said the other automatically.

The General Manager stared at Gerson with his clear blue eyes, as though exorcising an unpleasant optical illusion. 'Well,' he said eventually, 'I hope to God you're wrong.'

'I hope I am, sir,' said Gerson, complacent at having at length justified his work on the file, his appointment with Matheson, his patient approach.

'Of course, I'll have to put this request for a suspension of capital repayments before the directors.'

'Yes, sir.'

'See that it goes on the agenda for the next Board.'

'Yes, sir.'

'And before then we shall want an up-to-date valuation

of the place. Blackledge will arrange for it—consult with him on that, will you, Gerson?'

'Yes, sir.'

At this moment the General Manager's secretary entered with a little tray bearing Matheson's mid-morning pot of coffee and a plate of chocolate biscuits.

'Thank you, Doris,' said the General Manager as the tray was put conveniently on the desk to his right hand. Even in this moment he observed with satisfaction that the biscuits this morning were coated with milk chocolate. He stole a glance at the *Daily Mail* to confirm it was still there to accompany the coffee-drinking rite. All he had to do to enjoy the next twenty minutes was to dismiss Arnold Gerson.

'Well, Gerson, I think that's about it,' said the General Manager. He saw that Gerson nevertheless still looked expectantly at him and he felt an unusual pang of sympathy for this emaciated, industrious figure whose suits, he noted, still always looked too big for him though long ago Matheson had introduced him to his own tailor. 'Good bit of work,' added the General Manager.

'Thank you, sir,' Gerson rose, holding the file tenderly.

'I shall mention the case to the Chairman before Board Day.'

'The Chairman.' Gerson's voice held only the merest hint of a question.

'Or the Vice-Chairman. Perhaps both.'

'I certainly think Sir Harold ought to have an opportunity of looking at these figures,' said the Accounts Manager and moved silently away with his habitual walk that made him seem as though he were, like a mountaineer, fitting his feet into previously cut footholds.

Before he was through the door, Matheson had poured himself out a cup of coffee, and then his hand was left poised for a few moments over the biscuits while he pondered over Gerson's last words. For Gerson they were very daring, containing as they did not only a criticism of the Chairman's competence to deal with the West End House affair but also the expression of Gerson's independent opinion in the presence of his General Manager. Matheson had always valued Gerson as a completely reliable subordinate who would pass nothing that ought not to be passed, work like a black and keep those affairs of the society within his purview in meticulous order. But he was never wont to criticize or even comment on matters within the scope of his superiors in the hierarchy. By gum, thought Matheson as he at last selected a biscuit, perhaps Gerson was making a bid for the General Managership. There was no doubt that he was as thick with the Vice-Chairman in so far as it was possible for anyone to be thick with Sir Harold, and Sir Harold was certainly the man the successful candidate had to get on his side. Arnold Gerson as General Manager of the Saddleford Building Society: when one considered it it was not so absurd as it seemed.

Yet it was absurd, all the same. Gerson could not be imagined playing his part round the council table of the Building Societies Alliance, in the chair at a Dorchester Dinner, leading a deputation to the Treasury people. Those things eventually fell to the lot of any General Manager of the Saddleford. And who could see that dumpling Mrs. Gerson as the General Manager's lady? No, it was Blackledge—not so good as he thought he was; indeed, apt to be unreliable—who would take the step up. At least he wore his clothes well and could make a speech.

That, Matheson was sure, was how the Board thought; although, in its transitional stage, one could never be absolutely sure how the Board would act. And then, in spite of the comfort of the coffee and the biscuits, Matheson's own worry, like a sediment, precipitated itself into his mind. He was a man who had always told himself that he never worried. When he had come home late after a bad evening at the Conservative Club playing bridge for higher stakes than, in those earlier days, he could afford, he had taken his nightcap of scotch and gone to bed with hardly a pang. The secret of his life—unknown to the office, unknown in its disastrous scope even to his wife—was a passion for backing horses: he was almost totally inured to the bad weeks of his operations and could even contemplate wholly and rationally the absence of personal fortune that his gambling had caused. But now that he was older he sometimes woke an hour or so before it was time to get up and thought about his lack of money, and that would lead to the prospect of his retirement when he would have to try to live on the balance in his Superannuation Fund account—a balance that because of his long lowly years with the society and the inflationary era through which he had passed was almost derisory compared with his present salary. Unless on retirement he were elected to the Board of the society. There were precedents for it. Old George Sutcliffe had gone in 1910, for example.

But, admitted though he was to the Board's inmost heart, so far he had discovered no hint of its intention. The months passed, the early morning thoughts became more painful—worrying, he would have called them had he been a worrying man. The moment was not far off when, if the invitation from the directors to become one of their number did not arrive, he must try to resign himself to an idle and penurious old age. He looked round at the bow legs of his desk which ended in claw feet, the bow legs of the chairs, the heavy panelling, the turkey carpet, the silver cigarette box: no matter how high you get in the world, he thought, you're never safe. He opened his *Daily Mail* at the sporting page and took another biscuit.

Dear Mrs. Blackledge,

The innocent would start by imagining your surprise: the bold would assume that you felt no surprise. But I can think of nothing except addressing the envelope and sending its contents to the house of a man I call by his Christian name but to whom I would never send a letter. Writing a letter is easy even for the guilty, timid man: and he can often quite quickly bring himself to post it. But this letter implies the serious but absurd trappings of espionage: an envelope addressed on an untraceable typewriter or with the left hand, signed with a false name—'your loving aunt, Ada'. Perhaps—no, I'm sure—you've often had letters in circumstances like these and find all my guilt, procrastination, sense of fate, incomprehensible. After all, you'd say, the envelope wasn't disguised, except in so far as it was in a handwriting you didn't know; and its contents aren't, so far as you know, in code.

A man briefly visits a family under a false name, makes love to the daughter, departs leaving no address. Later he wonders if she had a child and thinks for a few moments quite seriously of all the terrible consequences, of no effect on him, of his action. Or a ghost, with the most frightful effort, removes himself from the place of purgatory where he circles, to visit the living about whom in spite of his death he is still anguished: but none of them see him. How will you think of this letter?

Perhaps you will remember it later in the day, laugh, and go and tear it up.

P.W.

In fact, the letter lay quite harmlessly in the kitchen, taking the imprint of a milk bottle, until Stuart Blackledge had left for work and Rose went to make herself some more coffee. She had failed to observe the Saddleford postmark and had imagined (glancing at the envelope quickly when she had sorted the post) the handwriting to be that of the secretary of the Old Girls' Association of her school who had lately taken to pestering her for a subscription.

She read the letter at the stove, waiting for the milk to heat, comprehending it as little as if it had been written in German, a language to which she had devoted the spare periods of her last school year. She took her coffee to the debris of the breakfast table, read the letter again, and finally understood—as the victim of a disease can no longer mistake the persistence of his symptoms—that it marked plainly Philip Witt's desire to enter, to alter, her life. And immediately, without visualizing him as someone with corporeal, contemporary existence, she felt a growing unease, as though it had been her feelings that had led to the initiative of the letter. From where she sat she examined the furnishings of the dining-room with the eyes of a stranger, excusing the glass and wrought iron dumb waiter as a wedding present thrust on her by some unspeakable relation of her husband's, the reproduction suite by the exigencies of post-war shortages, and even being frightened of her own taste that a year or two ago had chosen the Scandinavian cutlery.

In the bedroom, putting on the first make-up of the day, she regarded her face with the half-unsatisfied, half-excited eyes of an amateur painter looking at the progress of his work, moistening the arched but rather thick eyebrows, trying to pinpoint the marks that time almost imperceptibly lays on a woman who has moved out of her twenties. And then, restlessly walking about the house, the folded letter in the pocket of her dress, her usual routine forgotten, she saw her whole life through the eyes of this other person that it seemed this morning had taken possession of her—the remote ardours of the war and her girlhood, the marriage that had seemed to her, like a sudden accession of wealth, to promise at once infinite comfort and experience, and finally the routine that had made the last few years pass so quickly that she could scarcely distinguish one from the other. Again she was frightened—that the character she had become could no longer support or inspire any real life: that she could, for example, converse of nothing but the topography or personages of the town; be herself only with Stuart, move slowly in the tracks that habit had dictated—to the hairdresser's, the cinema, the shops in Manchester where she bought her clothes. How, she asked herself, did she spend her time, the hours when she was alone that at this moment seemed for the first time to add up to an impossibly enormous total? Yet even now it was not that she was dissatisfied with her existence, but that it had become the existence of someone she had never bargained to be. She was at the sitting-room window and she drew idly in the faint film of Saddleford grime on the glass, seeing in the sunlight, with her usual distaste, the dark hairs on the arm revealed by her summer sleeves. She thought of herself, her flesh, and incredulously imagined it entering into a new relationship with a stranger.

It was not until she had admitted Mrs. Horrocks, heard that lady's opinion of the previous night's television and seen her finally to her tasks in the kitchen, that Rose realized that she might reply to the letter, and she went, with almost a feeling of dread in her chest, to search for her fountain pen. It was a measure of the seclusion of her life that she really could not guess where it was. She looked in one of the small drawers of her dressing-table, knowing it to be the kind of drawer in which a fountain pen might be found. She lifted out a belt with an unstitched buckle, a bundle of snapshots, an artificial flower from an evening dress long discarded, a worn handbag unfamiliarly flat, the pamphlet of propaganda and instruction from a tonic preparation she had once used to take, a flattened cigarette. There was no fountain pen, and she opened the twin small drawer, but seeing it crammed beyond her patience closed it again at once. In her soul she was orderly, imagining her belongings arranged in exquisite order: she had, she thought, too much leisure to translate this essential self into reality, for the ideal Rose had no leisure, no dissipation of aim, no notion at all of the paralysing procrastination that accompanies an unurgent existence.

She went along to the small room Stuart used as a study and sat at the desk. In front of her was the stand that held a fountain pen in its swivelling calyx—a smart apparatus that had been his wedding present from the society's staff. She took out a piece of notepaper from the little suite of drawers that stood on the desk and laid it on the immaculate blotter. As her fingers touched the pen she thought for the first time of her correspondent.

She saw the lean figure; the creaminess of the complexion with the moustache hard-seeming on it, like the moustache of a bronze bust, the large dark feminine eyes. Her thighs trembled slightly with an unformulated apprehension and she took out the letter from her pocket. At this hurried reading of it, it once again seemed almost incomprehensible but she put it by her paper, took the pen and wrote quickly: 'Dear Philip.'

Then she looked up, hearing guiltily the noise of Mrs. Horrocks using the vacuum, the noise that on normal days was an unappreciated background to her making the bed or her journeys to and from the garden. Round her in the room were the furnishings which Stuart had made a point of choosing himself, but this evidence of his personality, like the neat desk, had become quite alien, as though the years of their marriage had suddenly been cancelled. A vivid sense came to her of the impermanence as well as the potentialities of human relations, and she looked down at the unfamiliar name she had written with the proud feeling of one involved in the beginning of some cataclysm of nature, alarmed at the strength of the wind but willing it to blow still stronger.

As a woman learns of her pregnancy while her shape and health are quite normal, so the dubious state of the West End House account seemed to Stuart Blackledge at first hardly to concern him. He had been told of it by Gerson in the diffident, apologetic manner the Accounts Manager always assumed towards him, and he had immediately anticipated what he thought was required of him.

'We'd better have the place valued,' he said.

'Yes,' said Gerson. 'The General Manager wanted you to arrange for that.'

'I'll get on to Powell.' Powell was the surveyor attached to the society's London office.

'Yes,' said Gerson again.

Blackledge looked at him sharply, remembering the voting at the Joint Committee, visualizing Gerson's old Morris in the second garage space: he could not accustom himself to the possible idea of Gerson as a man with ambition or power. He remarked, tentatively: 'Let's see, I had something to do with the original valuation, hadn't I?'

Gerson moved his thin pale hand on the bulky file. 'It was a joint valuation by you and Powell.'

'Of course,' said Blackledge. 'I remember it now. When was it? '47?'

'1946,' said Gerson.

'Hm. We looked at things rather differently in '46. I don't suppose we shall find the same value there now, shall we?' Blackledge watched for the other's reaction.

Gerson settled his spectacles. 'I don't know,' he said. 'It's the company's accounts I'm a little concerned about.'

It was as he had always said, thought Blackledge: one could never get Gerson to express an opinion. And how could a man rise to a great executive position if he had no opinions? It was only because he moved in the dead world of figures that Gerson was able to match up even to his present eminence. 'I can ill afford the time,' said Blackledge, 'but I suppose I'd better look at the place again with Powell.' He felt, having come to this decision to exercise the full strength of his skill and concern, almost sorry for Gerson. 'Let me have the dope from the file.'

'Very good, Stuart.' Gerson rose.

'When is the G.M. going to discuss it with the Vice-Chairman?' Blackledge had already sat up in his chair and was moving other papers on his desk.

'Thursday, I think. So that it can go to the Board next week.'

'All right, A.P.,' said Blackledge, putting his pipe between his teeth, and looking up with a smile of automatic charm. Gerson made the little obeisance that was an irradicable habit of his long years of inferiority and went silently from the room. When he had gone, Stuart dialled his secretary's number on the internal telephone.

'Book me a room at the Dorchester for tomorrow night, will you, Maureen?' He blew through his pipe and then began skilfully to fill it, feeling as he so often did, that sense of perfect knowledge and mastery of procedure that was one of the chief pleasures of his life.

It was as though an aeroplane had quickly dispatched his familiar body and clothes to some country of known name but remote location, a place of geographical existence but for him unbelievable actuality. And yet his presence managed to weave the alien reality into the continuum of his living.

'Was it wrong to ring you at the office?' she asked.

'No,' he said. 'No.' The denial was inadequate: he wanted to reassure her with words that would have been absurdly fulsome for the occasion.

'I wondered if you would have known that Stuart was going away.'

'I didn't know,' he said. 'My department is a world of

its own.' He felt a foolish and curious obligation to try to make jokes, introduce quotations, and almost added: 'A little world made cunningly of elements, and an angelic sprite.'

'If you had known would you have rung me?'

'No,' he said immediately, though the question involved what seemed to him inexhaustible moral and personal considerations.

She said: 'Then you think I was wrong to telephone.'

'Wrong?'

'Deceitful. Impudent.'

'But it was I who wrote to you—who started it.'

'Would you have written again after my letter?' she asked.

All this time, ever since he had called for her at her house, he had made the effort of driving an excuse to himself for not looking at her, her presence indicated overwhelmingly enough by the strange faint perfume which accompanied his archetypal view of the Rolls' obtuse-angled radiator, the spot in the driving mirror where the silver had worn away, the passing Saddleford mills whose evocative names—Asia, Hawk, Joshua Kershaw—his childhood had made as tame as nursery rhymes. But now he glanced at her before turning his eyes back to the road and saying: 'Yes.'

'I said "Dear Philip".'

The name on her lips made him smile involuntarily. 'You did,' he said.

'Did you think *that* impudent? I wondered all the time if I ought to change it. Then when I'd posted the letter I was sure—sure I should have changed it. I thought it was as though when I was at school I'd used the headmistress's nickname—which happened to be her

Christian name.' She was silent for a moment and then added: 'I'm not the person you think I am. I'm a fool, really.'

'How do you know what I think about you?'

'I know the kind of person *you* are.'

They had climbed until the town lay smoking behind them in the fading light. In front rolled the tilted fields of coarse grass, the strange bright green of evening, the hills in the distance purplish blue in the last light. He stopped the car close to the blackened stone of the road's nearside wall.

She said: 'Those two occasions when we met gave you a wrong impression of me. They were too favourable to me. I've no—no third dimension.' She made a gesture. 'It's as I said—I'm just a fool. I can't give you anything at all—I shouldn't have answered your letter. I'm frightened to death even of the very smallest things that friendship with you might ask of me.'

'You aren't convincing me,' he said, offering her a cigarette as he looked at the inexhaustible unfamiliarity of her face. His interest in her life and character was so intense that he wanted to delay her revelation of it so that his pleasure could be drawn out. Their conversation seemed to him like some vast library into which he was stepping for the first time: it was even delightful to pick up and turn for a moment the most repellent volume. 'Will you tell Stuart that you've been out with me?' he asked.

'No,' she said immediately, as he had known she would. Behind the excitement in his chest he felt an apprehension as inevitable but as remote as next term at the start of the holidays.

'Do you feel this is wrong?'

'Absolutely wrong or wrong to Stuart?' she asked.

'Wrong in any way.'

'Yes, it's wrong,' she said.

'Because Stuart would be hurt if he found out?'

'Why are you asking these questions?' she cried. 'Two letters—these few miles . . .'

The car was full of cigarette smoke: he lowered the window. 'You said you were a fool. I'm a coward and so I can't ask anything of you. The brain, the talent—those things don't matter, don't give me any status in real life. You must have seen in my letter how despicable I am.'

'You mean because it was left to me——?'

'To do something?' he finished. 'No, not exactly. Because my letter was stilted and priggish and about myself, not you.'

'No,' she protested.

'And my calling in this car and our driving away.' He felt an irresistible wish to tell her the last detail. 'To you it seems quite normal. But I had to ask my father's permission to take the car, as I always have. And I sat all afternoon wondering when the time arrived whether I should really be able to keep myself from telephoning you and making an excuse not to come. Even now, you see, we've stopped on our way.'

She sat silent before the bewildering choice of topics. Then she said: 'But it's not normal for me, either.'

'The abnormality is normal.'

'And—and . . .' She struggled for the phrase. 'Isn't here, where we've stopped, where, in a way, we were going?'

'Don't you mind,' he said, 'if we don't go to the Moorcock?'

She grinned. 'So that's where we were going.'

Still he could not relax. 'I changed my mind coming

along in the car,' he said seriously. 'There may be some Saddleford people there. Where could we go?'

'If we went on to Shapley,' she said, 'we could buy fish and chips and eat them in the car.'

He considered whether or not to admit that fish and chips were a food his digestion had long since refused to accept. The life that the journey in the car had assumed seemed suddenly to be beyond his powers—it was too complicated and arduous for his feeble body and will. He saw her strong hands lying gracefully across her thighs, slender looking under the silk dress, and a poignancy filled his throat as though she were already lost to him.

'Rose,' he said, using her Christian name for the first time and immediately trying to define for himself the delicious sensation: taking the cellophane off a packet of cigarettes, using a new razor blade, a new typewriter ribbon?

'Are you thinking about the future? What's going to happen?' she asked anxiously.

'Yes,' he said, not knowing if it were a lie or not; but certain that her breathing, perfumed presence, like the outbreak of a war, gave even the commonest objects of his existence a strange significance, so that when he saw her pull down the sleeves of her cardigan and was prompted to raise the window, he thought that never before had he realized what it was truly like to be in the enclosed space of a motor car. 'Yes,' he said, laughing and turning the ignition key. 'I'm thinking of those fish and chips.'

The Vice-Chairman took off the mean little spectacles he wore for reading and said, without emphasis: 'Your valuation is slightly above half what it was in 1946, Blackledge?'

'If you read the beginning of my report, Sir Harold,' Blackledge began.

'I don't pretend to understand the science of valuation —or is it an art?—but I do know a little about figures. £33,000 has apparently vanished into thin air.'

'No, Sir Harold, the society only stands to lose——'

'I know that, man,' Sir Harold spoke testily for the first time, and the colour leapt to Blackledge's face. '£8,750 with the current interest—if your valuation is to be relied on.'

'I'm sorry, Sir Harold. I thought you were referring to the difference——'

Sir Harold interrupted him again. 'What the Board will want to know, Blackledge, is how you and Powell in 1946 arrived at what seems now to be the astronomical figure of £70,000 as the value of the freehold.'

'Well, Sir Harold, the company paid £72,000——'

'I never thought that purchase price had more than an adventitious relationship to value,' said Sir Harold. 'But this is hardly the time for generalizations: you will have to try to make your peace with the Board at a later date, Blackledge.'

The bastard, Blackledge was thinking; the smug bastard. Had he himself never been guilty of a bloomer? Blackledge felt the sweat gumming his shirt to his back and the blood throbbing in his temples, conscious that the General Manager and Gerson had, during his grilling, only emphasized their surprise and interest by their elaborately assumed air of unconcern and needless study of the documents they had before them. He had never, since some catastrophic escapades of his schooldays, been in this embarrassed, indefensible, oppressed predicament. He had gone to London, enjoyed the luxury of the pullman and the hotel, met the deferential Powell. He had been somewhat astonished at what he had found at West End House, rather more astonished when he and Powell had arrived at their valuation figure, but even then he had regarded the decline as an inevitable result of post-war conditions and ill-management. It was not until he had sat down at this conference and seen the papers in front of Sir Harold's unfriendly brown eyes that he began to realize the extent of his own responsibility. During the last quarter of an hour the realization had grown to a monstrous and horrifying size and it was no longer possible to escape the conclusion that the original valuation (Powell's share in which he must also shoulder) was a grave error of judgement—an old man of the sea who was going to lie on his back for months, even years. It was intolerable—nightmarishly unbelievable—that this should happen to a man in his position.

'If the society ever has to realize this security,' the Vice-Chairman was saying to the room at large, 'on these figures the loss will be of such a magnitude that we can't possibly let it appear silently in the accounts. The shareholders will have to be told of it explicitly at the annual general meeting, and given a full and proper explanation.'

Everyone was silent, thinking of the covert jubilation and even the direct jibes of the Saddleford's rivals in the building society movement, at such a public admission of sin. They thought, too, of an officious and offensive shareholder called Jonas Barlow who made a point of asking difficult questions at annual general meetings even about innocent and prosperous accounts.

'It doesn't, therefore,' Sir Harold continued, 'need me

to emphasize that our aim must be to avoid realization. We must watch over the company's affairs, try to ensure that it vastly improves its standard of management of this property. After all, the building is in the West End where there's plenty of brass about: there is absolutely no reason why any part of it should be empty.'

Blackledge began to sweat afresh until he realized that he was the only man in the room who understood that, despite its name and the postal number of its address, West End House was not in the West End. It was, not to put too fine a point on it, in Paddington, in a district quite unattractive to those who might wish to live and eat at fair expense. This was something, he had to confess to himself, that he had quite failed to understand in 1946.

'The directors of the company must be gee'd up,' said Sir Harold. 'Someone from here must sit in at their meetings until they've put matters on a proper basis. They'll respond, I feel sure, especially when it's forcibly pointed out to them that they stand to pay over £8,000 out of their own pockets.'

'£8,000 out of their own pockets,' repeated Gerson questioningly and apologetically.

'As guarantors of the society's mortgage,' said Sir Harold with ostensible patience.

'They are not guarantors, I'm afraid, Sir Harold,' said Gerson.

Sir Harold tested the strength of his chair. 'Who *are* the guarantors, then?'

'There are none,' said Gerson, looking at the General Manager.

Matheson roused himself. 'There are no guarantors in this case, Sir Harold,' he said needlessly.

'I don't understand,' said the Vice-Chairman, in a choked voice. 'Is it not the society's practice in the case of an advance to a company to require the directors of the company to join in the mortgage deed and give their personal covenants to repay the advance and interest?'

'Yes, Sir Harold,' said Matheson ingratiatingly, 'but in this particular mortgage the society apparently thought itself sufficiently secured with the property and waived the requirement of the directors' covenants.'

The Vice-Chairman laughed ironically.

'The advance was authorized by the Board itself,' put in Blackledge.

'Then I must have been absent. I certainly would never have allowed the directors to escape their proper obligations.'

The silence fell again.

'Who are these fortunate gentlemen?' asked the Vice-Chairman at last.

Gerson said: 'Mr. Douglas Black. Mrs. Black. Mr. Sikowski. They are the London directors, one may say. And lastly Mr. Cecil Hepworth——'

'Hepworth?' said Sir Harold. 'He's a local man, isn't he?' He turned accusingly to Blackledge. 'He's the friend of yours who wants to borrow money on flats.'

'Yes, Sir Harold,' said Blackledge, feeling his colour rise again and recalling vividly that awful and disastrous day in 1946 when he had said to Cecil Hepworth: I'll see that we shan't require your guarantee, old man.

'He'll never have another penny piece out of this society as long as I'm alive,' said the Vice-Chairman. He turned to the General Manager. 'Matheson, the Board will want a full statement about the company's affairs.'

'Yes, Sir Harold.' Matheson relaxed a little, visualizing at last the end of this terrible meeting.

'Gerson had better meet the directors in London. He must take Witt with him to watch the legal aspect. And he must press for the directors to appoint a first-class firm of West End estate agents to take over the management of the place.'

'Yes, Sir Harold,' said Matheson.

The Vice-Chairman folded his hands under his pregnant-looking stomach. 'This case was mishandled from its inception. I'm scarcely surprised that it has gone bad on us. The Board will be extremely displeased, I can tell you, gentlemen.'

He said no more, and the three executives, after allowing a decent interval of quiet to give him the impression that his words had gone to their hearts, gathered up their papers and left the Committee Room. In the corridor outside they stood for a moment paralysed with their own thoughts. Then Gerson said, 'I'll arrange right away with Philip Witt to go to London on Monday.'

'Yes,' said the General Manager indifferently. He had an uneasy feeling that because Gerson had come well out of this mess his own position was that much the worse.

Gerson moved off along the corridor. Blackledge tried to think of something to say to hide his embarrassment and guilt, but the only idea that came into his mind was that the cocktail bar of the Queen's would now be open and that if he wanted he could walk out of this oppressive building into the atmosphere of comradeship and pleasure.

'Well,' said the General Manager, 'I expect things will work themselves out in the end.' It struck him that the whole thing was like a bad bet: the trouble was that the loss continued to hang over one instead of decently receding into oblivion.

'The Vice-Chairman was present at the Board Meeting that authorized the West End House loan,' Blackledge said suddenly.

'Of course he was,' said Matheson with a sigh.

'And he knew at the time that we weren't taking the directors' covenants.'

'Yes,' agreed Matheson, 'but he didn't make that valuation.' The General Manager walked slowly towards his office, wondering whether it had been wise to go, as Gerson had pressed, to the Vice-Chairman instead of the Chairman: there was, after all, a good deal of sense in delaying until the last possible moment the extraction of an unsaveable tooth.

VI

In the rack above him, on top of a new brief case as yellow as a duck's foot, lay Gerson's bowler hat, an article of clothing assumed only on such occasions as this. At the side of his plate was a neatly-folded copy of the *Financial Times*, which was the reading matter he had brought to while away the four-hour journey. Philip Witt observed that although Gerson's hands were well-scrubbed, dirt was ingrained along the grasping surfaces of index fingers and thumbs: was it from gardening merely, he wondered, or did he also help Mrs. Gerson with the rough housework? Philip had a sudden insight into Gerson's mind—the mind that visualizing the disasters of illness and old age willingly sacrifices his youth to guarding against them.

The steward leaned over and spooned some pale sprouts on Gerson's plate as though they were truffles. Witt said quickly: 'None for me, thank you.' Gerson began to eat—circumspectly, but with determination. Hedges and blue skies passed outside.

When Philip had been told of the critical state of the West End House mortgage he had felt an exquisite pleasure. It was not entirely—or even at all—the pleasure felt at another's misfortunes; and, indeed, from Gerson's colourless recital of the situation he had not completely grasped the enormity of Blackledge's offence in the initial valuation nor the full flavour of the odour the latter was in. It arose obscurely out of Philip's constant if largely unconscious hope that the society would be injured, that its borrowing members and employees would revolt against it, that its massive millions and its part in the social fabric of the times would somehow or other be undermined. The hope could scarcely bear analysis in rational terms, since the society's ruin would mean the ruin of his own status and independence. Perhaps the hope only existed because the society's position was virtually unassailable. That he felt it at all was the measure of the difference between himself and Gerson, Blackledge and even Matheson, whose loyalties were simple because not disinterested.

Hearing from Gerson that he would be required to journey to London to reason with the West End House directors, Philip's pleasure in catastrophe was tempered by the dread which always attended his anticipation of being moved out of the routine existence which a thousand habits of thought and action had made bearable for him. He would never have considered challenging the proposition that it was his duty to assume whatever repugnant and difficult task the society thought fit to impose on him. Instead, his whole *psyche* was directed to trying to exorcise, by imagining the details of the journey, the people to be met, tbe report to be written, the spectre of his unwished burden.

While Gerson had scarcely finished speaking of the Vice-Chairman's instructions and still sat modestly forward on the chair by Philip's desk, the telephone rang. Philip picked up the receiver and heard a voice say: 'Hello. Is that Mr. Witt?' It was Rose's voice. He said: 'Hello. Yes,' in what he hoped were neutral tones and glanced with covert apprehension at Gerson. But Gerson, with his excessive deference, had already risen to his feet, prepared at a sign to go out of the room. Philip shrugged his shoulders and gestured hopelessly at the telephone receiver. Gerson smiled and made his little bow of departure. As he went out of the room, Philip said to the telephone for Gerson's benefit: 'I'm sorry, I didn't catch what you said. I had someone with me.'

'Shall I ring off?' asked Rose.

The door closed. 'No,' said Philip softly. 'I'm free now.'

'I couldn't 'phone tonight and I wanted to tell you that I can see you on Monday evening.'

He wondered with alarm whether the girl on the society's switchboard was listening in or whether she had recognized Rose's voice. 'Alas, I have to go to London on Monday and.I shall be staying the night.' Like the writer of a message in code, he had to try to convey a meaning in phrases almost impossibly stilted.

'Are you going alone?'

'No,' he said, his nervousness increasing. 'Look, I think I'd better write to you about this.'

She said firmly: 'I'll find a way of telephoning you tonight.'

'You may get my mother or father.'

'Don't worry,' she said, and he was amazed at the intimacy and knowledge behind the two simple words. 'It will be after eight o'clock,' she added.

'All right,' he said, surrendering his fear into the hands of fate.

She said good-bye and rang off. At night, instead of making the after-supper journey to Christine's or his own room, he had stayed with his parents in the sitting-room so as to be near the telephone. His mother, when she had realized the change of routine, had with ostensible self-sacrifice asked him if he were really not desirous of working. His father had taken rather longer over his reading of the evening paper, as the eater of an egg begins on the white. But when the telephone rang they were well into their game of solo.

When he answered it and gave his number he heard her press the button of a public call box and then Rose's voice. He said: 'I'm sorry I had to be so impersonal on the 'phone this morning.' He spoke in a low voice, though he had shut the sitting-room door.

'Did you really mean it when you said I had to tell you when I could see you?'

'Of course.'

'I could go to London on Monday.'

A dozen objections sprang to his lips, killing the desire. 'I shall be with Arnold Gerson. We have meetings.'

She was silent. It was quite impossible, he thought,

and immediately his pleasure at knowing he would not have to experience a difficult and extraordinary series of events compensated him for the missed pleasure of being with her in a strange city. He said: 'I don't see how——'

'I hate these telephone conversations,' she broke in.

'Yes,' he said.

'Do you want to see me again, Philip?'

'Yes,' he said again, wondering if he was speaking the truth.

'Now?'

'What do you mean?' He looked round fearfully at the hallstand with its mushroom-like knobs, the barometer, the stained glass of the main front door.

'I'm in a call box near the Plaza.'

'The Plaza?' he repeated incredulously. It was the dingy cinema almost across the road.

'You ought to know the Plaza,' she said, amused.

At this moment his mother walked out of the sitting-room and gave him on her way to the kitchen the half-apprehensive smile he so detested. 'Where will you be?' he asked, when she had disappeared.

Rose said: 'Lurking at the entrance.'

He said, very softly: 'I may be a little while.'

'All right,' she said and replaced the receiver.

He went back to the sitting-room. The three hands lay on the card table, half played, and he took his up and stared at the meaningless arrangement of suits. His father was sucking a sweet: he shifted it into his cheek and called: 'Mother!'

When Mrs. Witt returned, Mr. Witt said: 'It's your lead, Mother. You're playing a *misère*.'

'Yes, my dear,' she said. They played a few cards.

Philip said: 'I think I shall have some fresh air after this hand.'

Mr. Witt studiously ignored this statement. 'You can't get it, Mother,' he said, laying down the three of spades.

'I've just put the kettle on,' said Mrs. Witt reproachfully.

'I shan't want tea,' said Philip reasonably.

'You've got to play to the three of spades, Mother,' said Mr. Witt.

'I'm sorry, my dear.' She played the five.

'Philip?' Mr. Witt inquired.

'I haven't got a spade.'

'I know you haven't.' Mr. Witt laughed cleverly. 'Pay up, Mother.'

'Where will you go to, Philip? Christine's?' Mrs. Witt inquired anxiously.

'Of course not, Mother. I'm only going round the block,' said Philip, thinking that it would be best if Rose had tired of waiting, for his life did not permit of him to give her anything.

'He's going round the block,' said Mr. Witt, finding amusement in this word.

But when he had crossed the road, curls of cotton dropped by lorries on its cobbles, Rose was there, looking at the stills of cowboys. He took her arm, feeling its slenderness under the thin tweed coat, and they walked down the narrow street at the side of the cinema.

'How can you go to London?' he asked.

'My parents live there. I go quite often. I could go on Monday.'

'I could never get away from Arnold Gerson.' He wanted to ask her what he could not bring himself to ask —what were they to meet in London for?

'Couldn't you let him come back and stay on alone?'

'I've no excuse. He knows my business as well as I know it myself. So does Stuart.' The name chilled him with guilt.

They had stopped by a wall which bordered a waste plot where children were still playing among the bricks and iron rubbish. At the back of the plot were the tiny gardens, the washing, the lit windows of a row of terrace cottages. 'I used to come here when I was young,' he said. 'A boy once made me eat a worm here.'

'Eat it?' she said in horror.

'As I remember,' he said. It was fear that had made him, when he saw children approaching him from far off, turn round in his tracks or slip up an alley; it was only the adults he knew that he had similarly avoided, his motive being shyness. 'I've always been oppressed,' he went on ironically.

'I wish I weren't such a simpleton,' she said. When he laughed she added: 'You don't contradict me.' She dug her hands in the pockets of her coat. 'Being with you like this is like reading a famous book you've always heard about. You open it at last and find it quite different from how you'd imagined. And you don't understand it.'

'I'm the simpleton,' he said.

'If we were away from here, and had time, we could understand each other.'

'It's the longing to be understood,' he said.

'What is?'

He was going to say love but instead said: 'Friendship.'

'The day of the dance at the Sports Ground,' she said, kicking a stone, 'my cat Ludo caught a bird.' She told him the story and he saw, as he remembered seeing the night he was with her behind the pavilion, her eyes brighten with the moisture of emotion. 'What I can't bear,' she ended, 'is the thought of the bird looking all day with bread in its bill for the young one.'

Even while he truly shared her horror he was thinking that it was time for him to return, before his parents began to suspect, because of his too-long absence, that his life had started to contain something of which they were ignorant and therefore must plan to learn about. Appropriately, a woman appeared at the back gate of one of the cottages and began to call for one of the playing children.

'I think I must go,' he said. He realized that he had not asked her how she had contrived her own, more dangerous absence; realized, too, that it was cowardice that prompted his incuriosity. For him her real life had somehow to be ignored, like the thought of a fatal disease in someone one loves.

'So we shan't meet in London,' she said, accepting it.

He turned away from her in disgust at himself. 'You mustn't bother with me,' he muttered, the words coming out against his deepest wish. 'It's no use. It was criminal of me to have written that letter.'

'No,' she cried, and he felt his hand seized. He gripped hers with the feeling that he would never, he thought, be able to show to her in any other way or at any other time.

'It's no use,' he repeated. Even in this moment of abandonment to emotion, he was capable of gauging the effect of that abandonment on what he had come to know as her eager nature. The double vision increased his self-nausea.

'No,' she said again. 'We must go on. I can't give it up.'

He wondered momentarily what 'it' was. A man in a trilby hat passed close by. Philip saw themselves through the stranger's eyes, the constrained, betraying, sordid public attitudes of private emotion. And then he was cognizant of the town's larger view—the Saddleford's solicitor, the wife of the Saddleford's Mortgage Manager, disporting themselves down an alley.

'I must go,' he repeated.

The head steward appeared with a tray of liqueurs which both men, for different reasons, refused. Gerson's hands, emerging like pale fins from his over-long sleeves, folded his napkin as though he were at home. He said, in a needlessly low and confidential voice: 'I think we ought to go over our plan of campaign.'

'I suppose so,' said Philip. A suffocating boredom swept over him.

'As I see it, we shan't at the outset of our discussion offer to suspend the capital repayments under the mortgage.' Gerson leaned far over the table so that Witt could clearly see the brutally severe shave and haircut to which Gerson always subjected himself. And so, he thought, this commonplace man was the reason why nothing lay at the end of the journey—no crises of action, no happiness, no misery. It seemed ludicrous that he had no mastery over such irrelevant and despicable elements in his existence. Of course, in a very real sense the prevention of his meeting Rose in London was not through Gerson at all, and he asked himself if it were not true that everything in one's life was symbolical of something else.

The permanent way curved, the train altered direction and the sunlight came through the window and fell on

Philip's face. He was conscious of his pallor, of the eye-sockets that betrayed the sleeplessness of the previous night: such things were like the proclamation by a poxed nose of the most disgraceful sexual secrets. Gerson's intent gaze on him was unbearable, and with a muttered word of excuse he got up and went through the car to the lavatory.

In the marvellous solitude of the little compartment he saw through the mirror, like one who has undergone plastic surgery, that after all his face was not impossible. He thought of Rose in Saddleford with her cat, her tweed coat, her copy of *Private Fall*, and suddenly the journey was given a meaning by becoming the prelude to his seeing her again, as for a child the long days before Christmas bear its reflected delight. The true happiness of anticipated happiness brought a frisson of excitement which automatically stimulated him to bring out his note-book from his pocket, and, leaning against the wash-basin, he opened it and read:

Imagine a society composed of two classes—the prosperous and the indigent. The classes have come together, drawn by self-interest, the prosperous to reap a profit by lending to the indigent, the indigent to exist by borrowing the wealth of the prosperous. But how were two such classes, their interests in mortal opposition, brought together and induced to persist in a calm and ordered relationship? The answer is that the machinery of the society consists of a third and much smaller class whose interest is merely to serve the interest of the other two classes. It is the third class which ensures that the needs of the indigent answer to the superfluity of the prosperous, that the profits of the prosperous are properly related to the capacity of the indigent, that the multifarious trans-

actions of the whole society do not exceed nor fall much below the society's means. The members of this third class are rewarded according to their relative importance in the machinery: thus, in their private capacity, they may either be members of the prosperous or of the indigent class.

But, you ask, are the two main classes really in equilibrium, does the third class serve them impartially? On a true analysis of the society is it not evident that the interest of the prosperous is paramount, that the machinery of the third class exists to preserve it, and that the members of the third class—even the privately indigent members—are necessarily, by virtue of their task in the society, permeated with the idea that, though while things go well a fair balance between the two other classes can and should be preserved, the protection of the possessions of the prosperous is their paramount duty? For, if those possessions are allowed to pass permanently to the indigent, will not the society ipso facto *be destroyed?*

Alas, these questions cannot be veraciously answered—at any rate by members of the society. Almost all of the prosperous and most of the indigent believe in the essential fairness of the society. Many of the third class have ceased to visualize the aims of the society, being unable to see beyond their own function as part of its complicated machinery. But one or two of this same class, though dedicating their whole lives to the service of the society, have in fact come to disbelieve in its proposed aims: these, beneath the veneer of their skill and devotion, are neurotic, unstable and unhappy, but fortunately they do not constitute any serious threat to the continuance of the society.

The Union Club was in Union Street, Saddleford's street of professional offices. Its stone façade, the double curving steps which led up to its pillared entrance, were black with eighty years of grime. The big smoking room was packed with hide furniture, its walls half panelled, half hung with a sombre blue and green Morris paper: in the middle an enormous table held periodicals in forbidding black binders and two dozen copies of the Saddleford *Evening Argus*. It was early and Stuart Blackledge sat drinking his whisky alone. An old member tottered in, said to Blackledge 'How do,' and immediately went out in search of better entertainment.

Blackledge wearily put down his own copy of the *Argus*. It was typical of Hepworth not to be on time: since the West End House affair had blown up, Hepworth's faults had become more remarkable. At first Blackledge silently defended him against the puritanical Vice-Chairman's insinuations: after more thought he had become suspicious of Hepworth's behaviour, even of his financial stability. To be tagged as Hepworth's friend seemed to him an unnecessary risk when, after all, the man meant little to him personally. And the benefits of their 'friendship' had been all on Hepworth's side.

When Hepworth at last threaded his tall figure through the furniture, Blackledge leaned rather embarrassedly forward and made a business of knocking his pipe out on his signet ring as though his thoughts, like wind broken in privacy, could linger and betray him. He ordered more whisky; Hepworth lit a cigarette and fitted it into a holder: the moment came when Hepworth expected Blackledge to bring up whatever business was the cause of his being asked to this venue suitable for the informal discussion of business and which he knew Blackledge did not otherwise favour.

Blackledge smoothed back one of his elegant grey

wings of hair. 'By the way, Cecil,' he said to his whisky glass, 'you never told me that the West End House company was in deep water.'

'Is it, old boy?' said Hepworth.

'You mean you don't know?' Blackledge looked the other in the face. 'But you're a director.'

'Not any more.'

'But you're a shareholder.'

'My building company was,' said Hepworth, ejecting the butt of his cigarette with the characteristically Hepworthian device concealed in the holder. 'We were paid in shares for some of the work we did on the place after derequisitioning. And the arrangement was I should go on the Board. But we sold out our shares a couple of years ago.'

'Very nice,' Blackledge said, hiding his exasperation. 'Unfortunately you've become associated in our own Board's mind with the loss we stand to make on this wretched property.'

'I'm not surprised that you anticipate a loss. The company never really had enough capital. The place soon got to look crumby and there was no spare cash to do it up. We were all a bit dazzled in 1946: I was tempted at the time to put some of my own money in the thing. Luckily, I've always been able to resist temptation.'

'The point is, Cecil, that this affair has cancelled out all the propaganda I've been feeding the society about your flats scheme. I don't see that I can get them to look at it now.'

'Well, that's bloody stupid,' said Hepworth. 'The society liked the West End House business when I brought it to them. It's no fault of mine it's gone bad on them.'

'They've never been keen on the flats idea. I was always battling with them about it.'

Hepworth reached out for his glass, revealing three inches of grubby white silk cuff. 'That's that, then,' he said, nonchalantly, and drank off his whisky. 'It won't be as pleasant working the scheme out with another society, Stuart.'

'Will you find another society to take flats?' Blackledge asked jealously.

'We've plenty of orthodox stuff to bait the hook with, old man. And that chap from the East Lancashire is always buying me drinks at the Golf Club.'

'The East Lancashire!' said Blackledge derisively.

'It's not the Saddleford, I know. But it's got the brass and doesn't ask so many awkward questions.'

'We didn't ask enough questions about West End House.'

Hepworth laughed his equine laugh. 'We've all got to swallow a peck of dirt in our lives.'

This interview increased Blackledge's distrust of Hepworth and when the latter had left him he began to think that there had been—though he could not quite formulate its terms—some kind of plot on Hepworth's part to induce him originally to put up West End House to the society. But the worst part of the affair was that his disillusion about Hepworth only confirmed the Vice-Chairman's views: he stood badly with both camps.

It was forcibly brought home to him that this was not the only plot against him. There was the garage business and the Joint Committee election. It might be that the plotters had no settled animus, no strong intention of injuring him—it would be absurd of him to imagine a world as evil as that—but it was nevertheless true that the fortunate—those who had looks, decision, ability—must expect in the natural order of things to encounter the envy and spite of lesser men. He came to this conclusion over the drink he had ordered when Hepworth had gone, and in his brooding solitude it seemed to him so startling and sound an extension of his knowledge of life as to afford him pleasure despite its melancholy content. Hitherto he had escaped the operation of others' wickedness, even the wickedness of nature. He had never been seriously ill; his business life had been all promotion; by the time the war came his managerial status had exempted him from service; he had married a bright and handsome girl. Conspiracy had taken him unawares, but so long as he recognized its authors and guarded himself against them, so long as he did not permit these setbacks to interfere with his destiny, he had little to fear. Talent could not, if it were true to itself, be diverted from its rewards.

He looked at his watch: he would be later home than he had told Rose but he was not disturbed—indeed, a sense of power came to him as for an instant he thought of her waiting for him in the midst of his well-run, well-equipped house. He finished his drink, got to his feet and found he had had more whisky than he remembered. On his way to the lavatories he paused before the open door of the billiards room, savouring for a moment its masculine, hieratic atmosphere. A face bent forward into the lights of one of the tables—the Chairman's face, the cue bisecting the walrus moustache. Blackledge stepped quickly from the doorway: he did not know whether Ambrose Halford had been told of the West End House valuation and either the Chairman's knowledge or his ignorance must make it painful for them to meet. Blackledge walked on, reminded again of his boyhood when he lurked guiltily in the house, uncertain whether or not his mother would, on his father's return, divulge to the latter the crime which he had committed so lightly and of which she had taken so serious a view.

By God, he thought, it was intolerable that the Club—like Saddleford House—had become a place in which he was not perfectly at home, where he had to divine what knowledge of himself and his affairs existed in those he met before he could enter into relations with them. Throughout his adult life he had often thought that existence would not be worth enduring were he not physically attractive; here was an analogous situation, and one which he had never contemplated as possible—some might despise him or pity him for his momentary loss of face, as though across his countenance there stretched an incredibly disfiguring birth-mark.

These exaggerated and gloomy fears vanished when he translated his whisky into action, driving his car very fast on the familiar road home. He wondered, as he so often did on this journey, whether it might be possible for him to make love to Rose immediately he got in the house; hoping he would find her in the sitting-room where his kiss of greeting could almost imperceptibly pass into the purposive series of actions he so desired. It was strange that upon such trivial domestic accidents as her whereabouts at his entry, or a cold rather than a hot supper, depended the possibility of the rich transformation of his evening implicit in his contriving to set her nakedness or half nakedness against the neutral, familiar objects of daytime existence.

It seemed to Rose that between her and her former life

some transparent but deadening curtain had descended, removing its immediacy and interest. She went through her normal routine with the detachment of one just wakened from a heavy sleep. Sometimes as she ate she was conscious of an excitement which almost inhibited her power of swallowing, but the excitement was unattached to her senses—as though somehow she was moved about a race whose result could have no possible effect on her. The motive of her existence had nothing to do with the house, her husband, the friends, which were still her ostensible occupation, but was directed towards making possible her infrequent meetings with Philip Witt.

These meetings—in his car, a café in Saddleford, the public shelter in a recreation ground near her home—she did not, for some time, recognize as the brief and unsatisfactory occasions they were. As soon as she was on her way to him the world became sensible and interesting. The most desultory encounter, the most ugly person, the most sordid aspect of the dark town, fitted easily into the pattern of goodness that her emotion made of everything. With him, her memories and opinions, her lust for knowledge of him, her own potentialities, seemed inexhaustible. Their interrupted but organically connected conversations took up all their time together, so that it was only when the moment came for them to part that she realized that she had never, as sometimes in the intervals of their meetings she had planned to do, kissed him; and they would grasp each other's hands fiercely as they said good-bye, as if they were about to be separated by half the globe.

She puzzled over the name to give their relationship. Had it been left to her she would have said that they were in love, but since the affair was unlike any she had ever known she was content to leave its character and limits to him, always conscious of the disparity between their intellects, constantly astonished to find that it was she who satisfied in him the need that she could not define. It was not until later in the summer, when she met him again after she had been on holiday with Stuart, that she began to see him as a character who existed apart from herself, with a life that persisted with its relations, pleasures, fears, even when she was not with him. She saw that beneath the glamour of his strangeness to her was a real strangeness, and again she was surprised, like a child with a blind father who discovers that not all fathers are blind. So she began to want to change him and their relationship.

Sometimes he left his car a mile from her house and then walked to his assignation with her in some quiet fields behind a small disused gasworks which had served the suburb in its days as a village. A scrap of wind-bent hedge was the landmark for their meetings: the time was always dusk or dark and he would wait for her, taking as much advantage of the hedge's cover as he could without making his concealment conspicuous, like a nervous soldier in a place of no real danger. Occasionally a solitary man would pass by, and Witt's heart would leap at the thought that it might be Stuart. When she arrived at last she always seemed smaller, stranger, more beautiful, than he had imagined her.

On one of these nights a drizzle began to exude from the warm grey still summer air as she came up to him. She said immediately they had greeted each other: 'I've been thinking about Christine.'

He was startled: it was the first time they had admitted

to her existence. 'Christine?' he said, and in Rose's presence the name took on an alien, even a foolish, sound.

'Do you see her?' she asked. 'As often as you see me? More often?'

'More often,' he said.

'But she doesn't know that you see me?'

'Of course not.'

'Do you love her?'

What does that mean? he asked himself, while his voice, without hesitation, said: 'No.'

'But you're engaged to her,' Rose persisted.

'I've had other fiancées, as my mother calls them,' he said, uneasily.

'Christine thinks you'll marry her, doesn't she?'

'I don't know.' It was the stupid answer of a schoolboy, and he added quickly: 'I'm not capable of marriage. Or of love.' He had a vision of his room at his parents' house: the notebooks on the desk, the alkaline tablets and *Anima Poetae* on the bedside table, the supply of paper handkerchiefs for his catarrh.

Rose said: 'Am I another "fiancée"?' When he did not reply, she went on: 'Why did you write? Why do we go on meeting—like this?'

'I've never made any secret of what I'm like,' he said, sadly.

'If you were the person you say you are we should never have been together, even here.'

He felt the rain on his face and a lifetime of conditioning told him that his health was being threatened, that he ought to be indoors. He half turned away from her as though that would induce her to see that they couldn't simply stand and get wet. 'No one can really be different from his own conception of himself,' he said.

She had her hands thrust deep into the pockets of her raincoat, and she said, almost stamping her feet with the vehemence of her uncertitude: 'Are we in love?'

'No,' he said again, without thinking, but seeing in that moment with such preternatural clarity the small glistening shapes of the leaves on the hedge that he knew his denial was a prelude to some agonizing feeling of loss that made it meaningless. The tears started to his eyes as he sensed a gulf yawn between them that his will was too weak ever to bridge. The explanation of his emotion about her—part relief at having escaped from her orbit, part anguish at having relinquished her—was too tedious, too tenuous, to attempt. He stood numb in his misery, his longing to escape.

She did not move. Nor could he detect any volition of movement in himself, but as, when a magnet slowly approaches its potential satellite and the metal, hitherto immobile, at the critical moment of its involuntary abandonment to the force of the field, flies suddenly to the outstretched arms, he found himself against her, pressing his lips on hers. His hands encountered the strange feel of another's clothes, her slimness was hard against him, and he thought incoherently: 'So this was all that was the matter.'

He whispered, his lips against her wet face: 'It won't do, it won't solve anything.' He felt the intense pleasure of knowing that his words were meaningless, of surrendering his intelligence to a more rudimentary mode of being, as a poet in the middle of cogitation permits his pen to write words he does not fully understand. When he kissed her again the cool unfamiliarity of her mouth was like some totally undeserved good fortune that it seemed as though he might be permitted to enjoy, and timidly, fearfully, anticipating his prospective happiness, he said: 'I love you.' And he saw that the word 'love' had not the meaning that formerly he thought it had, but was a word held in reserve to connote the specific abandonment of his existence to this real person he held in his arms.

'Yes,' she said, excitedly. 'Yes.' For the first time he heard in her voice what he realized had been always there but to which until now he had been deaf—the feminine catch and hollowness, the eternal threat of surrender—and he clasped her more fiercely, in awe of what she promised, fearful of losing what he had.

The following evening Philip came down from his room before his parents had gone to bed. They were drinking their tea and eating their evening snack.

'Well, this is a nice surprise, dear,' said Mrs. Witt. 'Will you have a cup of tea?'

'No, thank you, Mother,' Philip said, seeing out of the corner of his eye his father biting into a piece of the pastry stuffed with sugar and sultanas made regularly by his mother and that in their family was called 'flat Anthony'. It was unbelievable that he had once loved his father, rubbed his face against his stubbly jaw, thought him clever, knowledgeable, nestled close to him in bed. How monstrous that the family, suitable, progressive, for primitive man, should have survived to civilized ages! Though, of course, his mother and father were primitive still.

'Is it too late for a hand?' Mrs. Witt asked at large, seeking to communicate her sudden pleasure to her husband.

'We're not going to start playing cards at this time of

night, surely,' said Mr. Witt, sending out a few crumbs of flat Anthony. He had often commanded play at more advanced hours, but for some reason he wished to sacrifice his opportunity of enjoying himself.

'All right, dear,' said Mrs. Witt placatingly. 'We'll just have a little chat then before we go upstairs.'

But no one spoke. Philip began to sweat: the simple thing he had come down to do suddenly seemed outrageous. In the impetus of his love for Rose he had planned in the wakeful hours of the night the very phrases he would use to his parents, but, as always, he had not anticipated the stifling, impenetrable atmosphere they engendered, indefinable because compounded of no distinguishable elements and impossible for him, it seemed, to combat. Like a commander of forces hopelessly inferior, he threw his opening words to the slaughter.

'I'm thinking of taking a little flat,' he said.

'Oh, Philip,' his mother said as though he had stabbed her.

'I know we discussed it a few years ago,' he added quickly, 'and I remember the reasons you both had against it. The chief one was my health. But now my health is perfect.'

'You're still delicate, dear, you know you are,' said Mrs. Witt.

'The point is, Mother, that I need complete isolation for my work.'

'You have your nice room here, Philip,' said Mrs. Witt. 'We couldn't have made it more comfortable for you.'

'It's difficult to explain to you, but someone who is trying to work must feel a sense of freedom—to stay in his room, or to move about at all hours. . . .' He realized that they were not listening to him: they never listened to ideas that they felt were outside their comprehension.

'Who'd look after you?' asked Mrs. Witt.

He knew that the question was rhetorical, but he attempted a reasoned reply. 'I should have a housekeeper to come in every day.'

'To cook and mend and keep the place clean?' Mrs. Witt smiled pityingly. 'You'd soon find out the difference, dear.'

'Mother, I know that the move presents difficulties, but they can all be overcome.'

Mr. Witt spoke for the first time, leaning forward a little in his chair and addressing no one in particular. 'A little flat,' he said witheringly, and laughed at the evidently ludicrous phrase.

'Besides,' said Mrs. Witt, in triumphal argument, 'your Christine won't want to live in a flat.'

For a moment Philip was startled into imagining that his mother had by a slip of the tongue said 'Christine' instead of 'Rose', and knew of his liaison and the real reason for his desire to move. 'What has Christine to do with it?'

'You'll be getting married soon and be wanting a house. Moving into a flat now would be just a waste of money, dear.'

He began to invent a counter to this argument. 'But, Mother——'

'A little flat!' interrupted his father. 'Where will you find a little flat going in Saddleford? I've never heard of one.'

They were in the dining-room: the belly of the big mahogany sideboard was open to the room. It contained a wooden biscuit barrel hooped with silver, flanked on either side by the only books his parents possessed: Nuttalls' Dictionary, a Bible, a household encyclopædia they had acquired in the 'thirties through a newspaper free gift scheme, and an out-of-date A.A. Guide. When Philip was very young his father had sometimes jocularly put him in this space: he stared at it now, marvelling at the million threads which bound him to the almost insanely farcical life of this house. Just as his mother was about to speak again he got up and walked out of the room. From the hall he heard his father's voice raised in angry discussion and for a moment he felt the shrinking of the flesh that in boyhood had feared physical punishment. He let himself quickly out of the front door and got the car from the garage.

He drove it to Bellsgate and parked a street away from the Blackledges'. He walked on the opposite side, hugging the privet hedges, past the house. It was in darkness: the moon shone on the closed garage doors. The front door was hidden in the shadow of the porch and he willed Rose to come out of it. But perhaps she was already in bed. And then, as if he had remembered too late some disastrously neglected duty, the thought pierced him that she was possessed by another man. Automatically he started to run, so that his body could leave its pain behind. But his chest carried the pain along with him.

VII

It proved impossible to let the restaurant of West End House at an economic rent. The directors of the company conceived the idea of converting it into shops and approached the society for a further advance to cover the cost of conversion. This the society refused since some of the existing shops in the building were empty or occupied by tenants of dubious stability. The agents in whose hands the management of the building had been put had made little progress with it, and sent gloomy reports about situation and paintwork. The capital repayments under the company's mortgage had been suspended for two years, but even so it had failed to pay the interest due at the 24th June. Repairs and rates had swallowed up the current income, said the company, and there passed some correspondence between the managing director, desultory on his side, and Philip Witt on behalf of the society.

It became painfully obvious that the time was rapidly arriving when the society would be forced to exercise the remedies available to it under its mortgage deed. These could be boiled down to two practical alternatives: to sell, or to appoint a receiver to collect the rents of the place, pay the outgoings and apply the balance towards the capital and interest under the mortgage. Either alternative was distasteful to the society. A sale would certainly result in a large capital loss. The appointment of a receiver would postpone that evil day, but there seemed little likelihood that the receiver could manage things so that the net income from the property would service the payments required by the society's mortgage.

'The company is over-capitalized,' said Gerson, for the tenth time.

The General Manager sighed. 'It seems under-capitalized to me. It's got no brass, any road.' He had hopes that the thing could be kept ticking over until after his retirement. 'What about the bank?' The company's bankers held a debenture.

'The bank doesn't seem to be very interested,' said Gerson. 'They have probably said good-bye to their money already.'

'My bank never says good-bye to my overdraft,' said Matheson. 'Now if the company's bank were to advance them the cost of this conversion of the restaurant to shops and a little to spare for dolling the place up, we should have a very different proposition to sell in due course.'

'I don't think the bank would do it. There's so much due to the society they'd never see their money back.'

'My dear lad,' said Matheson, 'we wouldn't put it to them like that. We've got to sell them the idea that it's only for want of a little ready money that the place isn't paying its way. Carry out the conversion, smarten the place up, and you start bringing in enough income to service our mortgage *and* the debenture. It might even work,' added Matheson warmly.

'I suppose it could be tried,' said Gerson.

'It must be tried. You'd better ask Witt to go to London and meet the directors of the company and the bank people.'

'There are some very pressing creditors, according to the company,' said Gerson.

'He must see them, too, and tell them not to press. If the company goes into liquidation they haven't a snow-ball in hell's chance of seeing their money.' The General Manager touched his handkerchief to the roots of his silver hair. 'It's a proper worrying business, this.'

'It is, sir,' said Gerson.

'I think you enjoy it, though,' said Matheson, a little maliciously.

Gerson spoke out of a stiff face: 'I couldn't enjoy anything that damaged the society.'

There was no doubt about it, thought the General Manager: Gerson was becoming quite perky. The chilly character, that once had seemed only a nullity, had acquired a momentum. There was even something different about his appearance. Matheson eyed the Accounts Manager with more attention and saw that Gerson had different glasses. The old round horn-rims had gone: the new lenses were rather flattened, rimmed with gold along their upper arcs to which the thick horn ear-pieces were attached, the rest of the lenses rimless. Matheson was impressed with their smartness, opened his mouth to remark on it, but as though he had divined the coming embarrassment, Gerson rose, made his little bow, and departed.

The General Manager leaned back in his chair and from a paper bag in a drawer of his desk took out a sugared almond, a delicacy to which he was partial and which he never chewed until he had sucked right down to the nut, thus extracting pleasure from virtue.

After his first rash communication, Philip Witt had arranged with Rose to write to her at the General Post Office in Saddleford. Since their meetings were few she often called for his letters. Her journeys into Saddleford, formerly merely dutiful, became part of the expanding secret and nervous segment of her life. She grew to know the clerks behind the post office counter, to prefer that one rather than another, because of his sympathetic personality, should answer her self-conscious inquiry.

Passing through the town late on a Saturday afternoon on their way to a dinner engagement, Rose asked Stuart to stop the car so that she could make a shopping call. She knew that he would not be able to stay where she had asked him to draw up, and while he drove on and halted in a side street she slipped furtively into the post office and procured her letter before performing her errand. Back in the car she ostentatiously took the lipstick she had bought out of its package and reddened her lips, thinking of the letter hidden in her handbag as if it had a life of its own, like a normally inanimate object in a fairy tale, and might suddenly leap out proclaiming her guilt. She was aware of Stuart by her side, not as someone she knew intimately, but as a parent or superior officer whose desires, conception of life, ran counter to her own and who therefore must be deceived. In the mirror of her powder compact she saw the thinner, paler face that faithfully reflected her disturbed mind and appetite, the tension that woke her early, kept her on the edges of chairs.

She had tried to find in Stuart some venal quality to justify her abandonment of him. But it was only her own characteristics—the longing to be loved afresh, to find a sensitive probe for the neglected reaches of her mind—that could supply a reason for her action; characteristics that in the practice of the affair she could not approve, which seemed to her, indeed, in the depressed moments of her loneliness, smug and evil. Stuart was egotistic, committed too completely to success in the world of money and desirable social acquaintances, physically vain—but so had she been until the sheer accident of her love for Philip had made her qualities and situation irrelevant. The more demands that the relationship with

Philip made, the more eagerly would she strive to fulfil them, and the more guilty she would become. And she wondered whether there was any point at which her conscience—or her rational sense of self-preservation—would force her to return to the old, safe life, when it would be Philip in whom she would look for the flaws to solace her betrayal.

In this confused state she lived, striking out blindly towards the furtive and hard-won pleasures of a letter, a kiss, a walk at some dead hour of the evening, along factory walls and mean streets. This evening, when the bridge started that followed the dinner, she waited impatiently for the first time she was dummy. Then she went and locked herself in the bathroom and there, among the peach-coloured porcelain and the matching towels their friends had newly laid out, she tore open Philip's letter and tried to read it in one sweep of her eyes. Quick as she was, the cards for the next hand had already been dealt when she returned to the table, and for a moment of panic it seemed to her remarkable that none of the three players turned to accuse her of her secret life.

She had read in the letter of Philip's forthcoming stay in London: on the way home in the car she said to Stuart: 'I think I shall have a few days with Mummy next week.' And, after all her evening's dread of the moment, the words came out with no tremor, reasonable and convincing.

'All right, darling.'

She glanced at his face, faintly illuminated in the light from the dashboard, his words bringing home to her the fact of his increasing abstraction with her. She asked herself in alarm if he could possibly have an inkling of her disloyalty. But it was inconceivable that he could know and keep silent: he was too sanguine, insufficiently in awe of her, too intolerant of those with ideals and physique he considered inferior to his own. Perhaps, she thought with a little glow of joy, he had ceased to regard her with any serious emotion, and she said: 'You don't sound as though you'll miss me.'

'You know I'll miss you,' he said with more warmth. She was tempted, perversely, to go on, to drag from him an admission of her overwhelming importance to him. Before she could speak he took his left hand from the wheel and, with his eyes still on the headlight-pierced road, slid back the thin material of her dress until he found the bare flesh of her thigh. To her astonishment her body went rigid against the long-familiar caress and she felt a blush burning in her cheeks. She waited tensely for the minimum time to pass before her action could arouse his suspicion, and then eased his hand away by gently pulling down her dress. 'It's chilly,' she said, with a short laugh that frightened her with its manifest contrivance. But the hand went back obediently to the wheel. 'Shall I light you a cigarette?' she asked. It seemed to her the only concession she could make to him.

If she left him for ever, she thought, switching the lights on in the house that accommodated her like an old sweater, while Stuart was putting the car away, he would miss her because she was essential to the machine of his life. He would not be able, without unthinkable expense, scandal and inconvenience, to find someone who would combine in one respectable and commodious role the functions of housekeeper, lover, hostess, *objet d'art*. And yet, she continued, even in our walk of life, husbands and wives sometimes separate.

She undressed before him and was already in bed when he came from the bathroom. In the hollow formed by the curve of her legs the cat, Ludo, was curled up asleep. Stuart regarded the sight and said with a touch of exasperation: 'You ought not to encourage it to sleep on our bed.'

'I didn't encourage him,' she lied. 'It's just a habit he's got into. He'll probably go back to the piano stool in a day or two. Don't disturb him when you get in.'

'I can't think this a hygienic habit.' When he was in bed he switched out the light and said: 'Ready for sleep, darling?'

She simulated a stifled yawn. 'Yes, I think so. I'm tired.'

'It's Charley Mason's bridge. He's the slowest player I've ever come across.' She sensed him move into the attitude he always adopted for sleep. 'Good night, darling,' he said.

'Night, darling,' she answered. She cautiously extended her arm and felt Ludo stretch a little in his curvature at her touch and start a low purr. The dear guardian of her new chastity, she thought. Cats were the natural allies of women for they were like women—men only saw their subtly-motivated actions as whims and could never understand the delicate, demanding boredom of those compelled to spend their whole life in a house. She ought not to be annoyed with Stuart that he always referred to this real, mildly eccentric, beautiful, sensuous creature as 'it'. Then she began trying to imagine meeting Philip in London.

He could not have said whether or not his mention of his London journey to Rose had been a tacit invitation to her to meet him there. But as soon as he knew of her own journey an anxiety no less terrible for being unformulated started to gnaw him as though he were perpetually crouched at the start of a race he was in danger of winning. The evening he received her letter he went to his room immediately after his meal to try to reduce his vague fears to intelligible words. She could not have analysed, he thought as he took a sheet of notepaper, the possibilities of disaster that lay in their meeting. And, quite apart from the chances of their being seen by someone who knew them, the vast emotions that stretched beyond the first undisturbed hours they would ever have had alone, there existed the stupefying practical complications of time and place. Tonight was Monday: it had been impossible for her to see him. Tomorrow (she had written) was probably equally impossible. On Wednesday he must leave and they must travel by different trains, preferably on different days. There would have to be furtive, confused telephone calls. It seemed to him likely that they might both make the journey, their arrangements fragmentary or misunderstood, and never find each other in London.

He regarded these fears not without irony and a sense of their absurdity—as a madman might surrender to his recognizable mania. In all the distortions of his character there was a strong element of the conscious and therefore the avoidable. He remembered his last months in the Army—the cold nights in the Suffolk gun post; the cross-country runs; sitting in the Ipswich Y.M.C.A., his battle dress gently steaming, after an hour of wandering the streets in the rain; the strange food and the N.A.A.F.I. beer it had been a point of comradeship to eat and drink; the inanities of the army administration which he had taken seriously and therefore with horrible anxiety. All these had been avoidable. Even, he could almost think, the war itself. They had happened to him because his will had so demanded. In due time, his loss of weight, his sweats, his bad digestion, had presented to him the possibility of surrendering his body to the care of others. And so had started the long process which had ended with his discharge from the Army—a process he had never considered inevitable, for the very presence of the baccili in his lung had required his consent.

And, after all, there was nothing in his life or appearance which others could see that without his own confession could lead them to suppose he was other than he should be. It was he who was surprised when his acquaintances, as sometimes he learned they did, found him witty, sympathetic, kind, amused. The amount of suffering he betrayed was entirely optional.

He wrote: *You will have to fulfil some obligations to your parents and I shall have my meetings. It's too much to hope that our short free times will coincide. To avoid the bitterness of frustration and disappointment, ought we not, this time, to leave quite to chance whether or not we shall meet? Perhaps, walking out of my meeting—assuming that I have been able decently to shake off the men who tend to cling to one after such meetings, suggesting drinks or a shared taxi—I shall see you at the far end of the street, see that you, too, are quite alone and uncommitted.*

Suppose we were together on an uninhabited island: would we nevertheless form a society? Invent duties, taboos, fears, so that even there we could not, at all times, come together freely? Certainly two people can make a society, and not necessarily—or perhaps not possibly—so that it serves their desires . . .

And then, like the end of a long journey, it was as though there had been no anxiety, no tedium of arrangements, no threat of frustration, no ignorance of means, but that all had been inevitable from the start. Standing outside the store which had been surprisingly easy to find, he saw Rose on the opposite pavement, blotted out occasionally by buses unfamiliarly red, hands in the pockets of the cream-coloured raincoat, waiting to cross to him. Nor was it, as he had imagined, embarrassment that he felt as she came up to him and gave him her hand, warm from its pocket, but happiness.

'You were right,' he said, moving with her from the crowded pavement into the hushed shop, its lights glowing strangely in the morning air, 'it was possible.'

'And your first meeting isn't until this afternoon?'

'No.' He looked round. 'Should we have come in here?'

She laughed. 'I want to buy something. Do you mind? We can have coffee first in the restaurant.'

Among the hatted ladies, their parcels and handbags on the chairs at their sides, ordering in reckless self-indulgence cream cakes with their coffee, chattering under the low roof, Rose seemed to him all the more strange. Even her appearance he had forgotten or perhaps had never before had time to remember consciously—the light blue eyes set in lashes so thick that from a distance they grouped themselves in irregular masses as though badly mascara'd, the delicate hands that scarcely matched the vigour of her physique, the small gold earrings piercing the white flesh of the small lobes. They talked about the mechanics of their coincident arrival, and when they could see each other again, calculating the hours, appointing meeting places. He found himself astonished that this talk could be absorbing, inexhaustible, tender, at the power of love to transform, like metrical language, its common material. And his body drew in a strength that overpowered the hangover from his sleepless night of anxiety, so that he felt he could have assimilated coffee after coffee, cigarette after cigarette.

They walked at last down the staircase to a department that sold dresses. In the carpeted space between hanging clothes and curtained cubicles he sat rather embarrassedly on a gilt chair while Rose conferred with a blue-haired saleswoman. He was a little reassured to see, waiting on another chair, an elderly man of indubitable propriety and elegance. It came to him that Rose had planned this deliberately commonplace and purposeful hour of their meeting. What tortuous and tortured seriousness could have overcome them in other surroundings!

Passing him, in the wake of the saleswoman carrying an armful of dresses, Rose said: 'I'll try not to be long.'

He smiled and gestured, attempting to convey his understanding and so allay her anxiety that she might have gone too far in her effort to ballast their emotion. She disappeared into a cubicle with the saleswoman. He stared into the distance at the lifts, crossed his legs, reached automatically into a pocket for his pen, touched it but did not bring it out. He thought of the narrative in the notebook on his desk in his room at home, remembered the precise situation at which he had left it, but for once the creatures of his imagination seemed too unreal to capture his attention and he could not make out what they were up to.

Turning his eyes by chance towards the cubicles, his

glance fell through a few inches of space between the edge of a curtain and one of the ply-wood partitions. By some arrangement of the mirrors in the cubicle that was not clear to him, the gap was sufficient to reveal the reflection of a strange girl's back, its upper part bound with the thin straps of a brassière, then tapering to a slim waist. Out of the minute white drawers two long legs emerged, firmly planted apart. The girl raised her arms and a grey and black striped dress began to tumble down her length.

Philip averted his head, as guilty as though he had been deliberately spying, feeling his blood pulse. He feigned to examine the carving on his chair arm. He heard the swish of a curtain and Rose's voice call: 'Philip, do you think this suits me?'

He stood up and with astonishment and desire saw her standing in the open cubicle, flanked by the saleswoman, smoothing down the grey and black silk. Again he averted his head, frightened that she should see the blur he felt in his eyes. He uttered a few suitable words, thinking only how great his love for her must be since until this moment it had failed to take into its calculations the body that gave her her being. At last she reappeared in the familiar raincoat, the calculated rags that only serve to call attention to the princess's beauty; she wrote out a cheque for her dress and they walked to the lifts.

He said: 'Shall we go to my hotel?' He pressed the lift button with what seemed to him supernatural power.

'Is it all right?' she asked.

He said that it was, though when their taxi drew up under the glass awning and the commissionaire opened the door and saw them attentively through the portals of the vast foyer, handing them on, it seemed, to the eyes of under-managers, receptionists, inquisitive guests, he was seized with panic at the outrageousness of their conduct, and remembered how before he had left home he had discounted the possibility of Rose coming to his room. As he put his key in the lock he hastily formulated excuses should they find the chambermaid still there.

But the room was empty, the bed made, his two or three books neatly arranged on the side table and marking the place as his. He turned to her with relief. 'Isn't it a hideous room?'

She was automatically unbuttoning her coat: he took it from her and laid it on one of the chairs, seeing through the window a light rain coming out of the grey summer sky. When he looked at her again she was standing in the same place, smoothing back her hair. She said: 'I couldn't imagine this happening. But it has. It's this that one can't imagine'—and she touched the yellowish veneer on the bed-end—'and the precise time of day and . . . and oneself.'

The hammering started in his chest and since he knew that his hands were shaking he kept them behind his back. He said with ridiculous irrelevance, his voice skating on the top of tremulousness: 'You should have been able to imagine the fumed maple.'

She glanced at his brushes on the dressing-table. 'Trying on dresses is fatal for the hair.'

When he put his arms round her he was amazed at her slightness and softness and realized that he had never held her before without her coat. He drew away from her lips, highly conscious of the awkward three feet that separated them from the bed. He stumbled with her across the gap and somehow found himself outstretched on his elbow at her side. 'I really am a numbskull,' he said.

She laughed as though she knew what was in his mind, and put her arm round his neck.

'I can never think that anyone can love me,' he said, and saw his hand, with a skill that it did not seem he could own, begin to undo her dress. An absurd compulsion made him go on talking until at last she half sat up and, moving a little away from him, freed herself from the dress, and he saw with, as it were a sense of *déjà vu*, the brassière and the little drawers. Behind the desire his fear mounted, now that she lay so vulnerably unclothed, that someone in authority would come rapping at the door, challenging with undeniable justice his right to have her with him.

The meeting took place in the Victoria Street offices of the company's firm of accountants. It was conducted by a member of the firm, a Mr. Cawsey. He sat behind his desk, a pale cheerful man of thirty-five who in the intervals of a rapid lower-class London speech constantly produced a clacking noise from the back of his nose to clear his catarrh. He had done little to prepare for the comfort of his visitors. 'Put your file on the corner of my desk, if you like, old man,' he said to Philip Witt. Mr. Black and Mr. Sikowski, two of the company's directors, then entered. 'My God,' cried Cawsey, 'I think we shall need another chair.' He edged his way to the door and called along the corridor for his office boy.

Philip, seeing nowhere to hang it, had kept on his raincoat: the office was stifling. He had greeted the two directors on their entrance: now they sat together avoiding his eye, conspicuously without papers. Cawsey resumed his desk. 'Well, gentlemen,' he said, 'I think we're all here, aren't we? I'm not very sure myself what we're here *for*'—he laughed and clacked—'so I think the Saddleford Building Society ought to set the ball rolling.' He cocked his head on one side and looked at Philip.

Philip said: 'I hope we do know what we're here for. My society sent out copies of its letter to the company.' He thought of Rose saying she had not been able to imagine them together: certainly he had never anticipated this crowded, dingy office, his sweating body, the task of starting, from cold, to put the society's tenuous and almost certainly unacceptable ideas.

Black, who wore a moustache over a receding chin, heavy horn-rimmed glasses, and abundant hair brushed straight back, said, in his whining but irascible manner: 'For some reason I've never been able to make out, the building society has always been reluctant to make a further advance to my company for the urgent repairs and conversion.'

'Mr. Black,' said Philip, 'you know perfectly well that even the society's old advance is not secured on the present-day valuation.' He was surprised at his irritability: surprised and annoyed with himself—it was pointless to argue with Black, whom they had long ago discovered to be a weak man lamenting continuously over the thousands he had sunk in the company.

'The society would be far better secured if those repairs were done and the restaurant made into shops,' said Black, looking meaningly round.

'That is not as we've been advised,' said Philip.

Cawsey said cheerfully: 'Well, can we take it that there'll be no more money forthcoming from the Saddleford Building Society?'

'Yes,' said Philip. 'And I may say that we made that clear months ago.'

'Of course,' said Black, 'we should never have borrowed from a building society in the first place. We should have gone to people who would have been interested in our business, who would have helped us through these inevitable bad patches.'

'I really don't think generalities are going to help us today,' said Philip.

'No, no,' said Mr. Cawsey. 'Let's get back to practical politics.'

Mr. Sikowski, a middle-aged man in a brown suit, with a complexion a shade lighter, who hitherto had sat silent and unsmiling, opened a mouthful of black and gold teeth and said in a heavy accent: 'The place must look nice, you know, that is most important. It does not look nice. Also, the restaurant will not pay. It must be changed, you know, to shops. Then the place will make money.'

No one replied to these remarks. Cawsey said: 'The point as I see it is, is anyone interested enough to want the company to go on trading? There are several creditors who won't hold their hands much longer. Rates, electricity, fuel—very big bills.'

Filed in Philip's mind, waiting to display themselves during every lull in his attention to what was currently happening, were the pictures of the events of the morning and early afternoon. He yearned to prove those events accidental, uncharacteristic, capable of reversal. He relived every action, ending with the tying of his shoelaces, the false kiss, his exit from the room to come to this meeting, more hurried than the lateness of the hour warranted. He had even left her with the impression that the meeting was to take place earlier than its appointed time. He told himself that the few critical minutes could not affect the long-drawn subtleties of their relationship, but the relief was momentary: the poison of the fiasco penetrated again and again every thought he had about her. And if he despised himself how could he hold her against the force of convention that time would make stronger and in the end pull her back into her orbit? He saw with frightening clarity that with truer insight into himself he could more happily and satisfactorily have spent that hour in the hotel bedroom merely with his head chastely pillowed on the brassière, in the masculine dream of an eternal and balanced tension with an inviolable but desired protectress.

'I'm only the company's auditor, Mr. Black,' Cawsey was saying after some pointless exchanges, 'not its witch doctor.'

Philip made his effort. 'The situation, as we see it, is really quite simple. If we are compelled to realize our security now there will certainly be nothing left for the unsecured creditors. We ourselves stand to make a substantial loss. On the other hand we are prepared to be co-operative if we have evidence that West End House can be made to pay its way. We have already suspended the repayments of capital under our mortgage. I can't commit our directors, but I'm sure that suspension would be extended until the company was well on its feet—if we saw that it was really stirring from its present recumbent position. But at this moment the company is in arrears even with the interest under the mortgage, and, of course, if that isn't paid we shall be forced to realize. As you probably know, a building society must detail in its published accounts the mortgages it holds which are upwards of a year in arrears: a society of our size and reputation must avoid publicizing its difficulties over a mortgage as large as this.'

'At the moment we are not yet six weeks in arrears,' said Mr. Black in the tones of a Dreyfus.

'But without the slightest prospect, so far as we can see, of avoiding further arrears, let alone resuming capital repayments. Of course,' added Philip, wearily, 'all this is obvious. The real point I want to make is that we feel that a creditor might be found who would put fresh capital into the company to facilitate these repairs and alterations we've heard so much about, and with the object of enabling the company gradually to increase its revenue and avoid the sale by the society of what is its only asset.'

The solicitor acting for the company's bank, a small dark bald young man who so far had said nothing, looked up from an elaborate doodle and remarked: 'I can't help thinking that when you say "a creditor", Mr. Witt, you mean my clients.' He grinned amiably.

'If the cap fits, Mr. Gorman,' said Cawsey. 'Eh?'

'Certainly it has crossed our minds,' said Philip, 'that the bank would not wish us to realize our security. In that event the bank's debenture would be worthless. On the other hand, if the bank were to extend further credit to the company, it might in the end come out on the right side.'

'It might be chucking good money after bad,' said Gorman.

'That is for the bank to decide, of course,' said Philip.

'There is just one preliminary matter, Mr. Witt,' said Gorman. 'I was rather puzzled when you spoke of the worthlessness of the bank's debenture in the event of your clients selling West End House. My instructions are that the furniture and fittings in the building are of quite substantial value. There is the furniture in the furnished flats and the furniture and equipment in the restaurant——'

'But all that is included in the society's mortgage. We should naturally sell the building and its contents together, and even so, on the valuations we have, the proceeds of sale will fall very far short of the amount owing to the society,' said Philip.

Gorman looked at Philip with a rather studied, quizzical expression. 'I'm sorry, Mr. Witt, I'm still not with you.'

Philip experienced a slight feeling of unease: this man was not a fool though he seemed to be doing his best to appear one. 'I can't make myself any plainer, I'm afraid.'

'Then perhaps I'm at fault,' said Gorman with a self-deprecating smile. 'Not to put too fine a point on it, my clients claim to have a first charge on the furniture and fittings.'

'How?' asked Philip, conscious of his sweating body. 'Under what instrument?'

'The debenture.'

'But that is dated long after my society's mortgage.'

'The society's mortgage does not contain a charge on the furniture and fittings,' said Gorman.

'Nonsense,' said Philip, but the alarm rose hot in his throat.

Gorman imperturbably skimmed a document on to Cawsey's desk. 'Don't take my word for it. There's a copy of your mortgage.'

The hand Philip reached out for it was trembling. He began to turn over the pages, scarcely seeing the words as he tried to recall the circumstances in which he had drawn the mortgage, to discover a possible reason why he should have omitted to include the chattels. The society certainly had all along assumed that the chattels were a part of their security, but perhaps their instructions to him at the time of the loan had been faulty. That surely could be the only explanation.

'Clause four, Mr. Witt,' said the detestable Gorman. There was a silence while Philip read the vital words which was recognized as critical by everyone except Mr. Sikowski.

'It is no use,' he said, 'to try to bring nice tenants, nice people, to the place unless the place looks nice, you know. And a restaurant there is no good. The district is not rich enough, you know. But shops, yes, shops will do very well.'

Philip raised his flushed face. 'I don't agree,' he said to Gorman, 'that these words exclude the chattels.'

'Well,' said Gorman equably, 'I've advised my clients that they do.'

'I can see that there is perhaps a little ambiguity.' Once he had broken the ice he found that his voice was becoming firmer, his fear and embarrassment masking themselves with a veneer of reason and calm that he felt to be convincing. 'Of course, we shall have to consider the interpretation you are putting on the clause, Mr. Gorman. I haven't brought a copy of the mortgage down with me, so I shall have to write to you when I get back.'

'I don't think you'll find there's any doubt about it,' said Gorman.

Cawsey clacked. 'Now what does all this mean in words of one syllable,' he asked cheerfully, looking at Gorman as the man who obviously had the answer.

Gorman said: 'It means that my clients are not entirely without security. They will be quite content to let the contents be offered with the building when the society put it up for sale—and it seems to me that a sale by the mortgagees is the inevitable end of this matter. All that remains to be done is to agree with the society what proportion of the purchase price will be attributable to chattels and come to my clients.'

'In other words the bank is sticking at sixteen,' said Cawsey, amused at his own turn of phrase.

'Of course, I can't accept this,' said Philip. The car had ceased to respond at all to his steering. 'If the bank's interpretation of our mortgage deed is misconceived, it may want to change its mind about giving the company further credit.'

'Not a hope, I'm afraid, Mr. Witt,' said Gorman, already putting away his papers.

Mr. Black and Mr. Sikowski started speaking at once.

Their room faced the well in the centre of the hotel: very early in the morning Rose was wakened by clattering sounds funnelled up from below. Immediately she knew where she was, whom she was with, and yet an intense feeling of strangeness, almost terror, seized her. The white glazed bricks of the well sent the dawn light through the chink in the curtains and cautiously rising on her elbow (finding herself, because she had brought no things, vulnerably naked) she could see Philip's dark hair on the pillow beside her, the box of sleeping pills on the chest at his side, his brief case on a chair. As she had sometimes thought, in the face of a threatened, happiness-destroying event, of the conception of a God to whom conceivably she could appeal, so she thought now of the haven of conventional morality and wondered if evil really resided in the triumph of desire over the rules of human society. She saw, as one sees in the moments after breaking a valued possession, how easy it would have been to have avoided the events that had led up to the crucial, the irrevocable one; and it appeared to her that really she had wished to avoid it but that some fate foreign to her true self had compelled her on.

Philip's breathing seemed that of someone she did not know. She started to re-live the previous day: the time in Philip's hotel when the sudden, surprising familiarity of the final act had overwhelmed her impression of the individuality of the actor; the evening meeting, her telephone call of deceit to her parents, their coming to this hotel, the drinks, the dinner—the hundred irrelevant and unmemorable details which had nevertheless become a part of her deepest life and which she would always remember. Some time after they had drawn apart for sleep, she had heard him fumbling with the glass of water. When he felt her move he had said: 'I'm sorry. I shall have to take some knock-out drops.' And in answer to her unspoken question he had added: 'Nothing to do with us. I can't stop thinking about a horrible turn this West End House nonsense has taken.'

The milk churns, or whatever they were, in the bowels of the hotel were part of the whole awakening of the city that her long sojourn in the cosy provinces had made cold and antagonistic towards her. And now her conduct had destroyed her own home as a refuge. As always at the thought of a terrible gaffe she began silently to hum a non-existent tune, and then, not able to bear inaction, she crept from the bed to find cigarettes and matches.

'Rose.'

The sudden voice sent her pulses hammering. 'I'm only getting a cigarette,' she said, seeing through the gloom Philip poised alertly half-way out of the bedclothes. 'How lightly you sleep!' She lit her cigarette.

The match must have briefly illuminated her body for him. He said: 'You'll get cold.'

'No, it's quite warm.'

'Why couldn't you sleep?' he asked.

'Thoughts.' She laid the cigarette on the ash tray on the cupboard at her side of the bed and slid back between the sheets. Immediately she felt him clutch her hand.

He said softly: 'You're worried. Isn't my love enough?'

'Do you really love me?' she said uncertainly.

'Oh, Rose, it's I who ought to ask that.'

'Darling, I do love you, I do love you,' she cried.

'We must never come again to these awful places,' he said.

'No, it's not awful here now.'

'I mean the false names in the hotel register, and mixed up with the society's piffling affairs, and the fear of someone knocking on the door, challenging us.'

She said: 'No one can challenge us.'

His hand touched her. 'I loved you enough before I knew you were like this. I should have been content.'

'No,' she said. 'It will be all right.'

'Your cigarette,' he said.

She leapt up and stubbed it out. Then she leaned over him tenderly. 'It's you who worry,' she said.

'Yes.'

'You shouldn't worry about the society's affairs. They're beneath you.'

He laughed. 'Dear Rose.'

'I mean compared with your—your imagination, your writing. What made you concerned about that rotten company yesterday?'

'I've made a mess of it, I think,' he said.

'But it doesn't matter even if you have—it doesn't *matter*.'

'No,' he said. 'But it matters to me. I'm committed to not making a mess of it.'

'Why don't you get away from it—from Saddleford, the society, all those people you have to pretend are your equals?'

'It's too late,' he said. 'My parents taught me that life was making enough money, a place in society, and I've never been able to unlearn the lesson. I've only ever seen the world from a safe position. In the 'thirties it was my friends who were unemployed—sometimes I watched them from the window of the firm where I was articled, marching in processions, and I moved quickly away when they got near. Then the war started and I waited for my life to be changed for me. When I was called up into the Army it was changed and I thought I could never again go back to the old life. But I went back and it was just the same except that I had no friends who marched in processions—indeed, there were no processions—and my position in society was more assured.'

'But if you escaped now,' she said, 'you could live, you've enough money.'

'Not enough money to quench my fears that some day I shouldn't have enough money. Now I wait for my parents to die for my life to be changed for me.'

'And will you escape then?'

'What do you think? And what is escape? Whatever I

escaped to would still be something I should have to escape from again.'

She pondered over that and then said: 'All the same, there *is* something to escape to.'

'What is it?' he asked.

She thought: If you openly took me away from Stuart. She said: 'I don't know. I don't know the word. Not immorality.' She was amused at herself.

'Dissidence,' he said.

She moved his wrist so that she could see the dial of his watch. 'We've got four hours.'

His arms slid round her. 'My favourite toy used to be a rubber doll—the rubber quite hard, but resilient because the toy was only filled with air.'

'You see,' she said, 'you needn't worry.'

VIII

The first night of Rose's absence Stuart Blackledge dined alone at the Queen's. The other grill-room tables were occupied by couples with their heads together by the pink-shaded lamps. He read the *Argus*, talked to the waiter about the Saddleford Cricket Club's new professional, drank a double whisky with his steak and chips. After dinner he made the mistake of driving straight home.

He drew the sitting-room curtains against the disturbing light of the summer evening and got out a pack of cards with the intention of trying the *Daily Telegraph* bridge problem. The house was quiet and smelt warm and unused. He poured himself a drink and then, instead of sitting down with the cards, wandered into the kitchen, let the cat out, looked at his face in the small mirror over the sink. He whistled the tune he always whistled, a song from *Evergreen*, and went upstairs still carrying his drink. In the bedroom, changing into a sports jacket and flannel trousers, he smelt Rose's perfume, saw a white slip of hers he recognized hanging over a chair.

A mood came over him of years ago when he used to have a bachelor flat—a mood of intolerable restlessness in a familiar and boring cage. In those days he had sometimes drunk half a bottle of whisky while he roamed about the flat, playing the gramophone, eating, smoking, talking to himself; occasionally he had driven to a neighbouring city, visiting public houses and cheap cafés, and once or twice letting himself be picked up. Those depressed times had been when he had lacked a current amatory affair. At this distance his behaviour seemed to him startling, quite incompatible with his place even then in the society's hierarchy, his respected role in the town. He saw, too, how his marriage had saved him from the growing risk of scandals, from a reputation tolerated in a young man, viewed with suspicion in a middle-aged one.

The friends of his youth with whom he had drunk beer after rugby matches, driven in open cars, danced at the town's best dances, had already before the war found themselves wives and husbands and he had been forced to an older set, some of whose members had a faint air of disrepute. There was a bookmaker, a divorcée, a too well-dressed commuter between Saddleford and the West End of London whose prosperity was not fully accounted for by his business. Stuart could not doubt now that had his association with such people continued, his promotion in the society would have been prejudiced. The follies of his youth had lasted too long.

Then during the war came another era which he looked back on with a new sense of the risks he had taken. The confusions and uncertainties of the times had made it seem natural for him to do what he had never done before—involve himself with female members of the society's staff. The first had been in the Correspondence Department whose bosom had distinguished her for him from the ruck of girls who walked about the corridors of Saddleford House. Fortunately she had soon been called up into the A.T.S. The more prolonged affair had been with a telephonist whose husband was abroad in the Army and whom he had come to know in the spells of fire-watching duty he had democratically taken at Saddleford House. Sometimes in the evenings she had come to his office and he had locked the door, not caring if anyone should try the door and find it locked, concerned only that their sensuality should be uninterrupted. Even the husband's return might not have meant the end of that affair had it not been for his engagement to Rose.

His meeting with Rose—it was at the dinner dance organized by some prominent citizens to honour the departing Group Captain from the R.A.F. station outside the town—had brought out and emphasized hidden virtues. With her he seemed older and incapable of folly: and his marriage, his house, the stricter routine of his private life had, it seemed to him, added depth to his qualities of appearance, drive, leadership. Her fastidious, sometimes withdrawn, subtly-temperamental character kept his love for her always stimulated and aggressive, with areas, even in marriage, of denials and discoveries. And he was proud of her—of her appearance and, like an enterprising importer, of her London origins, exotic and foreign in Saddleford.

And yet at this moment in the empty house, when some hours of the evening still lay ahead, he felt in her absence a sense of freedom and opportunity that excited him—a precious sense, alien to his married existence, of unknown places and people open to his will. To walk slowly downstairs, to enter the sitting-room again, to pour himself another drink, was the exercise of a virtuous restraint. For a moment he thought of himself as he appeared to the world—a clever and rising executive—and actually got his brief case from the bench in the hall and went to the desk in his study. He took out a cyclostyled copy of the papers for the next meeting of the Board and began to read a report on salary scales for junior staff.

After no more than a few moments he rose abruptly and went out of the house. Getting his car out again was a no more boring preliminary than the cautious unbuttoning of a girl's blouse. Soon he was driving very fast under the sodium lamps of the bypass: in less than an hour he parked the car in a black cobbled street of warehouses in the city where he felt himself unknown.

Two streets away in the glare of neon signs, the lit entrances to cinemas, prowled the life he desired. He went into the saloon bar of a pub decorated with palm trees, green plastic leather and chromium, sat on a stool at the wet counter, ordered whisky, listened with benign alertness to the talk and laughter. The drink had surrounded him with an extra skin, at once numbing and sensitive. To the taste of the whisky, his pipe, his senses vigorously responded; he unhesitatingly arranged in order of desirability all the women presented to his gaze: but his rebarbitive concern about his West End House *gaffe*, his feeling that he had lost initiative and control in Saddleford House, seemed without hurting effect, the second jab of the cocaine needle. He thought about them as if some person other than the one inside his body were involved. The point was—and it came to him with a flood of happiness—the point was he did not care. The difference between caring and not caring was simply a habit of mind: it had no equivalent in reality. If he decided not to care, nothing and no one could destroy the happiness which quite obviously existed in himself not the world.

In a fish and chip shop after the pub had closed he got into conversation with two girls.

'What's happened to your boy friends?' he asked them.

One girl giggled: the other said: 'We've been tut pictures by us two selves.'

'I don't think much of the young men of this town if they leave two attractive girls like you to pay for themselves at the cinema,' he said.

The giggling girl said: 'He's tight.'

The other girl ate a chip or two reflectively and then said: 'Haven't seen you knocking about before.' Her round face with its formless features was very brightly made up.

'I'm the mysterious stranger,' said Stuart. 'Where does all the night life go on in this place?'

'What dust mean?' asked the round-faced girl.

'We could all do with a drink or two, couldn't we?'

'There's *King of Spades* on t' Manchester Road.'

'What are we waiting for, then? Let's go.'

'I'm going to no *King of Spades*,' said the giggling girl, fervently and not giggling.

'Well,' said Stuart, 'your friend and I will go by ourselves.'

The round-faced girl took a drink of her blood-coloured mineral water. 'Nay. I'm not going without Valerie.'

Stuart leaned forward seriously, as confident of his way through these familiar preliminaries as though they were negotiations for the finance of a building estate. The girls were impressed with the car when finally he led them to it, and since they both sat with him on the front seat, the round-faced girl was pressed hard against him. She did not flinch. On the journey he found that her name was Carole. He scraped a wing parking the car at the *King of Spades*, but leapt out without a thought about it. Over the gravel towards the sound of canned music and the flimsy floodlit building, he put his arm round Carole's waist. Her breast moved heavily against his finger tips and he thought that even after the first drink he would be able to persuade her back to the car.

'Of course,' said the General Manager, 'you can bet your boots that when one thing goes wrong another thing will go wrong. Stuart Blackledge made a ballsup of the valuation and now you tell me you've made one of the mortgage.'

Matheson's voice kept its usual philosophical calm, but in the General Manager's drumming fingers and vigour of language Philip Witt detected a concern and anger that affected him all the more for being concealed. He said again, like a foolish schoolboy: 'I'm terribly sorry.'

'It's a bit ironical when you think we insisted on you

and not the company's solicitors doing the job so we could be sure a ballsup wouldn't be made,' Matheson could not resist saying.

'It was inexcusable of me,' said Philip. His voice trembled; he felt utterly ignominious; and yet every word he uttered seemed fraudulent—the words of one who really desired to give the blow that proved in the end quite accidental.

'Now what exactly happened?' Matheson said. 'I want to understand it. I shall have to tell the Board this week. I shall get roasted alive.'

'I feel worst for your sake,' Philip managed to get out.

Matheson stopped drumming and eyed him carefully. 'You're looking a bit old-fashioned, lad,' he said. 'This is a bad do, but worrying won't mend it. Did you get any sleep last night?'

'I'm all right,' Philip said, and added quickly: 'I'll try to explain about the mortgage. It isn't in one of our printed forms, of course, because of all the special provisions. The society's instructions to me were quite clearly to include the chattels—the furniture and so on—in the mortgage security with the freehold property. I went to the precedent books for some of the mortgage clauses, naturally. Including this one about the chattels.' He took a copy of the mortgage from his file. 'There is a charge on West End House and then it goes on: "And also the furniture equipment and all the trade and tenants fixtures now in or about the said property (not being personal chattels within the Bills of Sale Acts) or which during the continuance of this security shall be brought in or on to the premises." '

'Well, that sounds all right,' said Matheson.

'It's not all right, I'm afraid. You see, a mortgage of

chattels by an individual has to comply with the formalities of the Bills of Sale Acts—it must be in the prescribed form, it must be registered under the Acts. So in the case of a mortgage of freehold or leasehold property by an individual you can only charge in the same document those chattels to which the Bills of Sale Acts don't apply. That's what the words I've read out are designed to do —get hold of as many chattels as possible without offending the Bills of Sale Acts. And so you have the words in brackets—"not being personal chattels within the Bills of Sale Acts".'

Matheson blew through his pursed lips. 'You'll have to write a report about this, lad.'

'It's a simple point really, as you'll appreciate when I come to it. So simple I can't understand how I came to pass it. You see, all that I've said about the Bills of Sale Acts doesn't apply to limited companies—didn't apply to West End House in this mortgage. The company could have charged *all* its chattels without offending the Acts. I used the wrong form—I used the form applicable to an individual mortgager not a company. I knew the law. It was sheer carelessness in the use of the precedent books.'

'Have we got *any* of the company's blessed chattels?' Matheson asked.

'Chattels within the Bills of Sale Acts are those capable of passing by personal delivery,' said Philip. 'So I'm afraid we haven't.'

'The bank's got them,' said Matheson. 'Under its debenture.'

'Yes.'

'What a ballsup!' said Matheson.

'There's just one possibility,' said Philip wretchedly,

'and that is that we might successfully maintain that the words in brackets are so obviously inappropriate in a mortgage by a company that they ought to be ignored in the interpretation of the clause.'

Matheson brightened. 'That seems plausible.'

'I thought we might go to counsel. Old Tibble might be prevailed upon to give an opinion on those lines and then we could flourish it at the bank. It would be a bargaining lever.'

'Go to counsel, lad.'

'I think it would be best for me to have a conference before I ask for his opinion.' Even in this moment Philip visualized the enormous emotional and travelling complications of another meeting in London with Rose.

Matheson brooded. 'You know what the valuation of the stuff inside West End House is?'

'Yes.' Philip looked away.

'£4,000.'

'Yes.'

'The Board will roast me alive.' The General Manager did not reveal what pressed most on his mind—that for both Blackledge's and Witt's bloomers he must, in the eyes of the directors, bear the responsibility, and at the very time of his impending retirement when they must decide whether or not to invite him to become one of their number.

'Who is she?' asked Christine, almost in tears.

'My dear, I can't tell you that.'

'I've a right to know.' Her fingers mutilated the tassel on the cylindrical cushion.

'Even if she had never existed we couldn't have gone on,' Philip said.

'Why not? Everyone thinks we are engaged. But it's not that. I can bear the things that people will say, and Mother wanting me to give reasons. That doesn't really matter. It's losing you to someone else I can't bear.'

'Christine,' he said unavailingly as she turned incoherently away from him. He saw the neat bun of fair hair, and thought of her white body as of a quite pleasant resort at which, nevertheless, one will never stay again. 'I told her that she had conferred a benefit on you.' She did not reply, so he added: 'By releasing you from me.'

'That's hypocrisy,' she said.

'No. When this evening is over you'll be glad that it happened.'

'I could never marry anyone else.'

He was drained of responses. He thought of the ghastly night, his forced morning confession to Matheson and now this emotional scene to which he had dragged himself without any emotion except fear.

Christine regarded him through glittering eyes. She said: 'We should have married long ago. You would have been happy—and well, too. I can't imagine why we didn't marry, why we went on . . .'

He saw how bitterly she regretted her unavailing guardianship of her virginity. 'This is not conventional comfort, but I think you'll start again now you're freed from me.'

She looked miserably at the two empty chocolate cups on the low table between them, symbols of their vanished relationship. 'No,' she said.

And perhaps, he thought, she wouldn't, but would merge imperceptibly into a middle-aged spinsterhood and old age, becoming awful and legendary to the children she taught. But the notion did not connect itself with the woman sitting here, and he felt sickened at the impossibility of true concern and sympathy for lives other than one's own. It was easy to believe that no one suffered save oneself.

The clock on the mantelpiece, which bore a silver plate commemorating its presentation to Mr. Eastwood for long tenure of some social office, chimed nine o'clock. Since he could not possibly bear to encounter Christine's parents, the situation for Philip now resolved itself into a matter of leaving the house during the next hour. They had become two more of those people in Saddleford whom his shyness, neglect or eccentricity impelled him to avoid.

The clock ticked loudly in the silence and he wondered if it would be outrageous for him to try to direct the conversation away from the subject which, like that of illness between one mortally sick and his visitor, seemed at once exhausted and without alternative.

'I'm sorry, Rosie,' said Stuart. 'I'm not hungry.' He began to fill his pipe.

Guiltily she put down her own knife and fork. Could he possibly know? And if he knew would he for the moment keep it to himself? 'I'm not hungry either,' she said. 'I'll get the coffee.'

'Did your father sell those Glaxo shares?' he inquired.

'I don't know,' she said, rising abruptly, as though the question were the innocent lead into others she could not support. 'I never asked him.'

'He should have taken his profit.'

'I'll mention them when I write,' she called, already out of the door.

When she returned with the coffee she had a question

prepared to keep them off the topic of her visit to London. 'How did you scrape the car?'

'You saw it? It was that low wall at the Queen's—some fool didn't leave me enough room.'

'Will you claim from the insurance?'

'No,' he said, going to the sideboard. 'I want to keep my no-claim bonus. Let's have a spot of brandy, shall we?'

'I don't think I will.'

'Come on. Cheer you up.'

It seemed to her that everything had its hidden meaning. And how strange it was that simply through her own defection the whole meat had been sucked from her marriage! Did he not see himself that everything they did was quite cold and dead, the motions and dialogue of two stand-ins? Yet all he said was: 'Shall we go to the cinema?'

'Yes,' she answered eagerly, seeing the problem of the evening dissolve. In her relief she said with almost genuine concern: 'You look a bit done in. Are you working too hard?'

He looked up quickly and said: 'It's the . . .' Then he stopped and finished his brandy. 'I thrive on work,' he said.

She got up, horribly conscious of her deliberate omission to press him to disclose what was in his mind, but quite unable to give him any more of herself and certain that what he had hesitated over was of no importance to her secret life. She said: 'I must go and get ready.' Only a few months ago she would have plunged into an analysis of his malaise of mind, gratified that he had hinted of it, anxious to deepen what was between them.

Repairing her lips in front of the dressing-table mirror, she was surprised and ashamed to see the brightness of her eyes, the glow in her cheeks. It was the sudden rain, she told herself, but she knew that her body realized its happiness in spite of her troubled mind. Though happiness was too simple a word to define the love that persisted and grew through the furtive encounters, the painful physical adjustments, the arduous chases after Philip's mind. The lipstick poised, her imagination leapt forward, over the impossibly tangled threads that her love had spun, towards a future truly happy.

She heard the car tyres snap on the gravel and glanced down through the window. She saw Stuart get out, go to the wing and pass his hand over the damaged place. In the fading light the hair above his ears looked almost white. She gazed back in the glass at her own and then remembered the long years she had in hand over him. Opening the wardrobe for a jacket she saw her clothes like a row of disguises.

'We would like you to leave for the next item, Mr. Matheson,' said the Chairman. 'And you, too, of course, Mr. Hill-Smith,' he added to the Assistant Secretary. When the two men had closed the Board Room door behind them, the Chairman said: 'The Vice-Chairman and I thought it was best to label this item "Chairman's business" in the Agenda to prevent any unfortunate rumours getting about in case we don't come to a conclusion today. Most of you know, gentlemen, that under this item we have to discuss the General Manager's retirement at the end of the year when he reaches retirement age.' He turned to the Vice-Chairman. 'You'll write the minute for the Secret Minute Book as usual, won't you, Sir Harold?'

Sir Harold nodded his yellow face.

From the position he had chosen right at the end of the Board table—the deliberately obscure class position of the obstreperous boy—Furness asked: 'Does the item include the question of the General Manager's successor?'

'I think so, yes, certainly,' said the Chairman, speaking as he always did at Board meetings, except about the most obvious matters, with his head turned only half to the front as though facing a biting wind, but in reality so that he could see any gesture of dissent or anger from the formidable figure of the Vice-Chairman at his side.

'Otherwise,' said Furness ironically, 'I see little point in the item. I suppose the General Manager *is* going to retire.'

'Well, of course,' said the Chairman, as though the question had raised a sudden doubt in his mind.

The Vice-Chairman said dryly: 'I don't think Mr. Furness is being entirely serious. He remembers, as we all do, the Board's decision two years ago to enforce retirement at sixty-five strictly in all cases—from General Manager down to office boy.'

A fat, jolly director said: 'How many office boys of sixty-five have we got?'

The Vice-Chairman did not deign to reply to this.

'The point about the item is,' said Dillon irascibly, 'as we all know in spite of these facetious remarks, that some of us would like to see Mr. Matheson on the Board.'

'Mr. Chairman,' called out Furness from a lolling position, 'my question was not facetious.'

'Of course not, Mr. Furness,' said the Chairman placatingly.

Dillon said, still in a bad temper: 'It doesn't need me to say that Mr. Matheson is a man of very wide building society experience, young for his years, who would be an asset to any building society board in the country. It would be a crying shame if our society were to lose his services at his comparatively early age.' He was conscious that he had put his case far too soon in the discussion for it to make its full effect, and his puce face moved round suspiciously trying to pin down the conspiracy that had prematurely led him on. In reality he had not the least belief in the justice of what he was urging, but he knew very well that the Vice-Chairman wanted to save the vacancy on the Board (which had arisen through the long-awaited death of an octogenarian director in the early spring) for a nominee of his own. And Dillon, besides disliking the Vice-Chairman, was convinced that he had already too much power.

'I would like to support those remarks, Mr. Chairman.' The speaker was an elderly director named Lees who rarely spoke and whose words had been prefaced by a painful throat-clearing. 'Mr. Matheson's appointment would give a real fillip to the morale of the staff. Mr. Matheson rose from the ranks. If he came on the Board the staff would know that in every clerk's brief case was a director's baton.' He smiled, pleased with himself that he had managed to get out what he had for several days planned to say. He saw the Chairman open his mouth to speak, and added quickly: 'I don't intend to vote on this question, if it comes to a vote, Mr. Chairman. But I thought it only right to voice my views in spite of my interest.' He referred to the fact of which everyone was aware that his sister had married the General Manager's brother.

'Very proper, Mr. Lees,' said the Chairman.

Dillon tried in vain to catch the eye of a director called

Buckley, an architect with prominent teeth and a tendency to side whiskers, who had privately expressed his belief in the desirability of Matheson's elevation but was now drawing an elaborate gothic façade on his blotting pad.

'Perhaps Mr. Barlow as the senior director in length of service would give us the benefit of his views,' said the Chairman. The aged Barlow, attached by the ear to the plastic deaf-aid in front of him on the board table, was finding inexhaustible interest in the sight of a glass of orange squash.

'You'll have to shout,' said Furness. 'He hasn't got his machine turned up far enough.'

'Mr. Barlow,' called the Chairman. 'What do you think . . .?'

The Vice-Chairman listened to these proceedings with noticeable patience. When Barlow had quavered his reminiscences and Dillon and Lees had repeated themselves he said: 'Mr. Chairman, to my mind this item cannot be separated from the previous item on the agenda—the disconcerting report we've heard on the West End House mortgage.'

'Hear, hear,' said Furness.

'Mr. Matheson has been long in the society's service and no one values his qualities more than I,' Sir Harold continued. 'Indeed, I was cordially in favour of his appointment to the General Managership seven years ago. But I had in mind then that his tenure of the office would necessarily be short. Frankly—and, of course, we are all speaking our minds on this matter in perfect confidence—he did not seem to me then of quite the calibre for the post. I am confirmed in that view by the state of the West End House account.'

'That is no fault of Mr. Matheson's,' said Dillon.

'It has happened under his régime,' said the Vice-Chairman. 'It is not necessary to be meticulous in apportioning the blame. Sufficient to note that there has been slackness and ill-judgement. Our society has a vast responsibility to its shareholders. I never want to hear of another West End House affair as long as I am spared to sit on this Board.'

'West End House was a freak,' said the Chairman fervently.

Sir Harold went smoothly on. 'Mr. Matheson has no professional qualifications. That is no fault of his, and his career has been all the more meritorious without them. Experience—however prolonged—is no substitute for a sound initial theoretical training and a life spent working to exacting professional standards.'

Many directors sat with mouths slightly open, dazzled as always by the Vice-Chairman's eloquence and force, and knowing, even against their previously formulated opinions, and in the face of their dislike of him, that his arguments were in the end unanswerable.

'Turning to the question of Mr. Matheson's successor,' said Sir Harold, 'similar considerations apply. We are looking for professional qualifications and impeccable soundness. I confess that I would like the qualifications to be those of a chartered accountant, but of course I am prejudiced.' Sir Harold's toadies laughed dutifully. 'A sound chartered accountant. The kind of man who would have looked at the West End House application long before it reached the Board and turned it down flat on the figures—in spite of plausible valuations.'

So, thought the more perceptive directors, in the Vice-Chairman's mind Blackledge was out of the running.

'I move, Mr. Chairman, that we set up a small committee to make its recommendations to the Board both on the question of the vacant directorship and on that of the General Manager's successor. That will save a lot of —I won't say aimless, but too general—discussion round this table. I hope you will choose Mr. Dillon, who has expressed his views so well today, to serve on that committee.'

Dillon could not help feeling mollified. Some directors who had been watching the clock and thinking of lunch spoke warmly in favour of the conception of a committee, which eventually was voted to comprise the Chairman, Vice-Chairman, Dillon, Furness and a director whose views the Vice-Chairman knew would coincide with his.

She had rehearsed the speech a score of times. 'Would you mind if I nipped down to Mummy's for a night? That grey and black dress isn't right.' But when at last she played it her audience was apathetic. After Stuart had uttered his three words of assent she had forced herself to check an explanation of her action—the expensiveness of the garment, the folly of shopping in London, the pleasure her surprise visit would give to her ageing parents—in case its very over-determination should arouse his suspicions.

She had caught the same train as Philip and they had engineered an encounter in the dining car. At St. Pancras they had left in separate taxis for the same hotel. Meeting again in their room the first thing he had said was: 'I've never thought of it before—Stuart must connect my absence at the office with your absence at home.' His agitation communicated itself to her: for long horrible moments she wished with all her being that she was back in the innocent unhappiness of her own house, out of the suddenly sinister walls of the hotel room, freed from the burden of contrivance and love. The feel of the plate glass on the dressing-table where she had momentarily rested her hand was at once insubstantial and haunting, like the milieu of a nightmare. Then she had embraced him and the different reality had slowly returned.

Once when she woke in the night the fear came back. Her brain, with the terrible clarity and logic of four o'clock, told her that since she had scarcely the courage for this deceitful life she would never be able to inflict the final hurt on Stuart. Like a child she lay as close as she could to Philip, hoping that he would wake and comfort her without her being guilty of the weakness of waking him. Hours later she opened her eyes and saw Philip leaning over her.

'Do you sleep with Stuart?' he asked.

A dozen questions and qualifications formed themselves in her still-drowsy mind. 'No,' she said, at random.

'How can you avoid it?'

'Not since . . .' She was suddenly conscious of the painful presence of his fingers round her arm and she grasped his wrist to pull them away. 'You hate me,' she said.

'You must leave him.' His face was clenched in an expression she did not know. It was slightly ludicrous though she could not really find it so.

'To come to you?' she asked disingenuously.

'You know I have nowhere of my own.'

They stared at each other with the forced calm of gladiators before the contest.

They left the hotel early. Philip had conferred with counsel late the previous afternoon and she went with him to the station. For safety she was to catch a later train. Under the gentle and huge glass arch of St. Pancras they gazed at the steam, signals and clouds framed by its further end, pretending, in case they were observed by any Saddleford traveller, to have accidentally met, and in reality feeling that what bound them was tenuous and false. Their true selves seemed to lie in the letters each had hidden away and in those which remained to write, when the hesitations and unfulfilments of their passion for one another acquired, by being expressed, the virtue of an art—as though belonging not to themselves but to fictional lovers reading of whose unhappiness made them, by purgation, happy.

Returning from London she had found Saddleford small and dark, its inhabitants pale and deformed, a dwarf and inferior racc. It was evening when she turned her key in the door. She had looked in the garage but the car was not there. Walking along the path a dry leaf had fallen from a tree and the street lamp had come on, blurred through the faintly chilled air. She looked in the sitting-room and the study in case the car was in for repair and Stuart had come home without it, and then, breaking a promise she had made long ago, she dialled the number of Philip's home. The voice, at once timid and curious, which she knew as that of his mother, denied his presence. Rose cradled the receiver with the mingled disappointment and relief of the thwarted telephonist, and remembered her beloved Ludo.

She found him under her dressing-table stool, after discovering a small patch of vomit on the bedspread. She picked him up and said fondly: 'Filthy animal! What have you been eating?' His coral nose against her cheek was dry. She was seized with remorse that he should have felt seedy without her indispensable presence to minister to his subtle needs. She took him to the kitchen and made a dish of milk and water the temperature he liked. When she put it near him he moved two feet away and remained still.

Later, as she was writing a letter to Philip, still in the kitchen in case Stuart should surprise her, she heard a sound as though Ludo had dilatorily decided he was thirsty. But when she looked she found that he had gone under the table and that it was a curious licking and opening and shutting of his mouth, as though he were trying to remove some stickiness from it, that had made the clacking noise. When this ceased Ludo gave a moan that set her heart beating, and then, moving jerkily backwards with convulsive heavings, he at last managed to leave behind a little pool of frothy vomit on the floor.

That was nine o'clock. It was almost midnight when she heard the car in the drive. She went to the door: Stuart seemed to her to take an unconscionable time putting the car away.

'Hello, darling,' she said to him when he appeared. 'I've been longing for you to come.'

'You shouldn't have waited up, Rosie.' He busied himself putting his hat and brief case in the cloakroom.

'Ludo's ill. Was he all right when you left this morning?'

'Right as a trivet,' he said, making for the sitting-room.

She followed at his heels. 'Is it too late to get the vet?'

'The vet,' he repeated, amused.

'Yes, it is too late. I should have 'phoned him earlier. Nine o'clock would have been reasonable, wouldn't it? Ludo's been sick twice since I came home.'

Stuart, standing by the tray of drinks pouring whisky for himself, made some indistinct remark.

'What, darling?' she said, going nearer to him.

'Have a nice trip?' he asked. He looked at her over the top of the glass.

'Not so bad,' she said seriously, and then saw that he was smiling foolishly at her. 'What's the matter, Stuart?'

'Have a nice trip?' he repeated.

'Stuart, are you drunk?'

'I defy you to prove it.' Very slowly he sat down with his drink. 'During the last few days I've evolved a new philosophy of life. Quite simple. You just decide you don't care. Then you're happy.'

'You shouldn't drive the car when you've had so much to drink. Is that how you scraped the wing?'

'I never thought I should marry a nagging wife.'

'Can you manage to get up to bed?'

'Go, if you want to. Go, if you prefer a cat to me,' he said.

Immediately he was in bed he fell asleep. She switched on the electric fire and put Ludo on a rug in front of it. By the time she was undressed the cat had moved from the rug and was crouching under the bed. She went on her knees and caressed and spoke to him. When she turned out the light she watched the rug, illuminated by the glow from the fire, hoping Ludo would go back on it of his own volition. In the end she fell into a light sleep from which she was awakened by the now familiar clacking sound. Her pulse beating fast, she switched on the bed-side light and leapt out of bed. Ludo was behind the curtains in the window embrasure. The clacking ceased, he uttered a heart-rending cry, and started his heaving retreat.

When the sickness was over she put him on the rug, but by the time she had cleaned up the vomit he was under the bed in his tensed, crouching position: she knelt for some time stroking the small black head with one finger. 'Darling Ludo,' she said softly. 'I shouldn't have left you.'

It was half past three. Stuart was on his back, his face very pale, a silver wing of hair straggled across his temple. Rose automatically folded the suit he had thrown off in his urgent alcoholic wish for sleep. Her concern for Ludo excluded every other feeling, so that Stuart's presence was no more to her than the presence of the familiar furniture and Philip did not enter her thoughts.

Three hours later she was awakened again by the sounds of the cat's sickness, and she rose weary but alert, thinking how quickly life could disintegrate into its essential element of death.

Often, at moments when he should have been happy—as now, taking Rose's letter to his room—the thought of his terrible mistake in the West End House mortgage dropped like a dagger into the pit of his stomach, and he was conscious of the magnificent subterfuge which enabled him to continue whatever outward action he was engaged on, like an actor who discovers the absence of some essential stage property. The enormity of his offence consisted not only in the revelation of his fallibility and stupidity, but also—and even more acutely—in its evidence of the failure of the duty he owed to the society that relied on his skill, maintained him and gave him his status. It became clear to him that his error arose out of his divided life—that he could not hope to serve the society as he should if he cared more for the imaginative creations of his leisure. And it was plain, too, that whatever he thought privately of the society, its functions, its ruling caste, its aims, since it had in good faith engaged his loyalty and skill, his error was an offence against a morality which he could not confine to his business life.

As one who criticizes æsthetically something he has carelessly smashed, he had tried, at first, to minimise his offence by setting the triviality of the thousands he had endangered against the millions in the society's reserve accounts, by recalling the sordidly mercenary motives which had brought the West End House company into being, and by despising the stained concrete and utilitarian outlines of the building itself. But the proposition that his own character, ideals and activities were self-evidently superior to those of the ordinary, ordinarily-motivated world, he could not persist in maintaining. His most secret, most cherished existence rested on an ambiguity which he could scarcely analyse—a child who would not have lived at all but for the act of the parents whose principles and persons the child detests, who did not ask to be born but whose birth cannot be cancelled, who would not have wished to be born, but whose life is precious.

He dragged his thoughts away from the details of his conference with Tibble—even the senile, kindly barrister, his life spent dealing with errors, had thought this one a monster: 'I'm afraid, Mr. Witt, that it is a fundamental canon of construction that all words in a document must be given their natural meaning: I cannot see anything at all in your contention that those words in brackets have no effect. . . .' Philip's last hope had faded in the dusty book-crowded chambers.

Rose's letter had come by the afternoon post: it had been in his pocket unopened through the evening meal. Downstairs his mother and father were certainly wondering whether or not he would emerge from his room before it was time for them to go to bed. Philip opened the letter nervously, fearing the greater candidness and authority of the written word, as though it were to reveal some truth about their second time in London—as a parent, forced to silence during the actual event, afterwards, sadly and not entirely unexpectedly, reveals the utter inadequacy of the child's conduct on a grave social occasion. He read:

Darling,—When I got back I found Ludo ill. I've just had the vet and he has diagnosed feline gastro-enteritis. My cat book says it is 90% fatal. Ludo has to have tablets —M. and B., I expect. The vet gave him one very skilfully but goodness knows how I shall go on. Ludo is very poorly. It is the worst thing—to see pain in someone you're fond of. You forget this and then it happens again and fills your whole life. I can't collect your letters, darling, so will you try to ring during the day? I love you. R.

Absurdly, Philip suffered a pang of jealousy that the cat should monopolize Rose's care and affection. Automatically he took out his pen to write to her and then remembered that he had to telephone her instead. As he sat in a stupor of inertia, there was a knock at the bedroom door. He hurriedly put away Rose's letter, and called: 'Come in.' To his astonishment, his father entered. Philip stood up, feeling his cheeks grow hot, not only at his father's mere presence but at the unrealized sin that must have precipitated it.

'I wanted to have a talk with you, Philip,' said Mr. Witt. 'Privately. I won't interrupt you for very long.'

'You are not interrupting me, Father. Sit in the armchair.'

Mr. Witt sat down and crossed his legs. On one foot the enlarged joint of his big toe had worn a hole in his felt slippers. Looking over the barrier of his own embarrassment, Philip saw, with surprise, that his father, too, was embarrassed, as though his authority and self-possession did not extend to this room. He had certainly not entered it since Philip's illness towards the end of the war.

Philip said: 'I haven't been able to start work this evening yet.' Even this neutral remark was, in their relationship, an enormous confession, a daring intimacy, for Mr. Witt had never in his life referred, in Philip's presence, to his son's writing. But in the awkward moment Philip searched about for any garment to hide the nakedness of his father's unease.

'Good. Well, in that case,' said Mr. Witt, 'perhaps we may get a hand in later in the evening.'

'Yes,' said Philip. Surely this momentous visit was not to sound him out as to the prospects of a game of solo.

'Your mother is very fond of you,' said Mr. Witt, as though this remark followed naturally from his last.

'Yes,' said Philip again, wondering apprehensively what new oppression was being hatched.

'When you had that touch of lung trouble she nearly went out of her mind. You know that. You're an only child. Except for the spell during the war she's always had you with her. Of course, she hopes eventually you'll be happily married, but she's always been very glad you've been able to live in this house, to be with her, for all these years. It's been a great pleasure and comfort to her. Even more so now she's not as young as she used to be.'

'Of course,' Philip muttered. As his father shifted his bulk about in the chair and became accustomed to the strange milieu, his robust presence dominated the room as effectively as that of a large and restless dog, and Philip felt his own personality shrink and with it his faculties. So he found difficulty in rational thought and even in the audible production of his voice. He added: 'I've no intention of marrying.'

Mr. Witt ignored this remark, as he ignored much of other people's conversation. 'You said a month or two ago, Philip,' he went on, 'that you were looking for a flat. Perhaps you weren't serious. I don't know. But it's been worrying your mother. She hasn't let on to you. It's been worrying her a tremendous lot.'

'I haven't found a flat.'

'I wish you could put her mind at rest, Philip. She knows that flat-life wouldn't suit you, and, as she says, although you've made a good recovery you've still got to take care. You've got your own room here—what you might call a one-room flat—and your mother to look after you. It wants a lot of thinking about.'

'Father, I haven't got a flat, you know.' Philip felt the familiar pressure of circumstance that kept always bottled up the words he really wished to say, permitting only a thin exudation of the commonplace. He was afraid, yes, but afraid not only for himself but also for the other person—afraid that the other would be hurt or disappointed or made foolish by being confronted with Philip's own desires. So that his character was forced to be deceitful: amenable and mild in public, in secret rebellious. Why, he asked himself in vain, should he be so desperately concerned about the feelings of others—of his father, for example, who oppressed him, who did not value his qualities, who knew him no better than a business acquaintance?

Mr. Witt at last addressed his attention to Philip's reply: 'Well, I knew you'd have difficulty in finding one. But that doesn't end the uncertainty of the position so far as your mother's concerned. Does it?' Mr. Witt was leaning a little forward in the chair, his great chest supported by his clasped hands, purplish like his compressed lips, his old man's eyes fixed on his son.

'I can't honestly say I shall live here for ever, Father,' Philip burst out, and moving on trembling legs out of the orbit of his father's stare. This comparative truth of expression sharpened the atmosphere like a smell.

'You've no need to say it,' said Mr. Witt. 'Your mother and I won't live for ever.'

Behind the hoarse, rough voice Philip suddenly perceived the intense and incongruous feeling. He turned to face Mr. Witt, realizing with baffled emotion that it was his father who feared most to lose him, that his was the motive of the visit, and his mother's concern, if not a total invention, merely a mask through which his father had been improvising. He said incoherently: 'You'll live—you're both all right.' His love struggled to free itself, to fly to its shameful object.

'In the nature of things, I mean,' said Mr. Witt. It was an essential part of the tortuous paradox of the relationship that in a real sense his father was not at all moved, that had Philip at this moment thrown himself on his father's knee, there would have been, on the parent's side, only bewilderment and contempt. And yet some element, instinctively a part of the father's life and yet wholly foreign to the crude character he had evolved for himself, yearned to possess the son. 'The last thing we want,' continued Mr. Witt, 'is to tie you down. We've only your good at heart.' His normal manner, brusque, bullying, insensitive, almost resumed control: 'Let's hear no more about that flat, shall we?'

To this question Mr. Witt did not expect a reply, nor did his son make one.

IX

The Saddleford Building Society's year end was the thirty-first of August, as it had been since its foundation. Its annual general meeting followed some two months later. One afternoon in September the door of Stuart Blackledge's office opened and admitted the General Manager. For Blackledge it was like the rather boring, faintly menacing visit of a distant relative who brings with him an aura of bereavement or sponging. He stood up behind the acreage of his desk and said: 'Hello, sir.'

'Don't disturb yourself, Blackledge,' said the General Manager. Blackledge sat down again but Matheson walked in his birdlike way to the window and stood contemplating the square, shining under a shower of rain. 'Do you know,' he said, 'I've never noticed before, in all my years here, that John Bright has one finger marking his place in that book.'

'You've got good eyesight, sir,' said Blackledge.

'Clever bit of work, that statue. The pages look quite real. But the Corporation ought to do something about the bird-lime.' The General Manager turned from the window and sat in the chair by the desk. His white head slightly on one side, he looked keenly at the Mortgage Manager. 'Don't mind me being personal, Blackledge, but it's struck me you've not been quite up to snuff lately. Been overdoing it a bit?'

Blackledge laughed and knocked his pipe against his signet ring over the ash tray. 'No. I thrive on work.' He was conscious that this was becoming a stock response of his and determined to think of some more convincing disclaimer. 'You'll think it quite absurd,' he went on, 'but I've been losing some sleep over our cat, of all things—it has gastro-enteritis.' And although as he said this he clearly visualized the strange domestic arrangements that Ludo's illness had brought about—the chair draped with a rug where it lay, the camp bed made up in the sitting-room where Rose insisted on sleeping to attend to the animal in the night, the box of earth on spread newspapers—and which he had to the best of his ability ignored, he could almost believe that he had shared Rose's vigils and inordinate concern to the detriment of his health.

'Nasty thing, I've heard,' said Matheson.

'Very nasty. It's a miracle that the animal has survived so far.'

Matheson was lighting a cigarette, sucking the end as delicately as he sucked sugared almonds. 'I've really come,' he said, 'to break a bit of news to you.'

Some whirling machine started up in Blackledge's breast. 'Oh, yes,' he said, screwing his signet ring.

'You may know already that a committee of the Board has been considering the question of my retirement,' said the General Manager. 'These things leak out however secret they are. When the Chairman was in today he told me that the committee had decided on its recommendations. It was a strong committee and one can take it that the Board will adopt its report.'

'Quite,' said Blackledge. With astonishment he had been realizing that this moment—despite its casual and rapid build-up, its background of perfectly ordinary objects, and such irrelevant considerations as the smut on Matheson's otherwise virgin collar—was one of the decisive moments of his life. Apart from a slight trembling of the lips he had suitably arranged his face and almost composed his voice, and his excitement as it grew seemed only to give him increasing control over the situation, as though his destiny had not yet been decided or that in some occult way he could alter past decisions with an effort of will. And at the centre of this nervous agitation, contradicting it, was the certainty he dared not admit to himself, the belief that the absurd little plots against his power and the accident of the West End House débâcle could not, had not, destroyed the universal recognition of his supreme fitness for the General Managership of the society.

'The announcement,' said Matheson, 'will be made at the annual general meeting, but of course the information will be common property long before then. I thought you ought to know right away. You're bound to feel some disappointment.' The General Manager stretched out to the ash tray and meticulously deposited a centimetre of ash in the middle of it. 'The vacancy won't be advertised. Gerson will be appointed.'

As one confidently and repeatedly misreads the simplest of names, Blackledge for a moment irrationally imagined that he was being told that Gerson was to be appointed Joint General Manager with himself, and immediately adjusting himself invisibly to the new situation, he said without a tremor: 'I foresaw that happening.' Scarcely were the words out of his mouth when he felt the blood quit his face and the enormity of his shame and jealousy rose in his throat, as burning and acidulous as vomit.

Matheson put his cigarette between his lips and got up and walked again to the window. He was shocked, almost frightened, at Blackledge's ghastly looks, and at his own under-estimation of the effect his revelation would make. 'I'm sorry to spring it on you like this, Blackledge,' he said. 'But better from me, perhaps, than anyone else.' No word came from the man behind him. 'It's the accountancy qualification, of course,' he went on, not knowing how to treat the terrible damage his blow had left. 'The bigger we get, the more important figures become. I suppose the top man of any organization of this size must be on the financial side—except when he's a relic of the past, like me.' This was true, he thought, but more decisive had been Blackledge's character—too confident for his ability, just on the wrong side of reliability—about which the man would never be told.

'Gerson knows?' Blackledge's voice emerged at last.

Matheson turned back to the desk. 'Yes. I hope you'll work loyally with him. He's a bit of a cold fish, as we all realize, but he does know his stuff.' The General Manager put out his cigarette with little dabbings in the ash tray and tried to think of something more to say. He did not look at Blackledge. 'I don't think you'll find that A.P. will interfere with your side of things,' he said, moving towards the door.

He was surprised that Blackledge could reply with moderate calm: 'No, I don't suppose so.'

Matheson opened the door, said: 'Ah well, change and decay,' and made his escape. It had not after all, he thought, been too much of an ordeal. He looked at his watch: in a few minutes it would be tea time and one of the pages would bring him the *Argus* and he would be able to see whether or not Dodo II had won the three o'clock at Wolverhampton. Under the circumstances he supposed he could hardly have expected Blackledge to show any interest in the question to whose resolution he had now almost become inured. No one could truly concern himself with the vital issues of another's life. The fact that the Board would not invite him to become one of their number, that his retirement would be into obscurity and comparative penury, would probably remain quite unremarked. He pondered on this on the way to his room, and suddenly wondered if there were really any pleasure in eating cream cakes and backing horses. He had begun to think of late that rich food did not suit him. Sixty-five: he was moving, if indeed he had not already moved, into the epoch of growths, bereavements, incontinency of urine. Near his office a young girl from the Correspondence Department, her skirt stretched tight over a ridiculously round bottom, swayed through the doors that led to the lifts: the General Manager saw her disappear and it seemed to him that he himself had never been young.

. . . *And I think that you cannot be in love with me—the person whose ribs are too clearly marked, who has a qualification as a solicitor, an inability to sleep—but with the idea of being in love with someone your inferior in health, capability, decision, as you might long to possess an injured animal.*

The sound of the front-door bell made him lift his pen and listen. After a few moments his mother called his name from the stairs and when he went down she said, with the mingled excitement and disapproval he knew so well: 'There's Miss Eastwood to see you. I've shown her into the drawing-room.'

He went in with sinking heart and smelt the dust burning on the electric fire his mother must have switched on. Christine was sitting on the edge of a chair. She did not rise, and when he greeted her she said very brightly: 'I'm sure I've interrupted your work.'

'No,' he said unthinkingly, 'I was only writing a letter.' The change in her face told him that she suspected that he had been writing to the woman who had supplanted her. The situation lay before him like a mediocre and previously-seen film. There was a silence which in the end he turned into something bearable by finding and lighting a cigarette for her.

'I had a meeting at the Oddfellows Hall,' she said, as though the proximity of that place excused her visit, as indeed it had come to do in the prolonged debate in her own mind.

'I'm very glad you called,' he lied.

'You're not really,' she said, suddenly betraying her emotions.

'Christine,' he said.

She saw that he was not moved and yet could not hold back the untimely approach she had planned. 'Are you happy, Philip? Are you going to marry her and be happy?'

'You mustn't distress yourself like this.'

She burst out at last with the only thing that was real to her, the expression of her own misery. 'Time makes no difference. Every morning I feel the pain just the same. I've tried to understand how you could be without pain, and failed, and I thought perhaps you felt you couldn't come to see me again. And if all that was separating us was pride or something——'

A footfall outside the door and the turning of the handle made her break off and dive into her handbag for her powder compact. Mrs. Witt entered with a tray.

'I had the kettle on,' she said, 'and so I made a cup of tea for you both.'

In the early interruption and the best tea service Philip saw the ambivalence of his mother's feelings. He kept his eyes on the poker-work motto hanging by the mantelpiece: it said: 'Hame's hame, be it never so hamely.'

'How very sweet of you, Mrs. Witt,' said Christine, removing the mask of her compact and revealing her eyes bright with unshed tears, her mouth imperfectly controlled.

Mrs. Witt marked the tension, and curious about it, envious of it, lingered a moment to straighten the embroidered crash cover on the settee. 'Of course,' she was saying, 'I've never known such weather for September.'

When she had, with almost ostensible virtue, left the couple to the privacy of her own contriving, Christine stared at the tray reposing before her on the brass and bamboo coffee table, as though it had been some unimportant but unignorable presence, a child, perhaps, that must constrain free intercourse. She glanced up at the grave, lean figure in the opposite chair who had uttered not a single word during his mother's interruption. 'Shall I pour?' she asked, feeling achingly that the words were the epitaph of her love.

A purchaser for West End House, building and contents, was found by the society for £34,000. Of this sum £3,000 was apportioned as the value of the contents to be paid to the bank. On sober consideration it was thought impossible to litigate on the interpretation of Philip Witt's misconceived drawing of the mortgage.

The news of the society's calamitous loss, like that of an illegitimate birth in a respectable family, filtered down through the hierarchy of the society's staff. Even Ramsden, imperfectly understanding the mechanics of the thing, apprehended the blow to Blackledge and Witt's prestige, and the embarrassment to those who must present the society's next accounts, trifling though the loss must look against the society's massive reserves. He found himself thinking of it quite often. 'Sixteen thousand quid,' he said to himself one morning, 'chucked down the drain, and they can't afford to put me in respectable quarters.' He stubbed out his cigarette and went to the store cupboard for towels, soap and toilet paper.

It was just after eight. Ramsden always attended personally to the replenishing of the amenities in the directors' and senior executives' lavatory. As he went to the lift he glanced into the garage: to his surprise he saw the third space already occupied by Blackledge's car. The bastard's putting in some overtime, he thought, and quite right, too.

He came out of the lift on the second floor, went in the lavatory and, with a start of surprise, found Blackledge standing with his hands on the edge of a washbasin. 'Good morning, sir,' Ramsden said. 'You're early this morning, sir.' Blackledge did not answer and Ramsden looked at him exasperatedly out of the corner of his eye while he deposited the toilet pads on the glass-topped table. As he looked he saw something heavy splash into the basin. He said: 'Are you all right, sir?'

When he went closer Ramsden saw blood on the porcelain and thought the Mortgage Manager's nose was bleeding. He looked in the mirror and saw a pallid face with a dabble of blood on the temple.

'I had a smash in my car,' said Blackledge, 'on the way here.'

Ramsden seized a towel. 'Sit down here, sir,' he said, pulling forward the chromium-legged stool. Blackledge obeyed. Ramsden wetted the towel and looked at the wound. 'It's just the surface of the skin, sir. Hold the towel against it and I'll nip down to the surgery and get a dressing.'

When he returned Blackledge had not moved. Ramsden applied the lint pad and the plaster. 'The nurse will be here at nine, sir. You ought to see her right away.'

'I will, Ramsden. Thank you very much. You've done a very good job with this.' Blackledge fingered his temple.

'What happened, sir?'

'It was my fault. The other fellow didn't stop. Probably thought he hadn't touched me.'

'I'll just sponge your jacket, sir,' said Ramsden. As he bent down he smelt spirits on the Mortgage Manager's breath. Automatically, he said: 'Shall I get you a nip of something from the dining-room?'

Blackledge shook his head. His face was still livid, his hair disarranged.

'You ought to sit down quietly till the nurse comes, sir. I'll give you a hand to your room.'

'I can manage, Ramsden.' The force had gone out of his voice, the energy from his movements. He stood up and did not refuse Ramsden's great hands which took his arm and ushered him out of the lavatory, across the corridor and into the leather-covered easy-chair facing his desk.

The room was chill: a breeze blew through the open window. In spite of this a familiar, unusual and momentarily unidentifiable odour smote Ramsden's nostrils.

'The cleaner ought not to leave your window open so late in the year,' he said, moving to shut it. 'I'll see it doesn't happen again, sir.' But Blackledge made no response, and on leaving him Ramsden went down in the lift to the garage. There he looked carefully over the Mortgage Manager's car. Some damage to the wing had been painted over with a red undercoat preparatory to spraying, but otherwise there was not a scratch. Ramsden walked incredulously to his despised office, rolling a cigarette with his nimble, hirsute fingers. There he sat down, struck a match, let it burn out, and said aloud to the nude back of the girl on his calendar, 'The bastard tried to shoot himself, and got the bloody deflection wrong.' And, he thought, without doing anything about getting him better quarters.

Ridiculously, it seemed to him, he allowed them time to have dinner before he called, as though the routine and commonplace parts of their lives were more important than the crises. As, indeed, they were, he thought, standing frightened outside the front door, otherwise existence would be unbearable. Rose opened the door to him. She had not switched on the hall light, and when he did not enter she peered out at him and cried: 'Philip, I thought it was Stuart and he'd forgotten his key.'

'Isn't he in?' It was inconceivable that the resolution

that had caused him so much agony should be thwarted by such a circumstance.

'No,' said Rose. 'Is it some office matter?'

'I thought he was bound to be in after his accident.'

'What accident?' Rose came closer to him.

'He had a slight collision in his car on the way to the office. Didn't he 'phone and tell you?'

'But he left early to go to Birmingham this morning.'

'He must have changed his mind after the smash.'

'He hasn't been home. I thought he must have been kept in Birmingham.'

'You sound worried about him,' said Philip. He saw the dim outlines of the hall and its furnishings, a part of Rose's life he could never appropriate, and his jealousy ached in his chest.

'Was he hurt?'

'I didn't see him,' said Philip. 'Someone told me about it at lunch. He got a little bang on the head.'

'Will you come in?' Rose asked.

'If you want me to.'

She turned and went back into the hall and put on the light. He followed her, shutting the front door behind him. He put his arms round her. She said: 'He may come back any minute.'

'I came to tell him I loved you.'

She freed herself from his arms. 'No,' she said.

'I should have come long ago.'

'You are doing this for me,' she said. 'What will happen to us?'

He had a strong sense of unreality—the unreality of an explosion or illness when time and the world's material become more powerful than oneself. 'We shall go away,' he said. He thought of the hotel bedroom behind Piccadilly, the loud speaker, the thick glass tumbler, the notice about meals and laundry.

'You'll leave the society?' she questioned.

He took her hand. 'Do you love me?'

'Yes,' she said. 'Yes.'

'Enough to leave this?' He looked over her shoulder at a pair of gloves on a chest, a softly lit room beyond an open door.

She said: 'Suppose he has known all the time.'

'Stuart known, and kept silent? Impossible,' he said. 'Why do you say that?'

'Because he's changed. And how can you know how someone will behave about something that touches him deeply?'

'But Stuart is simple—a humour, a humour of a business executive. How has he changed?'

'He drinks more. And he's silent.'

'That's the West End House business. And now Gerson.'

'What do you mean?' she asked.

'Hasn't he told you?' Philip explained Blackledge's part in the West End House comedy.

She said: 'He was too proud of himself to tell me. What is the thing about Gerson?'

He began to feel a deep despair. 'Gerson has got the general managership.'

She went to the telephone. 'I must ring the Queen's. Stuart may be there. I hope he is.'

'You must have loved him when you married him,' said Philip. 'You still love him.'

'I don't love him. But I must——' she was already dialling the number and broke off to listen.

Philip went into the sitting-room and closed the door so that he could not hear the conversation. There was a fire burning in the grate: in front of it was a chair protected from draughts by a rug. On the chair lay a cat, which raised its head when it saw Philip. By the chair was a bowl of water. What will she do with the cat? he thought, and there seemed to be no answer to the apparently ridiculous question. Perhaps it would die: perhaps Stuart would die, and his parents, and then there would be no obstacles in the way of his love. Immediately he was prompted with the sickening memory of West End House: the mechanics of the sale which he himself had to carry out, as a child by its heartless parents is made to clean up its own filth.

Rose came in and said: 'He isn't there. Hasn't been there at all tonight.'

'What are you afraid of?' he asked.

'I don't know,' she said.

He thought of his fiction that tried to comprehend the terrible events, absent from his own life and society, that nevertheless he knew were characteristic of human existence.

'Are you going to wait, and tell him?' she asked.

He saw with sudden relief, the excuse he always found to escape pain, decision, involvement. 'Do you think it would be too cruel to tell him now?'

She sank down on a chair. 'If it's cruel at all it will always be too cruel,' she said. 'And Arnold Gerson general manager! Stuart can never stay and work under him.'

He sat on the arm of her chair and clutched her hand: 'I'll wait until he comes in and then . . .' he said. Her fingers seemed not to belong to anyone he knew, nor alive even, but to be like the hand-rail of a vehicle about to plunge into dizzying convolutions and descents.

'All right,' she said.

As desperately as if he were having to fill in the last moments of seeing someone off on a train, he said, 'How is Ludo?'

'I don't know if he's going to make it,' she said, with the false nonchalance of one to whom a crisis has become habitual. 'He hasn't eaten for three weeks and he won't drink.' She told him in detail what her notes had only indicated—how the vomiting had occurred at longer intervals, how sometimes after the worst sickness was over Ludo had actually purred at her touch, how the vet had started injections, how she had constantly swabbed away the discharge from Ludo's mouth—indeed, had sponged the whole fur since he was unable to clean himself. It was a symptom of the disease that the cat should crouch for hours over or near a bowl of water, thirsty but unable to lap.

As she spoke she watched his worried, beautiful face and thought, yes, he was concerned but he could never feel as she did who alone had the responsibility and love for the creature. For him, perhaps, the tortuous but inevitable process of the illness was an image: for her it was nothing but reality which she must suffer without consolation—as the cat himself had suffered, crawling away from useless sympathy, to crouch waiting in vain for the pain to be removed, or lying dumb with a needle sticking in his belly while the vet refilled the plunger with the glucose that against nature was to attempt to nourish. It was amazing to her that it was only three weeks ago since she had come home and found Ludo sick: she could not imagine a time when the progressions of her thoughts did not time and time again run sickeningly against the pity and terror and hopelessness of his illness.

'I couldn't have borne it,' he said, becoming frightened of what lay in the hooded chair. 'You're stronger than I am.'

'How could you have not borne it, darling?' she asked. 'It's only other's suffering we can't bear.'

'Yes,' he said, 'but the suffering I bear, my own suffering, is absurd. Isn't it absurd for a gregarious animal to be shy, one designed to sleep not to sleep? And to choose always to do the thing one doesn't desire?'

'Does that mean we are never going to be together?'

He hesitated, trying to see how this would end, but seeing only her book open on the chair arm, a shadow moving as the fire flickered, his shoe making the airy pattern it always made when he sat talking. From behind him there came a small, strange, persistent sound whose momentary unidentifiableness alarmed him. 'What's that?' he asked sharply.

She was leaning forward, her finger to her lips. Very cautiously she rose to her feet and moved so that she could see behind the be-rugged chair. After a moment she held out her hand to him without turning her head. He went quietly behind her and over her shoulder saw in the shadows Ludo with his head in the bowl of water lapping. He heard her let out her breath very gently. At last the cat moved away from the bowl and stood, the water dewy on his beard.

Rose laughed uncertainly. 'It's the first time he's drunk. Darling, if only you knew how long I've crouched with him over that bowl.' She seized a scrap of cotton-wool and bent down and began to wipe the cat's mouth and whiskers. 'I think he's going to make it,' she said. 'Dear, clever Ludo.'

A dark curl had fallen over her white brow: as she sat on her heels he could see the white gleam of her thigh. A vast desire for her possessed him, and since he could not translate it into action it was transformed into a tenderness that could be content with nothing but a lifetime devoted to prolonging her happiness and beauty.

She said: 'I must try him with something to eat.' She stood up. 'He's very partial to the fat on boiled ham. Do you think that would be too rich?'

'You give him some boiled ham fat,' he said fondly.

When she went to the door the cat followed her. 'He's coming after you,' he said.

'I think he's going to make it,' she said. 'Can you see?—he's only a bag of bones.'

'He's all right. He heard you talk about the ham fat.'

She opened the door. Ludo walked slowly across the hall and down the corridor. They followed him. 'He's never been out of the room before,' she said excitedly.

'You shouldn't love so deeply.'

'How can you help it?' she asked. 'And how could he have lived if I hadn't?'

Like society, he thought, love enables man to exist, to resist his environment, at the cost of his freedom. He said: 'First you loved the victim—the bird, you know. Then you loved its destroyer.'

'But I loved the destroyer all the time,' she said.

The business of buying the rubber tube demanded all his attention. The diameter and length had to be determined, and then he had to drive to another town and try several shops. When the task was accomplished and he returned to the car he had almost forgotten what he wanted the tube for. He poured some whisky into the plastic top of a thermos flask and drank it off before he started to drive. Perhaps it was the drink that made everything appear remote—everything except this rather arduous mechanical routine of self-starter, clutch, gear lever, brake, which seemed more real than usual, as though his body had shrunk. It was miraculous that he could successfully guide this little world in which he lived out of the town and on to the very road leading to the place which, a very long time ago it seemed, had come to him as the place where he would stop the car. Miraculous, too, that he had evaded the plots and plotters who would certainly not have permitted him this perfect freedom.

In middle age one's grip on life slackened, so that it was difficult to point to any part of life as indispensable. And there came a moment when one could detect life itself saying: you are of no further use to me.

His temple hurt. He thought of his surprise at the amount of noise made by what was after all little more than a toy. It had been apt that he had used a toy, because he had only been playing. In a way he was still only playing. The manual labour of measuring, walking round the shops, stowing the parcel the tube made in the car boot—these could not constitute the prelude to anything serious. Besides, at any moment he could stop playing and resume the ordinary role of himself.

But the point was—and he came back to it again and again, as a man keeps on fruitlessly feeling for the cigarette lighter he has left at home—that he had no ordinary role to resume. The soul had left the body for one of its nocturnal excursions and returned to find the body broken, disfigured, incapable of re-entry.

The light was going as he left the last village behind. The road ran along one side of the long valley: across from him the low naked hills were patchily brown, like the hide of some captive ruminant. In between, the heather and bracken stretched unbroken by house or man. He ran the car off the road, along a tumble-down wall of black stone. When he got out the eastern sky was already dark. He took the parcel from the boot and fumbled patiently with the knot.

The end of the tube, as he had thought, came conveniently into the car through the little ventilation window by the driver's seat. He put a duster in the gap and remembered to take out the envelope and rest it on two of the dash-board knobs. He was pleased with his skill which, of course, had to be exercised, like that of a pilot in a storm, against a background of terrible noise and danger. On the envelope he saw that he had written the name of a flower. Each thing he had done that day (and each thing was in itself commonplace, the enormity—which he did not contemplate—being in the accumulation of things) from the earliest moment of his waking in the morning darkness, had sealed off his life, so that even if he had wished—and he could not wish it—there was no possibility of return. He pressed the starter and the engine came sweetly to life.

Since Gerson was still working at ten-thirty, his wife had brought his bed-time drink in to him. He had a desk in the breakfast room or, rather, a bureau which had a glass-fronted top for his books. He sipped the drink. Once they used to have cocoa at night but now it was a patent, chocolate-flavoured drink of which he had at first slightly disapproved but whose tonic and elegant virtues he had eventually seen to outweigh its expense.

At five to six the Vice-Chairman had telephoned the office to find out if the contract for the sale of West End House had been signed. He had asked for Blackledge and Witt in turn, as the officials directly connected with the sale, but neither of them was in the building. At last he was put on to Gerson to whom he had complained of his difficulty in obtaining information at what he regarded as an early hour. 'Thank goodness someone works in Saddleford House,' said Sir Harold. Gerson had also been able to supply him with the facts he required.

Arnold Gerson was aware that by some his conscientiousness and thirst for knowledge was thought to be only a design for finding favour with his superiors. But those of that mind did not understand the principles of loyalty and industry. Man existed to serve his fellow-men, and all who worked for the society had the great privilege and opportunity of serving through the society. Here was an organization which helped to preserve the community, brought stability and thrift into the lives of many to whom those qualities might otherwise have remained alien, and for itself made only such profit as was consonant with preserving its existence infinitely.

And now, the proof of the right conduct of his life lay in the fact that soon he would have no superiors in the society—except the directors, whose being was naturally on another plane to his. Gerson put down his beverage and could not resist opening the doors of the bookcase and taking out a volume called *The Building Societies' Who's Who*. He turned to the Gs, found his own name and visualized the changes which his coming promotion would necessitate.

He shut the book and put it back, conscious that the action had been a little foolish, proud even, certainly unworthy of the honour that had been done him. He had intended all day to spend a few minutes thanking God for the fulfilment of an ambition that once had seemed presumptuous in him. He returned all his papers to their folder and then, carefully taking off his still unfamiliar and costly spectacles, closed his eyes.

THE HOGARTH PRESS

This is a paperback list for today's readers – but it holds to a tradition of adventurous and original publishing set by Leonard and Virginia Woolf when they founded The Hogarth Press in 1917 and started their first paperback series in 1924.

Some of the books are light-hearted, some serious, and include Fiction, Lives and Letters, Travel, Critics, Poetry, History and Hogarth Crime and Gaslight Crime.

A list of our books already published, together with some of our forthcoming titles, follows. If you would like more information about Hogarth Press books, write to us for a catalogue:

HOGARTH FICTION

The Colonel's Daughter by Richard Aldington
New Introduction by Anthony Burgess
Death of a Hero by Richard Aldington
New Introduction by Christopher Ridgway

All in a Lifetime by Walter Allen
New Introduction by Alan Sillitoe

Epitaph of a Small Winner by Machado de Assis
Translated and Introduced by William L. Grossman

Mrs Ames by E.F. Benson
Paying Guests by E.F. Benson
New Introductions by Stephen Pile

A Day in Summer by J.L. Carr
New Introduction by D.J. Taylor

Beat the Devil by Claud Cockburn
New Introduction by Alexander Cockburn

Chance by Joseph Conrad
New Introduction by Jane Miller

Lady Into Fox & A Man in the Zoo by David Garnett
New Introduction by Neil Jordan

Born in Exile by George Gissing
New Introduction by Gillian Tindall
Will Warburton by George Gissing
New Introduction by John Halperin

Saturday Night at the Greyhound by John Hampson
New Introduction by Christopher Hawtree

All Day Saturday by Colin MacInnes
June in Her Spring by Colin MacInnes
New Introductions by Tony Gould

Extraordinary Women by Compton Mackenzie
New Introduction by Andro Linklater
Vestal Fire by Compton Mackenzie
New Introduction by Sally Beauman

Her Privates We by Frederic Manning
New Introduction by Lyn Macdonald

Morte D'Urban by J.F. Powers
Prince of Darkness & other stories by J.F. Powers
New Introductions by Mary Gordon
The Presence of Grace by J.F. Powers
New Introduction by Paul Bailey

Mr Weston's Good Wine by T.F. Powys
New Introduction by Ronald Blythe

The Revolution in Tanner's Lane by Mark Rutherford
New Introduction by Claire Tomalin

The Last Man by Mary Shelley
New Introduction by Brian Aldiss

Boston Adventure by Jean Stafford
New Introductions by Anita Brookner
The Collected Stories of Jean Stafford
New Introduction by Ian Hamilton

The Island of Desire by Edith Templeton
Living on Yesterday by Edith Templeton
Summer in the Country by Edith Templeton
New Introduction by Anita Brookner

In the Days of the Comet by H.G. Wells
New Introduction by Brian Aldiss
Marriage by H.G. Wells
New Introduction by Victoria Glendinning

Frank Burnet by Dorothy Vernon White
New Afterword by Irvin Stock

Memoirs of Hecate County by Edmund Wilson
Afterword by John Updike

J. F. Powers

Morte D'Urban

New Introduction by Mary Gordon

'This is the book for which his many admirers have long been waiting' – *Evelyn Waugh*

Father Urban Roche is a formidable golfer, raconteur and star of the preaching circuit – no ordinary priest he. Hardly surprising that he harbours less-than-meek ambitions of inheriting the highest of posts, Father Provincial to his Order. Then, banished to a deserted retreat in the wastes of Minnesota, this man for all seasons is forced to confront the realities of life on earth which, through a sequence of events at once uproarious and moving, he triumphantly does. A novel about a priest, a special priest, *Morte D'Urban* is a parable of the straitened role of belief in a secular age. It is also one of the comic masterpieces of our time.

Roy Fuller

The Ruined Boys

New Introduction by Jeremy Lewis

'Very funny and beautifully written' – *Observer*

School is a world most of us are glad to escape from – and yet there is an awful fascination in returning as adults (in fiction, at least) to those rule-bound, bell-echoing, cabbage-smelling corridors. Roy Fuller guides us back through the eyes of Gerald Bracher, innocent new boy at Seafolde House; and charts, with tenderness and comic irony, Gerald's evaluations of the memorable pupils and staff – to the entire upset of his moral notions.

J.L. Carr

A Day in Summer

New Introduction by D.J. Taylor

This, J. L. Carr's first novel, displays the same rare gifts as later works such as *The Harpole Report* and the Booker-shortlisted *A Month in the Country* and *The Battle of Pollocks Crossing*.

It is a festive summer's day when Peplow, a quiet bank clerk, arrives in Great Minden to shoot the killer of his son. But his task is complicated when he meets a couple of old wartime colleagues – only two of the townsfolk with problems of their own. Written with a wry understanding of the tragedy and folly of everyday lives, this is a blackly comic thriller, moving towards an ominous climax – for little can the folk of Great Minden suspect how their day will end.

T. C. Worsley

Flannelled Fool

A Slice of A Life in the Thirties

New Introduction by Alan Ross

This is the story of one young man's rude awakening from the innocence of a prolonged childhood (where hitting a six had been his wildest dream) into the turbulence of contemporary Europe – the rise of fascism in Italy and Germany, the purge of homosexuals, turmoil in Spain, and scandal at home. Like J. R. Ackerley's *My Father and Myself, Flannelled Fool* is remarkable for its rueful self-awareness, its hilarious anecdotes, its mirror to a whole generation. Long recognized as a classic portrait of youth in the Thirties – rushing with all its illusions and self-confidence into the crisis ahead – this haunting memoir is frank, funny and unforgettable.

Walter Allen

All in a Lifetime

New Introduction by Alan Sillitoe

'One of the most magnificent literary portraits achieved by any modern novelist' – *Daily Telegraph*

A classic of working-class fiction, *All in a Lifetime* is a history of a life, but also history as it is lived, in all its strangeness and magical ordinariness. The story of a retired silversmith, born in 1875, this novel is not concerned with world events, but with personal struggles and triumphs in friendship, marriage and political convictions – a moving, powerful testament to a whole way of living in this century.

Michael Wharton

The Missing Will

'Not to be missed' – *Sunday Times*

Michael Wharton – 'Peter Simple' of the *Daily Telegraph* – has for years been writing the most consistently funny and perceptive of newspaper columns, described by Kingsley Amis as 'a treasure house of truth, fantasy and wit'. The same can be said of this masterly slice of autobiography. From early life in Bradford, through a lamentable career at Oxford, army service in India and debauched years in post-war Bohemia to his desk in London, Michael Wharton hilariously charts the making of a remarkable satirist and a 'state-registered melancholiac'. 'Everyone should read his book who wants to know how an intelligent and civilised man can survive in the modern world.' *(Auberon Waugh)*